The Dreamer

❧

THE BEGINNING

By E. A. Meigs

Dreamer Literary Productions, LLC

2018

For information regarding this novel or permissions
to reproduction selections from this work, please visit
Dreamer Literary Productions at:
www.dreamerliteraryproductions.com

ISBN: 978-0-99812 59-3-0

First Edition Paperback

Cover photo by my friend, Paula Krugerud
www.PaulaKrugerudPhotography.com

I dedicate this book with much love and heartfelt thanks to my Aunt Carol; her wise counsel and moral support have meant so much to me throughout my work on this project.

 Fonts used in this novel 

Papyrus was created by Chris Costello in 1982.

Garamond was designed by Claude Garamond in the early 1530's.

The Dreamer

ⓒ૪ૐ

THE BEGINNING

 **Introduction** 

When the last Ice Age was well underway approximately 40,000BCE (Before Common Era), nearly one-third of the earth's surface was hidden beneath a thick layer of ice. Since a substantial percentage of the planet's moisture was frozen solid, the world's oceans receded and coastlines were greatly expanded. At that time the Eurasian landscape consisted of vast wind-scoured tundra and small pockets of woodland which were populated by at least two groups of people: the Neanderthal and the Cro-Magnon. These populations probably coexisted in parts of Europe and Asia for only a relatively short period of time, geologically speaking. They lived a seasonally nomadic lifestyle and each hunted the same game. We can only guess at what their lives would have been like: their languages, their social behaviors, their spirituality. Due to the passage of time and the impermanent nature of most materials they would have used in their day-to-day lives, there is little to tell us about their existence besides the tantalizing clues left by their remains, their tools, their art, their burials and…their refuse.

Analyses of fossilized Neanderthal skeletons show that the males averaged five feet, five inches to five feet, six inches. The tallest Neanderthal man found to date was five feet, nine inches. The females were five feet to five feet, one inch. Their bones were about one-third stouter than ours. They were heavily muscled and had tremendous upper-body strength. The Neanderthal had the largest brain size of any known humans. Initial DNA tests showed that they likely had fair coloring: red to auburn hair, green or hazel eyes, and pale, probably freckled skin. Later genetic research on Neanderthal individuals found in different parts of Eurasia revealed that some had brown hair, brown eyes, and dusky skin.

The Neanderthal roamed the earth for roughly 200,000 years before their trail went cold around 37,000 to 42,000 BCE. That said, the Neanderthal may have persisted to eke out a living for some time after that, but we have no evidence of it at this writing. However, since most modern humans outside of sub-Saharan Africa share between one to four percent Neanderthal DNA it is almost certain that the Neanderthal are still with us even now, albeit in diluted form.

The Cro-Magnon first appeared in the European fossil record around 42,000 to 47,000 BCE. Over a period of tens of thousands of years, they migrated out of Africa, gradually making their way into Eurasia. They were anatomically constructed more or less the same as most modern men and women. Cro-Magnon men averaged about five feet, nine inches in height, but it is thought that some taller individuals may have been upwards of six feet, five inches. Like the Neanderthal, their brains were also bigger than those of today's people. They are believed to have had dark coloring: dark brown to black hair, brown eyes, and tan or olive-toned skin. (Blond hair and blue eyes are a relatively new development in modern humans, having first appeared about 6,000 to 12,000 years ago, long after the pinnacle of the Ice Age, but possibly coinciding with the end of that last great glacial period.)

* * *

It is my humble opinion that after so many years of existence in a world which often presented extreme challenges, these intelligent beings would have been at the top of their game in leveraging the available resources in order to ensure their own comfort and the continuation of their species. Some indications suggest that early man was potentially much more advanced than is generally credited (more on this topic in the author's note at the end of the book) and it is my guess that we will continue to be surprised by what is revealed when ongoing and future anthropological studies peel back layers of time, as we search for ourselves in the lives of our ancestors.

An animal index is presented at the end of this novel for the convenience of those who are unfamiliar with the Ice Age animals of Europe. It gives basic information about most of the animals mentioned in this book. It might be useful to know, for example, that a wisent is a European bison, and that the animal to which North Americans refer as a moose is called an elk in Europe.

* * *

The Dreamer - The Beginning is the first in *The Dreamer* series. This saga follows the life of a young Neanderthal man as told from his perspective, at a time in history when Eurasia was experiencing brutal climatic changes and man's position on Nature's food chain was indeed perilous. This is a work of fiction and it is not intended to hold up to scientific scrutiny. I merely seek to tell a story that is set amid this ancient backdrop. I have peopled it with those whose lives—when broken down to their most basic elements—would not have been so different from ours: sharing care and concern for loved ones, enduring all life's hardships, and reveling in serendipitous moments of love, beauty, and joy when they grace us with their presence.

Tris, the Dreamer

Chapter One

The peace of the lonely grasslands was shattered by a deep, menacing roar as the near-by brush exploded with the onslaught of a large hairy body and a ferociously gaping maw.

I bolted upright from a sound sleep, shaken and unable to rid myself of these terrible images. I had experienced vivid dreams since I was a small boy, but the clarity of this nightmare was startling. For a few moments my mind fought to bring me back into my body, to return me to this place and time. My heart was pounding and I breathed as though I had run down a wounded deer in the bush. Gradually, the powerful thumping in my chest subsided.   The darkness prevented me from seeing much of my surroundings, but the familiar smells of home and the soft rumbles of our dog's snores were a comfort to me.

I was soon able to think calmly and rationally, but I was not relaxed enough to go back to sleep. An urgent need to relieve myself was making itself more apparent the longer I sat there, considering whether or not I should arise for the day. The urgent need won out. Pushing back weighty fur bed coverings in the decidedly cool air, I quickly secured leggings to the thick leather strap that held my loincloth around my hips. Then I added a sheathed bone knife, lacing it to the ties at my right side and next, wrapped my wisent-hide cloak around my shoulders. I found my wonderfully warm boots where they had been left to dry by last evening's fire and carelessly stuck my feet into them, not bothering to lash the boots to my ankles before walking out into the chilly early morning air. As I donned these additional layers, our elderly dog Rooph was awakened from his slumbers. He groaned as he heaved himself to his feet and then accompanied me out-of-doors.

We both stopped just outside the entrance of our cavernous home to smell the air and listen. Our breath turned into vaporous white clouds in the moonlight. The full moon was still shining up amongst the stars, illuminating the glittering crust of frost on the ground.

A cold wind whispered across the landscape, making just enough headway to rattle the still-naked branches of the trees. Spring may have begun its reign over the land, but winter had been slow to release its icy grip. In the distance, I could hear the deep hoo-hoos of a male owl and the answering calls of his mate. We walked out to the boundary that our family had been marking with urine for many generations, in a mostly successful effort to keep large predators from visiting our compound. Rooph and I contributed to the cause, and then trudged back to the welcoming hearth. There, I stirred up the coals from the previous night's fire, adding some small sticks and slivers of birch bark to tiny flames as they eagerly devoured the fuel.

"Well, old dog," I said to Rooph, ruffling the thick gray fur on his head affectionately with one hand while laying incrementally larger pieces of wood on the fire with the other. "How did you sleep last night? Better than me, I think." Rooph sensed my mood and nuzzled my bearded cheek with his big wet nose, whining quietly. "I know how you feel," I admitted. "I am uneasy too." Rooph's intelligent amber eyes looked intently into my face, but he issued no further comment. My mind struggled to grasp the meaning of the vision that kept replaying itself in my head. Dreams were important. Sometimes they were an echo of something that had happened in the past, but at other times they were a glimpse of events as yet unknown. They were a powerful message and such tidings were not to be ignored. Rooph and I sat companionably for a moment, gratefully soaking up the heat from the fire as I continued to feed the greedy flames.

There was no sign of my family awakening at this early hour, only the sounds of their deep contented sleep. I looked in on the huddled forms of my brother and sisters. My brother Ty was twelve winters of age and he was curled up in a ball with just his face exposed from the cocoon of furs. His complexion looked ashen against his deep red hair. He was just beginning to show signs of adulthood, but he had three more winters to go before he would be considered a man. Ty was nearly as tall as our Puh now and filling out well, his upper lip and chin sprouting soft russet whiskers. My sisters Saree, Twie, and Ru, who ranged in age from three to thirteen winters, were snuggled up together on a sleeping platform within a pile of soft fuzzy blankets. Ru, the eldest surviving sibling after me, had a protective arm around her younger sisters. Ru was mature for her years, both physically and mentally. Muh depended heavily upon her to help with all the household tasks that kept us fed and clothed. Ru was also a second mother to the younger children. The littlest sister, Mi, a plump and lively nine moons old baby, was with Muh in the small sleeping chamber that my parents shared off the main room of our home. There had been other offspring as well, all long-mourned: two babies who had not survived infancy and my brother Dak, born one year after me but sadly, was killed last winter.

I was both hungry and thirsty. I guessed that the sun would not rise for a while yet so I decided to visit our food cache, which was located in a series of rooms at the back of our earth-bermed home. We resided in a dwelling that may have once been a bear's den or wolf's lair, but had been dug out and enhanced over many, many years. My family had inhabited this domicile during the cold weather seasons for longer than anyone knew. Even my great-grandmother, my oldest living relative, had no idea how many generations had lived here. Several years ago I made my own modifications when I hollowed out an alcove in a wall for my bed chamber. It was little more than a shelf on which to sleep, but it gave me a place of my own that was off the cold floor. Previous ancestors added rooms and enlarged crevices on which we could place our oil lamps and store belongings. They had also built a hearth and constructed a chimney hole in the ceiling to allow smoke to escape the fireplace.

Before I slipped through the two layers of reindeer hides that covered the doorway to the cache, I pulled a long-sleeved elkskin tunic over my head for warmth and lighted a small oil lamp to illuminate the way. Our lamps were made from tiny clay pots with a braided fiber wick and fueled with various oils, but seal blubber oil was the most plentiful. We did not render much oil, so our lamps were only lighted when we absolutely needed use of them.

The food cache consisted of several chambers that were kept at a cooler temperature thanks to the double-thickness reindeerskin panels which insulated the rooms from the warmth of our living quarters. Of the many storage areas, I walked past the first one that contained all our winter snowshoes, hooded topcoats, and leggings, plus an assortment of finished hides, each awaiting the time when Muh, assisted by Ru, would assemble them into a garment, bag, or boots. Most of the bulky cold weather clothing was aged. Muh's hooded topcoat dated to a time before she was paired with Puh, but it was still a beautiful article of clothing, constructed of reindeer hides and garnished with a thick wolf-fur ruff around the hood. My siblings' coats were passed down from child to child. Because Ru had attained her full size, she would soon receive a new coat that would probably last her for the rest of her life. Puh's hooded topcoat, in contrast, was only a year old, because his was sometimes damaged beyond repair during hunting expeditions and therefore needed to be replaced almost every season.

I, too, had recently received a new coat and winter leggings, since I had outgrown the markedly tattered ones I had worn during the last few years. I looked forward to at last wearing garments that actually fit.

The next compartment, almost barren of stores now, held piles of empty baskets and leather sacks, small amounts of dried fruits, mushrooms, and herbs, various nuts, a basket of wizened apples, and two baskets of grains. Another room held baskets of tubers, garlands of onions and other root vegetables that were layered in dirt and dried grasses to help keep them from withering. Yet another room held sacks of sun-dried and smoked meats, most of which was harvested from hoofed animals but also included fish and seal. Some of this hoard was not only from last year, but from several years' past. These meats were our most plentiful food source in the winter and, while we were sometimes a little over-ambitious in the stocking of our pantry, you never knew when weather patterns, injuries, or illness would limit the season's hunting. So, it was always a good idea to put away as much food as we could—especially considering how much an unusually large family like ours would consume. We often kept other meat hanging up over our fire pit where the smoke preserved it, but as of now, the chimney area was empty, and all we had left to eat was the last of our winter stores.

* * *

Puh had left our home with the coming of the new moon to meet with his older brother, my Uncle Mror, to go up to the wide plains that were frequented by larger game. They had gone in hopes of bringing down perhaps a few early wisent calves or maybe an ibex or antelope or two so that our households would have succulent fresh meat instead of the chewy dried meat and fish that we had been eating throughout most of the winter. We had survived the cold and unusually snowy season quite well, but now that spring was upon us, I strongly suspected that Puh just wanted to get out and enjoy the freedom of being in nature after long dark periods of enforced confinement. Thanks to a persistent west wind off the ocean which brought plenty of warm moist air, this winter was not as bitterly cold as some of the previous. But it was a season of deep snows that kept us trapped on or near our family compound for many days at a time. We used shovels made from modified giant deer antlers to clear the snow away from the smoke hole in the roof, shovel paths to areas where we stored some of our wood and relieved ourselves. Sometimes Puh and I took our shovels down to the frozen creek a n d removed the snow from the icy surface so we could then chop through the ice with stone axes to get at the water that flowed freely underneath. We were grateful that the snow provided more water than we usually had most winters, since it could be easily scooped into gourd cups and melted. This was a welcome convenience when only a small amount of water was needed and a cold winter's day trek to the creek seemed a little too daunting. But on the negative side, the snow also made it harder to reach any nearby game. Winter hunting usually meant braving the biting winds and dry intense cold, but this season Puh and I instead trudged along in snowshoes. It was a relief to see the snows gradually lessen and to at long last, finally leave our snowshoes at home.

Puh would return with a load of fresh meat before the moon disappeared again, but in the meantime, I grabbed several large pieces of dried fish for Rooph and a stick of dried venison for myself. Next, using a large shell, I scooped a quantity of plumped grains from where they were soaking in water, took a small wrinkled apple from a basket, and then returned to the fire. Carefully I poured a little more water from one of our water bags into the shell, stirred it into the grains, and set it on the cooking hearth stone that jutted into the blazing fire. Then, settling down on my haunches, I used my bone knife to cut the apple into chunks, dropping them into the shell, and occasionally used the knife blade to mix the apple into the grains. I threw the inedible parts of the apple into the flames.

Rooph edged a little closer to me. The sight of cooking food made him drool. Rooph had already finished his own breakfast but he knew he was always allowed to have the last few bites of my meal.

"Puh will be back soon," I whispered to him, stroking his large furry ears, one of which habitually drooped to one side while the other stood upright. "Then we will have real meat, again! I do not even care what kind they bring home, so long as it is fresh."

Rooph licked his chops, still staring at the food.

Puh and Uncle Mror were proficient hunters. They were forced to learn how provide for their family at a young age and although they did not hunt together very often, they did try to plan at least one outing each year. Sometimes they were accompanied by our neighbor, Black Wolf. As we grew old enough my brothers Ty, Dak, and me, and Uncle Mror's sons as well, were sometimes allowed to join them. It was exhilarating to watch these powerful men in the prime of their lives as they demonstrated the skills we would one day need to support our own families.

Suddenly, my dream took on a new significance. What if it was a sign of something that might have befallen Puh and Uncle Mror? The thrum in my chest began again.

At that moment, Muh appeared at the entrance to her sleeping chamber. She smiled sleepily at me, smoothing the front of her mid-calf length deerskin gown and pushing her straggling but usually well-kept hair out of her face.

"Oh, dear Tris, you have already made your breakfast. What has brought you out of bed before the sun has come up?" She bent to wrap her arms around my shoulders and give me a quick squeeze, and then brushed the hair from my face as she kissed my forehead. "And you have a blazing fire going! It was so pleasant to come out to a warm room." Muh retrieved her tall boots from the hearth and tugged them over her bare feet and up well past her knees until her feet were seated over the soles. She then donned an outer garment which would protect her clothing from being soiled as well as help her to retain a little more body heat.

"I arose early because I was awakened by a terrible dream." I said, half-heartedly returning her smile. "I am not sure what it means."

Muh looked at me carefully.

"Hmmm," she said. "Your great grandmother is known for having extraordinary foresight. Maybe you take after her. You are at the right age for the Dreams to start."

Great Gran was known for more than having visions. In her old age she was also infamous for her eccentricities, one of which was keeping squirrels for pets. Muh's mouth twitched mischievously, but I knew that she was partly serious. I took a moment to consider.

"I think I would prefer to take after you and Puh."

Muh and I smiled again. Although we were members of the Old Ones, those who were sometimes looked down upon by other people for being lowly and primitive, I was proud of Muh and Puh and our clan. Even if Great Gran was a bit squirrelly, her grandson Tor, my Puh, was intelligent and well-looking, in a scarred lean angular sort of way, and mightily built. He was average height for a man of the Old Ones, with red-gold hair that was here and there shot through with early stands of white. Puh had light green eyes and freckled skin that was deeply weathered on his face and hands where it was exposed to the elements. Muh, whose given name was Awna, was tall for a woman —as tall as Puh—with deep red hair and vibrant dark green eyes. Her fine speckled skin was still fair and smooth.

In some ways I took after Muh, whose family tended to be tall, but as my Great Gran always told me, my face was the image of Puh's younger self. I had to take Gran's word for it, since I had never seen anything other than the wobbly and indistinct watery reflections of my own face. At first, I had a difficult time reconciling Puh's battered countenance to how I imagined my own younger visage might look.

I was somewhat skeptical that we might share much resemblance to one another. When once I mentioned this to Gran she seemed to assume that I was balking at the comparison. Although it is rare amongst our people to speak harshly to children since many do not make it to adulthood, she had chided me.

"Do not wish to reach your Puh's age without accumulating the signs of having lived. And *always*, always remember: every scar your Puh wears he has earned while providing the necessities of life for his family."

But, in actuality, I scarcely noticed Puh's outward appearance to be anything other than ordinary. It was just that he looked rather old to my eyes. I had always held my Puh in the highest regard and even thought that he was a handsome man for his advanced years, despite all the evidence of hardship that he bore on his face and body. I tried to reassure Gran that I was not at all reluctant to be compared to my father. After all, in everything I did I strove to be just like him.

* * *

Muh poured a little water into one of our many shell bowls. Every summer we left our home for the span of at least one moon and trekked to the sea where we can not only harvest much food, but also escape the inland heat. We always brought back an array of shells to be used for a wide variety of purposes, such as to string on lengths of leather thong in order to produce a noise-maker that would amuse the newest baby, to eat from, to use as scoops and spoons, to cook in or, as Muh was doing now, to wash from. She rubbed most of the water onto the distinctive planes that made up her face. She was an attractive woman, but she had strong cheekbones and a firm jaw line that made her look somewhat severe in the deep shadows cast by the firelight. Muh then washed her hands with the remaining liquid and finally flicked her fingertips to throw the excess water into the fire where it instantly turned into hissing steam.

I watched Muh as she began take down her coils of hair. I knew, as all Old Ones knew, that having great masses of curly hair means that you can only do so much to keep it under control, but yet we still wore our hair long. Our stories told us that our hair provided a heightened acuity, an intuitiveness that helped us to sense the feelings of the fellow creatures that inhabited these lands with us. Therefore, our hair was never cut for the sake of removing length, but it was trimmed on occasion. Muh's hair reached down to the backs of her knees and it was beautiful, thick, and lustrous. However, since that much hair had the potential to pose a certain amount of inconvenience and possibly hinder one's function as well, she dealt with her hair by twisting the curls into coils and gathered them into a bundle at the back of her head where she used slender ivory rods to hold the heavy coils in place. Those ivory rods were a gift from Puh and he must have spent many days on their making. They were carved with delicate lines Puh had scratched onto the rounded surfaces and they were her most cherished possessions.

Now Muh looked more like herself. She appeared to be deep in thought, possibly pondering the implications of my Dream. Muh also took note of my apparent frame of mind.

"You look worried," Muh said as she moved to stand behind me and started to rearrange my sleep-tousled hair. Even though I had been fully grown for several years, Muh still did this out of habit. She divided my hair into many sections and then wound them into cords so that all the wispy ends would be twisted together. Next, she gathered the coils and lashed them together tightly at the nape of my neck with a long leather thong, continuing to wrap and crisscross the thong until there was just enough left to tie it off, leaving about a hand's length of hair free at the bottom where it reached to my waist.

"Many thanks, Muh," I said and I tried to recall the details of my Dream. "I cannot explain it. It was as though I was there. A large animal charged out of nowhere. I cannot shake the feeling that Puh and Uncle Mror are in trouble."

By now, Muh was in front of me again and her large eyes were wide.

"You truly think that this was more than a typical dream?"

I wished that I had some other answer to give her. "Yes."

Muh knelt across from me and looked down at her hands in her lap. She was thinking of Puh. Although I had not yet been paired with a mate, I understood that not all pairings were bonded with love. Uncle Mror seemed happy, but when he paired with Aunt Vee, it was in order to share in the territory that was held by her clan. Aunt Vee was the only surviving child of her parents, who were now on the cusp of extreme old age. She was a small, feisty, and fun-loving woman and she and Uncle Mror had developed a fond contentedness together, but that was due to pure luck and their determination to have happiness. That was more the norm: to have a family and ensure the survival of the family line. But Muh and Puh, they were truly devoted to one another.

Muh was trying to purge the unthinkable from her mind, but she was also formulating a plan. She rose to her feet and began to make the morning meal for herself and my brother and four sisters, but I could see that her mind was working. I wanted to hurry her thought process along.

"I could go after Puh, just to be sure that he and Uncle Mror are all right," I suggested.

Muh's lips drew tight, "Your Puh would be indignant if he thought we were checking on him."

This was true. For all Puh's good nature he would be chagrinned we so lacked confidence in his abilities to take care of himself. Muh and I were silent for a moment.

"When Black Wolf and his family were here several days ago," Muh began, "they said that they were going to travel to the mountains to visit his cousin Gray Elk in order seek out some new dogs. Maybe you could see if they have left yet and you could ask to go with them. They would be traveling down the same trails that your Puh and Uncle Mror would use—all the way up to the plains. You would have to run into them or at least see them in the distance. But they ought to be on their way home by now, or at least packing up to come home."

I saw the advantages of Muh's plan immediately. It was an open secret in my family that I was thoroughly besotted with Black Wolf's daughter, Morning Star, who had been my childhood playmate almost from birth. So it would come as no surprise to Puh that I would ask to accompany Black Wolf's family on an extended trip. It would be the perfect way to prove or disprove my disturbing vision without arousing Puh's suspicions. And it would give Muh some peace of mind. The other reason that Muh did not want me to go that distance alone was because of what had happened to my younger brother, Dak.

At sixteen winters old, Dak had just reached manhood the previous year. He was tall, sinewy in build, and he had the dark red hair that came from Muh's side of the family. Dak was an adept hunter; he frequently brought in small game in his determination to contribute toward the family's welfare. He chafed at his role as the second son, often ostensibly left behind to protect the family when Puh and I were away. Then, late one day, Puh and I returned from a hunt to find that Muh was frantic because Dak had not come home.

The day began with a rare bright sunny morning. After we had cleared away the previous night's new snow, Puh and I decided to take advantage of the good weather to see if we could bring in a deer. These conditions meant they were easier to hunt because they were weakened by lack of forage and the snow allowed us to more easily follow their tracks. And, the depth of the snow also meant that their speed was no longer a factor. However, that worked both ways. Even with snowshoes, our headway was so laborious that Puh and I took turns breaking a path through the soft thigh-deep snow. We forged on toward one of our favored game trails. This one led to a river so fast-flowing that it seldom had more than a skim of ice at its edges. As the only easy water source, it was an essential stop for most of the animals that lived in the area. This made the riverbank a prime location to ambush potential prey.

* * *

It did not take long before the condensation from our breath coated our beards with frost and formed small icicles that hung from our mustaches. We were nearing the river when we saw that a deer, probably a young red buck, judging by the size of the depressions its body made as it moved through the snow, seemed to be making its way to the water.

Puh put a mittened hand on my chest to stop me in place and he held my eyes for a moment. He then subtly jerked his head toward the side of the trail. Without exchanging words, I knew this meant *Stay here. I am going to try to get ahead of the deer and drive him back to you.*

I nodded. We had done this many times before, except now that I was fully grown and the larger, heavier man, our roles had changed. These days, Puh was the one who could move faster over the snow. I watched Puh break from the path and although the trees soon shielded him from sight, I could hear the steady shush-shush of his progress through the forest. Then all was silent, except for the sounds of nature. I also removed myself from the trail, taking cover behind a large tree. There, I stood immobile to await the next stage of the hunt.

I watched a few birds as they sang and flitted from branch to branch, their lively actions occasionally making small amounts of snow fall on me from the tree limbs above. I took note of the position of the sun and the slow movement of the shifting clouds overhead. Slowly, the cold began to seep into me.

Finally, Puh's shrill whistles met my ears. This was my signal that the deer was approaching. I soon heard its panting and the sounds of the deer's struggles through the deep snow. I could picture the buck trying to reuse the path it had already broken on the trail, but this time coming from the opposite direction. This would give the fleeing animal a little more speed, but it would still be difficult for the deer to move forward efficiently. When I judged that it was within striking distance, I poised my spear for the assault. I waited until I could just see the buck's nose before darting out and thrusting my weapon into its side. The buck had run half a body length past me by the time my spear made contact. It was a good hit. I felt pretty sure that I had at least ruptured one of the lungs. As I twisted the shaft of the spear to maximize the wound Puh rejoined me, breathing hard. He buried his spear in the other side of the deer and in a moment, the buck passed from life.

We gutted the deer, afterwards using handfuls of snow to cleanse the steaming body cavity and wash the blood from our hands. We would need a long branch or a sapling to carry the buck home. By the time we lashed the buck's feet to the sapling and shouldered the burden to commence the trek home, the day's temperature had begun to drop and the gusting winds were thick with large fluffy snowflakes.

Puh and I were pleased to arrive well before nightfall. We had just hung the buck outside our dwelling when Muh suddenly exited our home. We were surprised at her sudden appearance and the fact she had not bothered to put on any layers of outdoor clothing. Muh ran to Puh. She then put her hands on his shoulders and looked desperately into his face.

"Have you seen Dak? Have you seen any sign of Dak?" she asked urgently.

"No," Puh said, shaking his head. "Has he been gone all day?"

"Yes," Muh replied. She was quickly becoming covered with snowflakes and shivered with both cold and fright. "He left shortly after you and Tris."

Puh leaned closer to give Muh a hug and kiss and then he guided her toward the hide-covered doorway of our domicile.

"We will go out and look for him. Go back inside and stay warm. Try not to worry. Have Ty come out and take care of this buck. We will soon be back." Puh kissed her once more and pushed her indoors, but Muh's final glance begged us to bring home her son, safe and sound.

Puh and I searched for Dak in the drifting snows and gathering darkness without success. Disheartened, we were forced to return home. Puh and I set out again as soon as the sun rose the next day, when we could once more attempt to find his tracks. After a long morning of snowshoeing through the woods, we were finally able to pick up Dak's trail when we had found some sheltered foot prints where the wind had not yet swept them away. We followed the intermittent tracks in the blowing snows to the point where it became apparent that he had been stalked by wolves. We eventually found the place, marked by a gathering of crows, where the attack had taken place and he had made his stand. Dak had known better than to run. He faced them with his spear and knife and he had managed to slay one of the wolves before they took him down.

It was a horrific sight and one that I would never forget. It haunted both my waking moments and my sleep for many days and nights to come. We knew what the scavenging birds signified as soon as we saw them and ran to the scene, scattering the crows as we approached. Puh dropped to his knees and rocked with an intense but silent grief, and I thought he seemed to age before my eyes. It was the only time I had ever seen him to weep. Although it was an unspeakably devastating find and hard on all of us, it was hardest on Muh. And it reminded us all too well that our loved ones were beyond precious and never to be taken for granted.

* * *

I began to fill a pack with the things I would need for the trip with Black Wolf's family: a piece each of flint and iron pyrite for making fire, a flint knife, some extra spearheads, bee's wax, used for making glue to set new spear heads, a hammer stone that doubled as a whet stone, antler pummel and antler tip pressure flaker for making minor adjustments to the cutting edge of my spear, knife and hatchet, a coil of cured gut for hafting, and some lengths of leather thong. I added a small water bag, some shelled nuts, a few apples, and stuffed in several sacks of dried meat and fish. I briefly considered taking Rooph, but then realized that he was too old. Sadly, he would attract predators who would consider him to be easy prey. Rooph had once been a fine protector and I had no doubt that he would still defend his family to his last breath, but both he and I would be safer if he were left at home.

Before I tied the pack flaps closed, I placed my hatchet at the top of the load. There, it would be quickly accessible and its weight would ride easiest. Next, I prepared my boots for travel. My thick elkskin tunic, deerskin leggings, and chamois-skin loin cloth would keep me comfortable enough now that the sun was clearing the horizon, but keeping my feet warm and dry was quite another matter. My winter boots were made of a combination of animal hides: the soles were tough bearskin treated with birch tar; the outer pieces were constructed of elkskin, and the liners were made of reindeer fur that tended to shed a little fluff each time they were used. In addition to this, two layers of reindeer hide, cut in the shape of a rough outline of my feet, were inserted into each boot.

Even so, this wet muddy season meant that my footwear had to have their various layers disassembled and dried every night. I took off the outer boots I had slipped on my feet earlier, put the boots back together, and fastened them to my feet by tying them at the ankle. In other years, when the severe cold and arid conditions meant that we had little precipitation, we might use dried grass for additional insulation in our boots. But what with all the heavy snow this winter, any dried grasses or mosses we had put away last fall were saved for tinder or bedding.

Lastly, I slipped my arms through the pack's shoulder straps and selected a stout spear with a good blade. Muh was just taking the cooked grains off the hearth to cool. She reached for my cloak, bundled it up and placed it over my left shoulder.

"If Black Wolf has already left," she began, "we will have to think of something else. But, if you go with him, know that my thoughts will be with you always."

Muh then embraced and kissed me.

I smiled at her, "And mine will be with you. Do not worry, Muh. Maybe it *was* just a dream."

Chapter Two

As the sun continued its ascent over the horizon, the frost gradually melted away and disappeared into the damp spongy earth. Dried leaves from many autumns past crunched under my feet as my strides took me down the path to the home of our friends.

Black Wolf and his family belonged to one of The People from the East's tribes. Some of The People from the East did not accept the Old Ones because we are different in appearance and traditions. The People tended to be taller than we Old Ones and slighter in build; they had straight dark brown or black hair, flesh the color of a tanned deerskin, and dark brown eyes. We have what we consider to be real names, while they were named for things. They sometimes stretched out spoken words as they told their stories. They called it *singing.* It was interesting and sometimes beautiful to hear, but it took a while to become accustomed to the sounds. They were a good-looking people and many, like Black Wolf and his kin, had become allied to those of us of the Old Ones.

Black Wolf was a longtime close friend of my Puh and Uncle Mror. We had visited back and forth, hunted together, and traded goods with one another for as long as I could remember. We children were companions throughout all our years as neighbors, completely unaware that we were of different peoples until we heard the hushed whispers from adults when we became older. It was then that I realized my long-held assumption that Morning Star and I would someday be paired was never to be.

When I learned that my hopes were futile, I hid from sight the seashell necklace I had been making for Morning Star. We of the Old Ones did not wear much in ornamentation. Making ornaments took time away from providing food for the family, cutting firewood, producing clothing, tools, and other household essentials. Plus, wearing the clunky rattling jewelry that we sometimes saw on The People also meant that you made more noise as you moved about, which was surely detrimental to a hunter. In my clan, ornamentation was reserved for special occasions and usually consisted of feathers, which were light and most importantly, noiseless when worn. But I had seen that Black Wolf's mate Little Fawn sometimes wore a necklace made of shells and polished pebbles, and that had inspired me think that Morning Star might desire a necklace as well.

I was only ten winters old when the idea came to me while my family was at the coast one summer. Those warm days of living near the ocean were pleasant as we harvested and dried fish and seal meat, rendered seal oil, foraged for berries and other small fruit, dug for shellfish, and gathered driftwood under a friendly sun, wearing little and feeling so free after a long cruel winter. Except for missing Morning Star, who was far away at home several days' hike distant, it would have been idyllic. When wandering the beach, I would collect numerous small shells in a variety of shapes, matched for size and color, and I set to work on the gift I hoped would show my great love and esteem for her. I used a stone awl to drill holes, painstakingly enlarging the naturally occurring holes where another snail had bored out the previous inhabitant—or if there was no preexisting hole—creating one with the awl. It took just the right pressure on the tool to keep from breaking the fragile shells. I still had the partially completed project hidden away in the dried grass padding under my bedding, but I could not bear to look at it. It would serve only to remind me of what was never to be.

The Dreamer~ THE BEGINNING

The passing of time only increased my grief as she grew into a rare beauty—a smart and spirited woman of The People. I tried to come up with scenarios in which I was able to prove my love and worthiness to her, but none of them seemed plausible. How could I ever hope to gain her as my mate? Even if she was open to the idea, surely her parents would never allow it.

Pairings between The People and Old Ones were rumored to have occurred, but I had never heard of one taking place, myself. This was all the more important because there were few potential mates for young men in this area. The only other Old Ones within reasonable traveling distance were Uncle Mror, Aunt Vee, and their three sons.

Once upon a time there had been many more Old Ones. More than you could count, claimed Great Gran. But many, including Puh's younger brothers, Zor and Kror, left when the People from the East began to settle in the vicinity. Many were killed in accidents of one kind or another. Some did not survive the perils of childhood. And others, who lost the services of the strongest members of their families—the hunters of large game—to illness, injury, or death, were unable to prepare for the long winters and they starved or froze to death. To find a mate I would likely have to travel somewhere very far away. But Morning Star was the one who dwelt in my heart. I did not want to travel to become paired. I wanted her.

* * *

I had been taught that when you walked through the forest it was vital to be aware of your surroundings. So I dragged my heavy thoughts from Morning Star, my concern for Puh, and the uncertainties of the future. I recalled Puh's words: *You must have a firm, self-assured step and you must appear large and strong, especially when alone. You must appear to be a predator and not the prey.*

But the cheerful sunshine and twittering birds were a welcome distraction after so many moons of seemingly endless gray days. I noted that the leaf buds on the trees and bushes would soon be ready to burst open. Some were in flower.

Without consciously deciding to do so, I checked the patches of early spring greens as I passed by: ferns, asparagus, plantain, dandelion, cabbages, and many others, to see how they were progressing in the warming days. I did not slow my pace; I just noted their state and tried to make guesses at how long it would be before we could harvest the tender new vegetation.

It had been so long since we had any fresh greens that we all craved them. Well, except for the cabbages, which could stay in the ground as far as I was concerned, but Muh would want them. She believed that they contributed to our well-being. She tried to disguise their flavor and smell by soaking and cooking them with lots of herbs, onions, leeks, and anything else that might make them more palatable. But despite her efforts, I did not find that cabbages were a happy addition to our meals.

I carried only a few swallows of water in my water bag, just enough to make it to the stream that was the halfway point between our compound and Black Wolf's home. Then I would not have to deplete my family's water supply, since I knew that they would have to go to the nearby creek to refill the bag often enough as it was. The little stream still had ice at its edges, but it was swollen with melting snow as it flowed vigorously down the slope, jogging out here and there like a silvery gurgling wet snake bent on escape. I stopped to fill my water bag, then made the easy leap across the stream and continued my way down the foot-worn trail.

* * *

As morning progressed and the bright sun warmed the air, I was beginning to sweat, especially where the pack rode on my back. Despite lingering signs of winter where soggy puddles of snow still stubbornly clung to the shady areas, I became hotter yet. I loosened the strings at the neck of my tunic but I could still feel my perspiration as it began to run down my back and down the backs of my legs. I would be arriving at Black Wolf's lodgings before long and I did not want to appear to be a dirty sweaty contemptible Old One in front of Black Wolf or, more importantly, Morning Star. Fortunately, a lake was close at hand and although the beautiful light blue glacier-fed waters would be mortally frigid, I was determined to stop there to wash.

The path to Black Wolf's forged straight ahead, but I took the fork toward the sparkling aquamarine waters. Upon arriving, I laid down my spear and pack and stripped off my clothes. The cool air was wonderfully bracing on my naked skin but the lake itself was painfully cold. The surface of the lake was still partially frozen. Only my fervent amour for Morning Star made me stay in those waters long enough to be sure that I was well scrubbed. I emerged from the lake almost as blue as the waters themselves. Shivering, I sat on my cloak while sultry breezes dried my goose-bumped skin. My cold-numbed brain and limbs slowly revived while I watched the flocks of waterfowl paddle around the surface of the water as they took in nourishment and rested in preparation for the next leg of their northbound migration routes. A large number of ducks, geese, and several pairs of swans were present. Vultures wheeled in lazy circles overhead in the brilliant azure sky, but there was nothing here to interest them. The migrating birds, the herons wading at the shore, the woodpeckers calling out and sounding on tree trunk, the turtles newly emerged from their winter dormancy and sunning themselves on logs—all were aglow with life.

At last, I took my clothing from the branches where I had hung them, dressed, and struck out down the path once again, feeling refreshed and much more presentable. Perhaps I didn't have the slightest chance of winning Morning Star, but I refused to be placed in a position where I might perpetuate the myth of being a squalid Old One if I could help it.

As I regained the main trail, I could hear the faint sounds of an axe chopping wood and smelled telltale aromas from a cooking fire. I quickened my pace, spurred on by the idea of seeing Morning Star and finally getting my mission underway. I rehearsed in my mind what I would say to Black Wolf about my need to find Puh and Uncle Mror. The People did not believe in dreams as we did, but I trusted Black Wolf to listen respectfully and offer his assistance. In our part of the world, it was an unspoken rule that a request for help was never refused. Regrettably, this was not always true outside of our lands, but it was invaluable to know we could count on it here.

Black Wolf's four dogs saw me from a distance and barked excitedly. They had known me since the days of their puppyhood. Although they were undoubtedly fierce with strangers, they were quite friendly toward those they recognized. The dogs charged down the path to meet me, still barking merrily. Upon reaching me, they vied for position to place their huge front paws on my chest so they could try to lick my face.

Black Wolf was outside his dwelling, hacking at a fallen tree with a large stone axe. It was evident he had been chopping for some time. Black Wolf had already limbed the trunk, stashing the branches to the side, where they would be used as tinder and firewood. He had just begun to work on the trunk, which would be lopped into manageable sections. Later, the hefty logs would be rolled to the wood-splitting area to await the attentions of Black Wolf's stone wedge and huge wooden splitting maul. Black Wolf grinned as he saw my approach. Even though my face had just been washed with dog kisses, I did not feel as self-conscious as I might have under other circumstances, since Black Wolf was winded and sweating profusely from his labors. As I dried my face dry with one hand and my sleeve, I could see that Black Wolf was also wiping the sweat off his face. We both grinned as we rubbed our damp hands on our leggings and then embraced.

"Welcome, Tris, welcome!" Black Wolf exclaimed. "What brings you here on a bright spring day like today? You would have missed us if you had come two days ago. We started for my cousin's place in the mountains but turned back because of a late spring snow shower. Little Fawn does not want to travel with our small ones in those conditions. But this heat will soon take care of any remaining snow. Can you stay a while? Where is your Puh? He has not returned, yet?"

Little Fawn was Black Wolf's mate; her name was ironic because she was nearly as tall as Black Wolf, who was very tall even for one of The People. Little Fawn had bland features and tended to be plump; she wore her long black hair in braids, usually in two or three plaits on either side of her head. Little Fawn always moved with a slow plodding gait, as though it required great effort to put her large body into motion, but she was also warm-hearted and affectionate, and took great pains to keep her family and household in good order.

Black Wolf, on the other hand, was a bit more suited to his name. He was an unusually large man with thick black hair worn in multiple plaits that were oiled and stiffened so that they stuck out from tops and sides of his head, giving him the appearance of wearing an enormous spider for a hat. His beard was long enough to reach his chest and most of it was woven into many thin plaits which were then intertwined into an elaborate pattern. Black Wolf had an open, heavy-boned face and an engaging smile. He was a successful hunter who seemed to possess an uncommon luck and he provided well for his sizable family.

Like my kin, Black Wolf and the members of his household preferred to live away from the village where most of The People in this area dwelt. We Old Ones did not go to the village since we were not always well received there. And besides, we liked our privacy and we cherished the peace of living far from the clamor that was usually associated a large gathering of people. Although Black Wolf's family sometimes visited a relative who lived in the village, they also valued their quiet life in the forest. We hunters enjoyed the freedom to seek game and fish to our heart's content; the women and children often pursued smaller quarry and foraged for edible vegetation. It was a good living. Our families were independent, but also interdependent at the same time.

As Black Wolf stood before me catching his breath, his muscular chest heaving and the furry black hair bristling out of the gaping opening at the neck of his tunic. I explained to Black Wolf my dream. He listened politely. He grasped the essentials of the situation immediately.

"So you want to go after your Puh? Well, do not go on your own…your Muh would never…um…we will be heading that way soon. Maybe tomorrow morning, if the sun does its work today. Stay here for now and we will figure it out." He smiled at me kindly. "I can see that you are worried. Do not think on it. If he is all right, there is no harm in taking a trek with us and if he is not, we will find him and do all we can." Black Wolf paused. "So, what do you say to taking that load off your shoulders, setting down your spear and helping me move this tree that so inconveniently fell across our doorway while we were gone? My boys wanted to assist but they are only eight and ten winters old, so I sent them off with Little Fawn and the others to get them out from under foot and to keep from doing themselves a harm. This is not work for children."

I accepted his proposal and borrowing one of his full-sized axes, walked around to stand on the other side of the tree trunk. Since cutting and bringing in firewood was probably our second most prevalent task after hunting, I was very familiar with this chore.

We took turns swinging until the cut was complete, stopping occasionally to touch up the axes' cutting edges. We then moved up the trunk and continued until the tree was cut into workable sections, which were finally rolled across the clearing to his wood-splitting area.

By this time, I was once again covered with sweat and I realized how ridiculous it had been to stop for that dip in the icy lake. Both Black Wolf and I had removed our tunics at some point and we were now well coated with the wood chips and other tree debris that had adhered to our moistened torsos, and which, in Black Wolf's case, had stuck to his profuse body hair.

"Tris, I am so glad you showed up when you did," Black Wolf said as he patted my back. "What with your strength and endurance, you have made this task so much easier for me and I am grateful. It would have taken me another day or two of hard work to finish this by myself. Let us see if we cannot wash away these wood chips." He shook his head as we walked toward the small pond located behind their home, both of us brushing at the wood chips as we went. "Little Fawn will be after me for taking off my tunic and letting those chips get caught in my hair. She will be telling me that they will be all over the house now."

At that moment, we heard the happy voices of Little Fawn and the children as they returned from an outing, each carrying what food they had collected. Morning Star was the first born and she strode in front of the group with her long dark braids swinging. She held a brace of ducks. She was not tall like her parents, but lissome and lithe and a pleasure to watch. Morning Star smiled as she looked our way and handed the ducks to her sister Petal before she ran up to meet us.

"Da!" she said. "Tris! Did you two take that tree away? You are both a mess!"

Perhaps I just imagined it, but despite her words I thought I detected a look of admiration as she looked in my direction and my chest swelled. I had never felt so grown up or so manly.

"Morning Star, that is not a very nice way to welcome your neighbor!" Black Wolf reproached her, but with apparent tenderness. "And yes, we did cut up the tree and carry it away."

"I am sorry, Tris," Morning Star said softly. "I was just so surprised to see you that I spoke without thinking. And Da, I am truly impressed that you and Tris managed to move that tree so quickly," she added with a sideways glance at her father, wrapping her arm around one of his and accompanying us toward the pond. "Is Tris going to stay with us for a while?"

"For as long as he wants," Black Wolf nodded. "He is going north with us. And what with this heat, all the snow on the trail will soon be melted, which means that we may be able to leave in the morning. So go and tell your mother what I have said and help her to prepare for our journey."

"All right, Da." Morning Star squeezed his arm and tiptoed up to kiss her father before turning to run away. She called back to me. "I will see you again at the evening meal, Tris!"

Black Wolf and I watched her graceful form dash back to their family compound.

"Ack, she is a wild one," Black Wolf lamented. "But also a beauty. Although, being that I am her proud father, I am not exactly an unbiased judge."

"She is indeed a beauty," I agreed, well aware that

I too could not be considered unbiased.

"I do not like to think on it," Black Wolf continued, "but she will be ready to be paired this year or maybe the next. Whoever gets her will have a handful. I am going to talk to some of the elders at the next tribal gathering and see if they can suggest any likely young men. I do not want her stuck with any of those layabouts from the village. She is much too good for them."

I could think of no response. I could only say "Oh". But I felt an acute pang that pierced me to my innermost core.

For just a fraction of an instant, Black Wolf looked sharply at my face. His expression became grim. He was silent, but he briefly put a hand on my shoulder and then turned to lead the way down the trail.

We walked to the water's edge, where we removed our footwear, untied our leggings and loincloths, and waded into the pond. Bathing with members of my own people was nothing new to me, but it did not prepare me for this.

I had never seen anyone with as much body hair as Black Wolf. We of the Old Ones have comparatively little body hair and what there is, is pale in color. Black Wolf, on the other hand, had a rather alarming appearance to my eyes. Except for his beard and the wild braids that sprouted out of his head, he had an almost animal-like coating of fur. It was perplexing. What was the point of all that hair? The stories said that The People from the East had traveled from warmer lands to settle here many generations ago. Did the hair somehow protect them from the heat? If anything, Black Wolf had sweated even more than I had while we were working, so that theory seemed doubtful.

Maybe it was possible that instead of growing a great quantity of thick hair on their heads as we Old Ones do, that they instead grew theirs on their bodies? Thankfully, the women of The People did not seem to share Black Wolf's propensity for growing vast amounts of body hair. I did not know if I could have felt quite the same way about Morning Star all this time if I knew that she was going to grow up to look like her father. I shuddered at the thought.

"Are you cold?" asked Black Wolf, "I am still roasting in my own skin. Ack. Look at this." He motioned to all the flakes of wood that stubbornly clung to his upper torso. "Little Fawn will be right…I am going to be dropping wood chips all over the house."

* * *

When we were dressed again, the sun was nearing the western horizon and the air was distinctly cooler.

The weight of clothing on my now-reddened skin made me realize that after so many hours under an open sky and strong sun, my tunic would soon be a painful burden to bear.

Black Wolf and I put away the tools as some of his children played in the clearing in front of their home. Then I picked up my pack, cloak, and spear, and followed Black Wolf to his door.

Black Wolf had built their dwelling into the side of a cliff that had a substantial rock overhang. Using tree trunks, branches, mud, sticks, and dried grasses, he had formed a large and comfortable two-room domicile with a connecting storage area for their food and firewood.

Little Fawn looked at Black Wolf and muttered something about wood chips and then she turned to hug me warmly, kissing my forehead as she did so. Little Fawn was quite a bit taller than I and her tight embrace reminded me that I was grateful to have reached my full height. When I was younger it was somewhat daunting to be crushed to that ample bosom.

"Welcome, Tris." She smiled at me and she called to her six offspring to greet me as well. The children included Morning Star's two sisters: Petal and Sky; two brothers: Swift River and Hawk; and ended with the baby, Dewdrop, also known as Little Rain Cloud in her more temperamental moments. They were all bright-eyed, boisterous, and friendly. This brood, along with their four large and unruly dogs, made for a lively household.

Whenever I visited with Black Wolf's family, the children treated me similarly to a favorite uncle. I was called upon to listen to stories of their latest adventures, allow them to climb all over me or sometimes just to provide a lap in which one of the younger ones might fall asleep. This time, as the elder siblings helped Little Fawn to prepare the evening meal, Dewdrop was placed in my arms. She looked at me solemnly, a finger stuck in her mouth as she drooled copiously.

When Morning Star came in from drawing water, she saw me holding the infant. After she hung the water bag in its usual spot, Morning Star approached us and held her arms out for the baby. I placed Dewdrop in Morning Star's embrace. Morning Star shook her head as she looked at me.

"I am sorry, Tris," she began. "Dewdrop is breaking in new teeth so she is a fount of running liquid most times, and now she has dribbled all over your arm."

Morning Star's apologetic smile dazzled me and I was vaguely aware that a spontaneous sappy grin had appeared on my face in response.

"It does not bother me. I am used to babies," I assured her. After all, I had survived the infancies of each of my brothers and sisters, and my littlest sister, Baby Mi, was nearly the same age as Dewdrop.

Morning Star gave me another broad smile and moved away, carrying the baby on her hip. I stepped back to withdraw from the lighthearted turmoil of meal preparations at the fireplace so that I would not be in Little Fawn's way. Several rabbits and ducks were herbed, stuffed, and spitted over the coals and I could see that there was an assortment of tubers and onions roasting as well.

The delicious aroma made me realize that I was very hungry. Little Fawn was soon satisfied that everything was cooking as it should and she gathered up several gourd cups and the water bag. Little Fawn motioned to Morning Star, putting one of the cups in her hand. Morning Star nodded and gave Dewdrop to her brother Hawk while she filled the vessel and pushed her way through the throng of family members to pass the cup to me.

"You must be thirsty," Morning Star said.

"Many thanks," I replied and drank down the water.

She was right. I was thirsty and, in fact, I could have drunk quite a bit more. Without speaking, Morning Star took the cup from my hand and refilled it several times. Black Wolf and I had not had much to drink all afternoon and we were quite parched. Across the room, Little Fawn was doing the same for Black Wolf as he gave her an account about my dream and my desire to find Puh and Uncle Mror. When at last we had our fill, Little Fawn and her older children carefully removed the tubers and onions from the fire pit to cool, arranging them on a birch bark platter. The rabbits and ducks were added to the heap of food. We all settled down on the layers of skins that covered the floor.

"Let us eat!" Black Wolf said.

Hawk still held Dewdrop and he, too, had noticed her unremitting drool.

"Dewdrop is producing enough slobber it is a wonder that she does not eventually run dry." Hawk laughed. "I think that she has been misnamed, Da. She should switch names with Swift River." He gave his older brother a mischievous smirk and Swift River scowled at him in return.

"Well," Swift River retorted, "I think that you should be re-dubbed *Lumpy*, because I am going to give you a few fresh lumps before nightfall."

Black Wolf gave the boys a stern look.

"There will be none of that. *Eat!*" he commanded.

No one spoke as we helped ourselves to the plentiful food. When all was consumed we each sighed with repletion and the conversation resumed.

"Many thanks," I said to the group, "that went down very well."

"You are always welcome here," said Little Fawn. "It is a pleasure to feed someone with a good appetite such as yourself. And we are so glad you arrived in time to help Black Wolf with that tree. It fell in such a bad spot. We knew that it was dead and that it would come down some day, but we did not know it would land across our doorway and that we would have to climb through a forest of branches to get in and out of the house until it was finally removed."

"Yes," added Black Wolf. "I would never have finished today without your help. Now we can leave for the North Country at first light and see if we can find your Puh and Uncle Mror on the way."

"We will find them," said Little Fawn kindly. I nodded in reply. "Then you can travel up to Cousin Gray Elk with us. Has your Puh told you about Gray Elk? He is famous for his dogs. Folks come from all around to trade for them. Maybe you will meet some of your people up there. After all, you are well past the age for pairing now, Tris. You will need to find a mate soon and start a family of your own."

I did not know how to respond to this. I could not very well choose this moment to announce to the family that I was desperately in love with Morning Star and had never even thought about the possibility of being paired with anyone else. I decided that the briefest answer was the safest answer.

"Yes, I hope so," I said after a moment.

This brought about more talk about our upcoming journey. I listened without comment to their conversations about the places where we would stop. We could make inquiries at the village where someone was bound to have seen Puh and Uncle Mror while they were out and about in the surrounding area.

Little Fawn mentioned that they had plenty of hides and pelts from all the animals they had brought in during the last season. Surely someone will want to trade their bone needles for some of those skins. And they would certainly stop in to see another of Black Wolf's cousins, Eagle Owl. Little Fawn had made a pair of boots for Eagle Owl and he would probably appreciate a gift of cured hides. As a stone knap, Eagle Owl used pieces of leather to pad his thighs and hands as he worked. And maybe they would be able to get some honey while they were there too. Bees were so disagreeable to deal with. It was better to let someone else brave their fury and then trade for the honeycomb.

I was surprised to hear them talk about bees as though they were so very dangerous. Puh and I had routinely gone out to collect honey every fall and although we had to take certain precautions, the bees were not nearly as bad as they made them out to be. Usually, the most difficult part of the process was climbing the tree to access the free-hanging combs which were sometimes affixed to limbs that were very hard to reach. And you had to make your climb with slow, steady movements that would cause no shaking or even slight trembling of tree branches, since bees are very sensitive to vibrations.

Here at last was a subject that I could contribute to.

"Actually," I began, "bees are mild-tempered if you approach them in the right way."

The family all turned to look at me in mute surprise.

"You just have to disguise yourself so that you do not appear threatening and then confuse them with smoke," I continued.

"What kind of a disguise would you wear to visit a beehive?" Black Wolf asked, smiling indulgently.

"Not much of one," I admitted. "The bees will naturally defend their hive from any animal, so the trick is to deceive them into thinking that you are nothing more than a whiff of smoke. Puh and I use sticks to carry a combination of smoking leaves, pine needles and grasses toward the hive, progressively leading the smoke closer and closer over a period of time. Then we leave a very small smoky fire just upwind of the hive, letting the smoke saturate the area before we attempt to take away any honeycomb. We choose a cool day so we will not sweat. We take extra care to wash off as much identifying scent as possible, just as we do whenever possible before a hunt. Then we promptly return to the hive, approaching it slowly from downwind, and stand amid the smoke until our skin is saturated with the smell." I paused. "Next we climb the tree. One of us cuts down a few sections of comb and the other takes the comb and puts it in a sack. The bees might land on us and walk around on our skin, but I have never been stung while raiding a hive."

"Tris, you and Tor are even braver than I thought," Black Wolf grinned. "I assume that you mean you do not wear anything but the smoke on your skin while you are employed at this chore, since you say any semblance of animal hide would bring out masses of the raging insects. How did I never know that you and Tor were tamers of bees? It must be the red hair…red as a fox…no red-haired animals take from the bees! But they see me coming and think that a big old bear is coming to eat up their whole hive anytime I get within ten paces!"

Everyone laughed. It seemed that I was not the only one who had noticed Black Wolf's furry animal-like coat.

"Well, it is not really a matter of courage, it is just the easiest way to accomplish the task," I said. "Besides, in this case there is an additional advantage to being unclothed. If there is anything worse than being stung on bare flesh, it would be having a horde of angry bees trapped inside your clothing."

"Ah," Black Wolf nodded. "Yes…I can see that would be so."

Little Fawn stood and laid the last of the firewood on the glowing embers.

"We will need some tinder and wood for to-morrow's fire before we go to sleep," she said.

"I will get them," I volunteered, rising from my spot.

I had often fetched wood for Little Fawn and I knew just where to go. I was glad for this errand; my legs and backside were becoming numb from sitting so long. I left the room, passing beyond the deerskin curtain to a hallway that led to the large cavern where their wood was stowed. A small amount of light passed beyond the gaps where the curtained barrier did not quite meet the sides of the opening, so I did not need a lamp. I gathered an armload of wood and a variety of tinder in the semi-darkness and retraced my steps to the hallway. I paused to shift the load in my arms to free one of my hands so I could raise the curtain, but stopped in place when I heard my name as Black Wolf whispered to Little Fawn.

"Do not talk about finding mates while Tris is here. I did not realize…I know they have known one another since Tris was a tot and Morning Star was a babe in arms…and his eyes have always followed her, but I thought that was just the natural way of boys who like to see a pretty girl. Today, when I said something about locating a mate for her, he looked so stricken. I feel badly about this because he is the finest kind of young man, but she will want…she will expect to be paired with one of The People. Everyone will expect that. And she is so innocent. I do not think she sees the effect she has on him."

"Yes. You are right. I did not realize this either. I will speak to Morning Star. She has been a woman for a few years now, and we have delayed making arrangements for her future as long as ever we could. Also, it is about time she starts to act like an adult and prepares for her eventual pairing. She still wants to run wild the same as her younger siblings instead of behaving with the decorum of a woman who will soon have a mate to please," Little Fawn whispered back.

I sunk against the wall of the passageway. The pressure of the firm surface against my back made my sunburned skin ache more than ever. There had been no escape from this discussion. I had caught these words even through the jumble of many conversations being held in the main room. The People often forgot that we Old Ones have much sharper hearing than they and I was sure that Black Wolf and Little Fawn had no idea I could hear all that they said. I closed my eyes as

I composed my despairing emotions for a few moments. I reminded myself that this was nothing I had not known for a long time. However, it was still deeply wounding to hear the words spoken, to have my worst fears confirmed.

I told myself I had to stop thinking about Morning Star and concentrate on our journey to find Puh and Uncle Mror. Muh and the rest of my family were depending on me. Puh and Uncle Mror could be dead or injured and it was imperative that we set out in search of them as soon as possible.

 **Chapter Three** 

The bear was intent on us. Snarls, roars, and hot dank breath in my face. Mror suddenly moves to stand in front of me, placing himself between me and the bear...

I awoke with a start, my heart galloping like a stampeding herd of wisents. I had fallen asleep on a mat laid out near the fireplace in the main room. I must have been very tired after yesterday's early start to the day and my tree-chopping labors, because I continued to sleep even after everyone else had arisen. I was alone except for Black Wolf, who was packing a sack by the light of the fire. The dogs whined as though they sensed my distress.

"Tris, what is it?" asked Black Wolf.

I rubbed the sleep from my eyes. My sunburned skin pained me more than ever. I wanted to groan with every movement, but I was determined not to complain. Now I knew why Black Wolf had all that hair. He was not sunburned in the least. I gathered my wits enough to reply.

"It was another Dream. There was a bear. I think Uncle Mror may be hurt. Perhaps badly. I could not see Puh. I do not know what that means."

"Try not to worry, Tris. We will find them soon. Everything will be fine."

"I hope you are right," I said with a nod.

I arose and went outdoors. The dogs were eager to get out as well, but they were waiting for their master to accompany them. The rising sun was brilliant orange and its slowly strengthening rays stained the clouds in soft shades of pink and lavender. An early morning mist was gradually dissipating as the heat of day worked to evaporate the moisture created by the melting snow. The thawing earth smelled pungent as it released all the odors that had been locked in winter's deep freeze. Capricious breezes still bore traces of the duck feathers that had been plucked in preparation for the previous night's evening meal, causing bits of down to swirl in the air around me.

Songbirds chirped happily as though to usher in

perfect weather for the day, but I was still plagued by my Dream. The bear! Uncle Mror! And where was Puh? Why could I not see Puh in my Dreams? What had happened?

Black Wolf came out to assemble their travois sleds: three smaller dog sleds and one large sled that would be pulled by hand. These were packed with animal skins and a variety of goods.

Morning Star then appeared at the head of the path that led to the pond where Black Wolf and I had washed yesterday. I could hear the sounds of the other family members who were still bathing there.

"Hello, Tris," Morning Star said. She did not smile. She looked older. Strained. "Sit down." Morning Star motioned to a chunk of the tree trunk that Black Wolf and I had worked on the day before. I was mystified at her request, but did as I was bidden.

She stood behind me and loosened my hair, much the same as my Muh always did, but that routine occurrence suddenly felt much different and brought about a whole new series of emotions. I felt Morning Star separate the strands into their usual sections and re-twist the curls into cords. I tried to focus on her words and not the fact that her hands were in my hair.

"Mother spoke to me this morning. I wanted to tell you..." Morning Star paused. "Mother says that I am a woman now and I must behave like a woman. I must be a credit to my family. I must do my duty for my family. But I wanted to tell you that you must not mind…you must not mind if I act differently." Morning Star gathered the many cords together into one thick bunch and retied the leather thong around it. "Because I am still me. I am unchanged, in both my mind and my heart. Never forget that."

I took to my feet again and spun to look at her. Morning Star slowly raised her head to meet my eyes and held them in her gaze as if she were searching for something within them. I returned her stare. She had such dark eyes, set in such a lovely face.

Then Morning Star lowered her head and turned, and quickly walked away.

* * *

It was not long before the packing was complete and we began our long trip. We hoped to reach the village sometime after midday. We planned to stop for the night at Black Wolf's cousin's home. Then we intended set out again early the next morning to embark on the next leg, which would last several days as we hiked through the forestland. On the sixth day, we would reach the open plains.

With luck, we believed we ought to be able to locate Puh and Uncle Mror at that point or soon thereafter. I would not allow myself think about what we might find.

* * *

Our group was strung out along the trail, Black Wolf at the front of the line with his lead dog, who scouted ahead for possible threats. They were followed by the older children, who took turns pulling the big travois sled. Next came the younger ones and Little Fawn, who carried Dewdrop in her arms. The sled-laden dogs and I brought up the rear. This protected the youngest and weakest members of the family by situating them in the middle of the procession.

There was little talk, just the pads of our footsteps, the panting of the dogs, and an occasional rattle as a sled went over a bump in the trail. Some of the first insects of the season were out, no doubt hatched in yesterday's warmth. We saw very few animals except the squirrels and other small rodents that quickly fled from us. The larger animals probably heard our approach and moved off to safe distances before we came anywhere near them.

By midmorning, the little ones were complaining of hunger and thirst, so we stopped just long enough to let everyone rest and take a drink. Then we each were given a piece of dried meat to chew on as we walked, and set off once more. Baby Dewdrop was asleep by now and she was lashed to the big sled where she could doze comfortably on the parcel of hides.

I was used to walking all day, but I was thoroughly miserable. My mind wrestled with the horror of my recent Dreams. My beloved was never to be mine. The weight of my tunic, rolled-up cloak, and pack were chafing my sunburned back and chest. My feet were constantly wet and cold from trudging through the occasional patches of mushy snow that covered the shady segments of the trail. I was glad to be at the rear of the group, where no one could see me and question my mood. I just wanted to find Puh and Uncle Mror and go home.

I did not even care if I went to the mountains. I did not care if we met with any dangerous predators. In fact, I felt an equal match to their ferociousness. Any lion or wolf would be sorely tested if it met with me.

* * *

I smelled the rancid smoke and heard the noises of the little community while we were still some ways off. Eventually, the village walls came into view. A long time before I was born, The People had begun to congregate in this place, erecting homes of whatever materials suited the builders. There were several good water sources nearby and the game had been plentiful. They prospered from sharing the results of communal hunts and foraging for other foods. But soon large predators decided that this sizable collection of humans was as attractive as a herd of antelope grazing on the prairie, so they began to attack the humans as opportunities presented themselves. The People then felled many trees and used the logs to build a tall fence. The barricade now looked somewhat the worse for wear, but at least new trees had started to sprout up again. For many years, the area in and around the village looked starkly naked since all the wood had been sacrificed to provide for the construction of The People's homes and for the great wooden wall.

Black Wolf's family began to chatter with anticipation. They were excited at the prospect of their visit with Eagle Owl, and also at the thought of seeing the many sights of the village. I had heard about this place so I was prepared for the piles of burning refuse, the overabundance of people, and the crowded quarters. The homes varied from large stick and mud houses to small hovels that were constructed of animal hides stretched over a frame made of fallen deadwood and mammoth bones. Some of the dwellings were abandoned and in various stages of decay. This was an abysmal departure from the lodgings I was accustomed to, where everything was reasonably clean and orderly. Even the remaining piles of snow were discolored with mud.

The inhabitants looked somewhat insubstantial compared to Black Wolf's robust family and although they were well dressed, they were certainly dirtier than anyone I had ever met outside of the village. This was because they had to leave the village each time they needed to refill their water bags. Evidently, they did not care to tote enough water home to bathe and nor did they often leave the village in order to wash themselves at any of the water sources. I knew that some of them looked down on me for not being one of The People, but I could not help but feel pity for them. They dwelt within their sprawling bulwarks for protection from the wildlife and the elements, but I did not think that they were better off for it and I could not imagine how they could bear to live here for even a day.

We marched straight to the home of Black Wolf's cousin, Eagle Owl. He was at least ten winters older than Black Wolf, gray-haired and slightly rotund, back bowed, and missing an eye. His thick, well callused hands attested to his trade as a stone knapper. Black Wolf once told me that Eagle Owl had been an imposing figure of a man in his youth, but he was badly mauled by a lioness while on a hunt. The scars from the punctures on the side of his face made plain for all to see where the lioness's teeth had pierced his flesh. Not as easy to see were the matching scars from the upper teeth that were hidden underneath the hair on his scalp.

Eagle Owl had been unable to hunt much since then, so he lived in the village—alone—because there was a shortage of nubile females and a man as broken up as he was unable to find a mate. But Eagle Owl was a kind and gracious man, and his reputation for his extraordinary work meant he could barter for food and goods to provide for his living. He had accumulated a large following, as anyone who wanted the very best spearheads and cutting blades had to trade with him. In fact, Eagle Owl lived in a large comfortable house and he was considered to be quite well off.

When we were all settled around Eagle Owl's hearth Black Wolf told him about our quests: mine, to find my Puh and Uncle Mror, and his, to travel to the mountains to see Gray Elk to inquire after new pups.

Eagle Owl looked at me closely with his one eye.

"Who is your Puh? Would he be Tor?" he asked as he scrutinized me.

"Yes," I nodded.

"I thought so. You look much as he did at your age, except that you must be nearly a head taller than your Puh. Tor was here last season to trade for various blades. I well remember his brother Mror also, although I have not seen him in some years. No one could ever forget him. I have heard that Mror became a Keeper of Stories. Your Puh and uncle were the first Old Ones I had ever known. It took me a while to get used to their ways. Especially the soundless laughter; and, as I understand it, you Old Ones also cry silently. As I am told, it is in your peoples' stories that to make noise when you laugh or cry is to attract predators that might attack you." Eagle Owl looked to me for a response so again I nodded.

"Both your Puh and Mror were great hunters," he went on. "So strong, and so fast, too! They liked to go after wisents in the spring to hunt down a couple of the new calves. They would wait until a pack of wolves or some other predator drew the cow's attention from her calf and bag the youngster before the cow knew what had happened. Hmmm, those calves are good eating…it makes me salivate just to think on it! At other times, they brought down deer, horses. And, on occasion, even a full grown wisent or aurochs… but, with two lone hunters, that is unusual because you would only take on such an animal if it charges and you have no choice but to kill it before it kills you…as I am sure you know. If we went as far as the mountains, we would sometimes see them hunting chamois, sheep, or ibex, too. I was there when your Puh received one of the scars on his face. A big ibex buck managed to slash his cheek with one of its long horns before they could subdue and kill it. They were just young men then. Their father had recently been killed in a bad fall. He took a ruinous tumble when they were bringing down a giant deer and he broke his neck. And this was just after their older brother Bror had been killed in another hunting accident. So Mror and Tor, being the eldest surviving boys of a large clan, were the sole providers for their family."

I knew most of this already, but still, I enjoyed

hearing Eagle Owl speak of my family. Again, he spoke of their youth, muttering almost to himself.

"They were so young, barely men." He shook his head at the memory. "We knew their situation, of course, what with Black Wolf being a good friend of theirs. Sometimes we invited them to share our camp with us. Tor was soft-spoken and quiet, like many of the Old Ones, but jolly Mror was talkative enough to make up for it. How I loved to listen to his tales!"

As Eagle Owl seemed to be lost in his reminisces, my thoughts wandered to what my Puh would have been like back at that time, only fourteen winters of age but sharing with Uncle Mror the onerous burden of procuring all the food and household essentials for their family.

Then, turning to Black Wolf, Eagle Owl continued.

"If you go out that way, watch your step at the head of the Canyon of the Cave Bear. Ever since last fall there have been reports of a rogue bear in that area. Most of those bears will avoid men when they can but not this one!" He shook his head. "This one will run you down and snap you in two as soon as look at you. The men have been making treks to the valley and fabricating traps to catch and kill the bear. He will be especially vile-tempered now that he is fresh out of hibernation. No one will be safe in that vicinity until it has been caught."

My Dreams began to replay themselves in my mind's eye. Black Wolf seemed thoughtful.

"Yes, if that bear is awake now—and I am sure he is—he will be on the move, looking for food," Black Wolf agreed. "In that case, I cannot take Little Fawn and the children through the grasslands on our way to Gray Elk's. It is too near the canyon. Tris and I will have to forge on by ourselves."

"Leave Little Fawn and your dear young ones here," Eagle Owl volunteered. "They would be most welcome company for a lonely old man like me. And thinking of having company, I will just step out for a little bit and call on some of those who have promised me foodstuffs in trade for the blades I have made for them. We must have a feast tonight to celebrate your visit!"

Although Little Fawn was not pleased to hear about the bear or Black Wolf's determination to travel regardless of the hazards, she and the children were happy at the prospect of spending some time in the village with Eagle Owl, who would delight in catering to their every desire.

Eagle Owl then left us briefly while he went out to make arrangements and have some special treats brought in for his guests.

"Before Eagle Owl departed on his errand, I asked him to inquire after your Puh and Uncle Mror while he is gone…" Black Wolf said as he took me aside, "but you look as though you have been thrown by a charging wisent. Are you ailing?"

"No," I told him. "It is just Eagle Owl's description of the bear. It is much the same as the one in my Dream. We will leave as soon as it is light tomorrow morning?"

Black Wolf nodded.

By now, Little Fawn had moved to the fireplace and was busily cooking some of the food we that had brought along. This was unnecessary, since Eagle Owl reappeared with a friend and both were carrying armloads of edibles: roast meat and vegetables, cored baked apples filled with a mixture of grains and honey. We all ate until we were too full to take in another bite.

* * *

That night Eagle Owl graciously insisted that Black Wolf and Little Fawn lodge his sleeping chamber and he slept out in the main room with the rest of us and the dogs.

We were comfortable on the soft floor mats while Eagle Owl entertained us with stories of his glorious days as a stalker of prey in the wilds.

"I used to know all the finest hunters," Eagle Owl explained. "It was through them that I learned which types of spear heads and tool blades work best and were the most sought after. I still talk with each of the men who stop in to do trade with me and ask if they have seen or heard of any new hunting tools or weapons so I can get ideas to improve my offerings. But there was a time when I could do my own field work. I did not live in the village then, but a few days' hike to the west. Great groups of us used to travel to the vast plains even farther to the west to hunt big game. Few people ventured that far, so not many animals had ever seen a human before and they scarcely noticed us at first. What a fine land it was! We brought down wisents, woolly rhinos, bears, and mammoths. Even a few lions before that lioness managed to take me down. When I moved to the village I did not bring any of the magnificent horns or tusks that we carried home and kept at the family homestead where my oldest brothers and their families still live, but I do have this." Eagle Owl pulled a cord that hung around his neck from under his tunic to show us the four lion's teeth hanging from it. "These fangs came from the lioness that ended my hunting career. Luckily, my father killed her before she could finish with me."

"I have never had much luck with females of any species." Eagle Owl sighed. "But there is no help for that now. I leave all that to the younger generation." He then smiled at me. "Like you, Tris. You have your whole life ahead of you. You will have a family someday. You are strong like your Puh and tall for an Old One. You have all it takes to be a great hunter.

Your father takes you with him sometimes? Have you made any big kills of your own?"

"Yes," I answered. "Sometimes as part of a larger hunting party but most of the time Puh and I just go out for the day on our own. I have brought down many deer—and a boar once, last fall—but those are the only single-handed kills of a large animal that I can claim."

"Ah! A boar! How big were the tusks?" Eagle Owl questioned eagerly.

I indicated that the boar's canine teeth ranged from the upper tusks that were about the size of my thumb, to the lower tusks, which were slightly larger than my forefinger.

"Good sized!" exclaimed Eagle Owl. "Did you save them?"

I shook my head. It had not been a kill that I was proud of. It was not a beast we would have pursued under ordinary circumstances. It was rutting season and the boar was incredibly musky and rank. The meat would have been so gamey that we only would have harvested it if we were facing possible starvation. Even if we had wanted to bring the meat home to feed Rooph, Muh never would have allowed that malodorous flesh anywhere near the family compound. When the boar charged at me, he came out of the brush from downwind and there was no time to do anything but react. I side-stepped him at the last moment and then whirled around quickly to thrust my spear into its heart, twisting the weapon after it rammed home and the boar dropped skidding to the ground.

It was an extremely fortunate hit. Puh had been close at hand, but by the time he reached my side, it was already dead. Although the boar would feed many scavengers, I felt that it was a terrible waste of a prime breeding animal.

"I suppose that they are still attached to the boar's skull. I know where it is, so I could retrieve them. Do you want the tusks?" I asked. "I would be happy to get them for you."

"Thank you, but no," Eagle Owl smiled. "I just thought that you might have wanted to keep them as a remembrance of your first big boar! Hmmm... if those tusk measurements were the size of the teeth while they were still attached to his head, with two-thirds of the tusk still embedded in the jaws, those ivories would be prizes indeed. Last fall, you say? That would have been during their mating season. Facing huge tusks that are perpetually honed as they plow up the earth to find their food, and wielded by a cantankerous rutting animal that is at least twice, maybe three times your weight is a serious business. That is no mean feat! I can just picture the scene! It is not exactly the same as taking down a bear or a lion, but it is still impressive for a young man!"

Eagle Owl was silent for a moment as he looked me up and down.

"Even for a young man of your size," he finally said. "I mean to say, you may not be exceptionally tall for one of The People; the top of your head reaches a little higher than Black Wolf's shoulder, but the two of you must weigh about the same amount…you have a massive build. Let me see your hand."

I held out my hand and Eagle Owl examined it, turning it over a few times. I had never really noticed before, but seeing my hand against Eagle Owl's made me realize how broad it was and how thick my fingers were in comparison to those of the men of the People.

At last, Eagle Owl laid our hands palm to palm and my hand was clearly of greater size in both length and breadth.

"This is not a hand!" Eagle Owl continued. "This is a paw! The paw of a brown bear!"

I withdrew my hand from Eagle Owl's grasp. I was starting to take offense. As a man of the Old Ones I was used to being thought of as somewhat different, but to be compared with so brutish an animal was beginning to be a bit much.

However, Eagle Owl soon made up for his remark. After adding a little wood to the fire and resettling himself comfortably, he cleared his throat before speaking.

"You must be a very formidable hunter indeed," Eagle Owl stated.

"I hope to be as adept a provider as my Puh," I said quietly.

"If you are not, I predict that you soon will be," Eagle Owl grinned. "No one can match the Old Ones for their predatory skills. And you have had the best mentor that a young man could wish for."

"Yes. I am grateful for Puh's careful tutoring," I agreed.

Eagle Owl seemed to be slowly fading. He kept himself propped up on his mat with one elbow, but his eye was half-closed and he was gradually leaning over more and more. Eagle Owl yawned.

"What I would not give to be back on the grasslands with my father and brothers once again," he spoke. "How I miss those days."

And with that, he lowered his head and drifted off to sleep, to dream of times past when he was whole of body and chased big game, and to re-experience the freedom and exhilaration that filled the life of a young hunter.

Chapter Four

I drive my spear into the brute again and again. The bear turns and takes a mighty swipe at me while hardly breaking his stride. I am running in pursuit.

My eyes opened to see the dimly lighted room and my ears took in the soft breathing of Black Wolf and Little Fawn's offspring, and the gentle din of Eagle Owl's snores. A few of the dogs lifted their heads to look at me, but other than my canine companions, I was the only one in the room who was awake. I rose and carefully stepped over the sleeping bodies to look out the doorway and gauge the day's weather, pausing for just an instant to gaze upon Morning Star as she slept peacefully with her sisters. Then I went to the hearth where my boots were left to dry after yesterday's hike and began to combine the many parts in preparation for today's trek.

I could hear the whispers from Eagle Owl's bed chamber, where Black Wolf and Little Fawn were quietly conversing.

"So," began Little Fawn, "you will head up to your cousin Gray Elk's after you find Tor and Mror and find out if he has any new litters? I hope he has a good selection of pups."

"Well, I do not know about that," replied Black Wolf. "What if either Tor or Mror is injured? We cannot just leave them. We will have to bring them back here or take them home to heal."

"They are dead," Little Fawn said flatly. This statement stopped me in mid-process of tying on my first boot.

"What? How can you say that?" Black Wolf's whisper was hoarse with emotion.

I quickly finished fastening my boot. I considered hobbling outside with just one boot on one foot and going some distance down the path before bothering to put on my other boot so I could flee from these words. I hesitated only because many of the villagers already thought that we Old Ones were odd enough as it was, without giving them more reason to question the level of our mental competence.

"I know you think that the Dreams are silly, but I have heard many tales of the Old One's visions and I believe that they are true. If Tor and Mror have met up with that demonic bear, they are dead. I will be very sorry for it, but there is nothing we can do to change what has happened. So take Tris up the mountain to see Gray Elk. Insist on getting him a puppy while you are there. You know how he loves dogs and he deserves one after working so hard with you the day before yesterday. You would still be clearing away that old tree right now if it was not for his help. He will need something else to think about besides his father and his uncle."

There was a brief pause in the conversation. I hurriedly finished putting together the next boot and I stuffed my foot in, fumbling at the laces with clumsy fingers in my haste to get out the door.

"I do not think you are right," said Black Wolf finally, "but if that is the case, I will do as you say. Give me a kiss now. I will be back as soon as I can." Then he must have given her an affectionate goose or something because I heard Little Fawn let out a shrill squeak that caused the dogs to stir; one lifted his head and uttered a soft woof.

"Go away!" Little Fawn giggled. "Oh, now look at what you have done! You have awakened the baby! If she begins to cry she will awaken the whole household." Dewdrop then began to whimper for her mother.

I sorely wished that I had not heard their discussion. I had both boots on by this time and I moved to stand in the doorway again. The dogs joined me. We peered outside at the slowly brightening skies. There was a glow off to the east where the sun would soon be clearing the horizon. A moment later, Black Wolf entered the main room wearing a mischievous smile on his face.

"I have already said my goodbyes to Little Fawn." Black Wolf said in a whisper as he scratched at his scalp. "She is busy soothing Little Rain Cloud so we can leave as soon as we are packed."

It did not take but a few minutes to gather our gear. Black Wolf did not want to carry food for the dogs, so he ordered them to stay. I wanted to turn back and look upon Morning Star once more but I could not do so without Black Wolf watching me so I simply went out the door.

Thus, we left behind those who were slumbering in the room, and all the sad dogs who sighed as they lay down to nurse their disappointment at being left behind.

* * *

Black Wolf and I set off at a strong pace toward the village gate in the cool early morning haze. Now that we began to put distance between ourselves and the village, I was very glad to be away from the stinky confines of civilized life and back out in the open again.

Black Wolf was still smiling to himself, looking ahead down the trail as though he was happy to be off on an adventure and ready to take on the world. I was relieved to finally be on our way to find Puh and Uncle Mror. We would be able to travel much faster and for longer stretches by ourselves than if we had been accompanied by Black Wolf's entire entourage, which included small children and straggling dogs weighed down with travois sleds. That meant our chances were good to reach the plains in two or three days instead of the four we had planned.

There was more snow here than there was at home but it was patchy, soft, and wet. My feet were soon damp again, but somehow it did not seem as irksome as it had been yesterday. At least my sunburned skin pained me less this morning.

"I meant to tell you," Black Wolf started, "when Eagle Owl asked around while he was trading for food last night, he was told that the last time anyone had seen your Puh and Uncle Mror was back around the new moon. They had passed near the village on their way to the prairie hunting grounds. This is no great surprise, but I thought you should know."

"Many thanks," I replied quietly.

"Aw, Tris, do not brood! It is a grand day and soon we will find your Puh and uncle, and you will see that there was nothing to be worried about."

"I guess I am brooding. These Dreams weigh me down. My Muh talks about visions as though they were a gift, but I would give anything not to have them. That is, unless I could see something pleasant for a change."

"Cheer up!" Black Wolf smiled at me. "You are a young man and you have a lot of wonderful things yet to experience in life. Sometimes it does not seem that long ago when I was your age. Here I am, on this earth for thirty-four winters now, so that would be about half a lifetime ago. Before you know it, you will be my age and you will wonder where all the time went…and where all those babies came from." He paused. "Well, I *know* where the babies came from." He sighed. "Don't I, though."

* * *

At last, we had traveled far enough from the village that the wildlife was becoming less wary of humans and therefore more visible. We turned a corner on the path and startled a herd of roe deer that was grazing on the newly budding leaves. At least forty or fifty animals hurtled across the trail to escape the sudden appearance of the strange two-legged creatures. We could hear them crashing through the brush for some while before the commotion stopped. When we left the path to drink from a small fast-running stream, we met with a very thin young brown bear that looked rather bedraggled. It must have been newly awakened from its winter's sleep and it had also stopped to slake its thirst. It did not linger when it saw us, but promptly turned on its heel and disappeared amongst the trees.

Back on the trail once more, we ate dried meat and a few old apples as we walked, our pace steady and brisk. Later, we saw a huge bull elk run down the path ahead of us, finally breaking from the trail and continuing noisily through the brush with its powerful high-stepping gait. It was just starting to re-grow the antlers that would be truly impressive by the fall rutting season, but even without them the elk was still a remarkable sight.

"All this game," Black Wolf said regretfully, "and no time to go after it."

I nodded in agreement. It did seem ironic that we would see so many animals on a day when we were not actually hunting them.

"We will need to find shelter soon," Black Wolf went on. "The sun will be going down ere long. I know of a nice dry rock overhang where we might camp if we can reach it before nightfall. Those building clouds look like thunderheads. They will likely bring rain and it would surely make sleep a lot easier if we were not stuck out in the open, getting wet all night."

Black Wolf was right. Soon I heard the distant rumble of thunder and the wind began to blow in gusts. My untended hair was now coming free of the cords Morning Star had so carefully arranged and most of it trailed downwind behind me like a wild burst of flame. Black Wolf gave me an amused glance. But I did not feel too embarrassed since his numerous stiff braids looked funny to me at any time that I was apt to contemplate on them.

We were relieved to finally arrive at the ledge before the main body of the storm was upon us. The ceiling was too low to be able to stand upright but it provided a well-protected spot from which to escape the wind and incoming weather. A ring of stones surrounded a depression in the dirt where many fires had brightened and warmed the enclosure over the years. We quickly gathered nearby fallen branches, twigs, mosses, and pinecones and soon had a blaze started. Black Wolf and I sat on our cloaks, rubbing at our eyes which stung from the wind-driven debris on the trail. The fickle winds also occasionally blew smoke in our faces, along with a few stray rain drops. At last the fire was burning well enough so that most of the smoke rose up and away from the enclosure. I reached for my hair and pulled loose the leather thong binding so that I could do something to tame the tangled mass, half of which now hung down in my face. The thong was nearly as long as I was tall, so I doubled it before using it to tie a rough knot around my hair at the back of my neck.

"Why do you not braid it?" Black Wolf asked.

"I guess I could. I can braid rope, so I reckon I can braid hair. We have always simply coiled our hair out of the way. It coils into cords on its own, so it seemed futile to fight nature," I said as I untied the thin strip of leather and, starting at the back of my head, began to weave my hair into one long braid.

"What are you doing? *One* braid? You will never get all that hair into one braid!" Black Wolf's wiry plaits bounced as he spoke. I stifled a laugh and continued braiding. It was not very neat and it was as about as thick as my wrist, but it would keep most of my hair off my face. As I finished tying off the end of the braid, I realized that through force of habit I was lashing it tight as though I was hafting a new head on my spear's shaft. I shrugged. At least the binding would not come loose for some time.

"If you choose to grow your beard longer," Black Wolf continued, "I will teach you how to plait it."

"Many thanks," I replied politely, but noncommittally, picturing the startled looks I would receive from Muh and Puh if I were ever to appear before them wearing a long beard and sporting the fantastically woven patterns that Black Wolf and many of The People wore in their chin whiskers. We men of the Old Ones only grew out our beards for warmth during the cold weather seasons. Other than that, our beards were shorn as closely as we could cut them without also cutting our faces, which was maybe a finger's width in length. Puh and I had ours trimmed with the coming of spring, so at present my beard was very short and I was rather enjoying the respite from having all that hairy bulk on my face.

* * *

The night sky was frequently splintered by flashes of lightning and the air was shattered with crashing claps of thunder. Rain plopped heavily on the ground outside the shelter as we warmed ourselves by the fire. The flames danced on errant puffs of wind, while the sparks of embers were carried upwards on an eddy of hot smoke. We sat shoulder to shoulder as we ate more dried meat, a few nuts, and some thoroughly wrinkled old apples. We had pushed hard in order to cover as much ground as we could and we were more than ready for a restorative night's rest. It was not long before we fell into a deep asleep.

* * *

I am cold and wet. A thunderstorm rages overhead. I desperately try to catch as many raindrops as I can in my mouth and in my cupped hands. I am hungry and still so thirsty. The earth keeps caving in all around me.

Unlike the Dream, the morning found me warm and dry. The thunderstorm had blown over, leaving cool air behind it. We groaned and stretched as we left the shelter, finally able to straighten up for the first time since we had arrived at the ledge the previous evening. Black Wolf and I packed and set out at a bold pace, eating breakfast as we walked.

"With luck," Black Wolf spoke, "we will find your Puh and uncle before nightfall."

"I am hoping for that luck," I said earnestly. "We must be more than half-way to the grasslands by now."

"We will come across another stream sometime after the sun reaches its zenith. There we can replenish our water bags and drink our fill. That will be the last place where we will be able to get potable water for a while. There are a few ponds on the grasslands but I dare not drink from them. The mammoths muck about in those ponds. Putrid waters. Ugh." Black Wolf made a face to show his distaste.

I paused as my nose informed me that we must be near a fire. Too, my ears were struggling to decipher faint sounds.

"I smell smoke. I hear voices," I said.

Black Wolf looked at me with mild astonishment.

"You do?" he stopped and listened. "I do not hear or smell anything. But if good fortune is with us, maybe it will be your Puh and Mror."

"Yes," I nodded, but I was doubtful that these voices, which were becoming ever louder as we drew closer, would belong to men of the Old Ones. Not even Uncle Mror at his most animated would get carried away enough to make that much noise. Then, sniffing the air some more, I added, "Someone has been roasting deer meat."

We walked a little distance. The sun rose higher in the sky. A couple of does ran toward us as though we were not there. We watched wide-eyed and with hands itching to thrust our spears as the deer disappeared into the woods behind us. By now, we both could smell the smoke and I had been able to distinguish words in the conversation for some time.

It was not Puh and Uncle Mror. It was a group of four men, men of The People, cooking their breakfast and chatting as they sat around their fire. They stood as they saw our approach, each one raising a hand in greeting. We returned their salute.

"These are men from the village," Black Wolf whispered to me. "I do not know them well but I do know them well enough to ask for information." To the group he called out, "Pleasant morning to you.

Have you seen any hunters or travelers while you have been in this area?"

They all shook their heads. They were wet and they stood around the fire, huddled under their damp cloaks in the chill morning air.

"We have not seen anyone else since we left the village five days ago. We have been doing a bit of hunting and will head back today. After that massive thunderstorm last night, it will be good to be home and enjoy the warmth of the hearth again."

"Yes," agreed another, "our lean-to blew over in the storm. We re-anchored it, but not before we and all our gear were drenched. It looks as though you two came through it all right, though. Sit down and share our breakfast. We have some leftovers from the deer carcass we roasted on a spit yesterday afternoon and we are baking some tubers in the hot coals."

"We cannot stay," Black Wolf stated. "We have to keep moving, but I do thank you for your offer of hospitality."

"Well then, have a good journey and be watchful if you plan on venturing near the Canyon of the Cave Bear at the head of the prairie. An especially vicious cave bear rambles around that place and it killed and injured several men last fall. I think that it likes all those caves and crevices in that rocky terrain. Some people think that this cave bear has even taken to killing its own kind. I hear that other bears were found up there…dead bears…killed by something big."

Black Wolf nodded grimly in response.

"Again, I thank you and I wish you a good journey as well," he said.

"Yes, many thanks. Good journey," I chimed in.

The men pointedly stared at me, but I was used to this. Because most of The People did not often see many Old Ones, we were a novelty to them. I did not mind their curious stares as long as there was no malice behind them. After all, I am apt to stare at something I have never seen before, too.

I was not surprised to hear what they said when they supposed we were out of earshot.

"Did you see that hair?" one began. "I have never seen that color hair before! It was orange-ish red! Tawny red as a summer fox."

"And in addition to that hair, he was huge!" remarked one of his companions. "I have never heard of any men of the Old Ones to be so tall! He must have stood nearly as high as you do, Red Buck. I knew they were built much stouter than we, but such a neck! I have never seen the like except on a bull aurochs."

"I did not know the Old Ones to be so pink," another added, having taken note of my sunburn.

"And he has such strange eyes…green as the leaf of a willow tree," still another piped-up. "How do you suppose he sees out of eyes such as those?   Would everything take on a green tint?"

"Bonehead!" the first said. "Does everything look brown to you because your eyes are brown?"

The rest of the words were lost to me. I was amused that they mentioned my height, but not Black Wolf's, who was considerably taller than I. I turned to look at Black Wolf. His blank expression told me that he had not heard their conversation.

"Well, Tris," he said to me. "It was not the right group of men, but we will soon find the ones for whom we are searching. I would think that your Puh and Uncle Mror should have started home by now. Maybe they are on the trail already."

"I expected to meet them late yesterday or this morning, but maybe they were delayed. Maybe they waited out the storm in a shelter somewhere."

"Possibly," Black Wolf agreed. "Your Puh knows better than to be caught out in a thunderstorm."

I smiled and nodded. That was true. My Puh was the smartest man I had ever known. Though he had a gentle presence, he was tough and strong. He had lived on, hunted, and explored these lands all his life. He knew the animals and their habits, their strengths, and their weaknesses. I tried to remember all those things and push the terrible Dreams out of my head. I told myself that Puh and Uncle Mror would be fine.

* * *

The air began to take on a different smell and the temperature was steadily dropping, but it was comfortable weather for hiking. Each time the trail took us through an open glen in the forest, we could see the white-capped mountains in the distance. There were still deep piles of snow in the shade of the trees but the rest of the ground was clear, although it was squishy under our feet due to the heavy rain and the snow run-off. We saw numerous tracks in muddy areas, mostly comprised of those belonging to small animals, but also many which were left by deer, elk, and even a wisent. Later, we identified some wolf tracks and one perfect imprint of a lynx paw. In several places, large animals such as bears and wisents had wallowed in the mud. But there were no signs of men. I comforted myself with the thought that the rain would have erased all but the most recent tracks.

When we reached our next planned stop at the stream, we paused to drink as much as we could. The water was incredibly cold but thirst-quenching. We unpacked our water bags and filled them as much as we dared until each was nearly the size of a man's head. After holding our water bags under the stream's surface to refill them our hands were blue and numb. We both blew on our fingers and rubbed our hands to warm them before attempting to tie the bags closed. Then they were inserted into small sacks and restored to our packs. We were back on the path again in a matter of moments. We were very aware that we would have to walk fast to make it to the prairie by nightfall.

As the sun was setting and we found ourselves still trekking through the woodlands, it was bitterly disappointing to realize that not only would we not find Puh and Uncle Mror today, but we had fallen short of our destination. The wind was gusting in heavily from the north, making the trees sigh and sway. The temperature fell still further.

"We will need to make a camp tonight," Black Wolf announced.

I pointed to a grove of birches that looked starkly naked against the dark green of the fir trees. The birches' few remaining desiccated leaves rustled and shivered in the wind.

"Over there," I said, and I walked to the spot.

Some of the birches were little more than saplings. I experimentally bent a few this way and that to find a place where they could be bowed to meet at their tops and then I lashed them together to make a frame for our shelter. Next, I used my hatchet to cut fir boughs to make walls that would block most of the wind and a floor to keep us off the soggy ground.

Black Wolf watched me for a few moments.

"I remember your Puh doing this when we were boys!" he exclaimed. He began to cut boughs from the fir trees as well. We started by placing branches at the bottom of the walls and worked our way up. It was a small enclosure and we would have to sleep curled-up on our sides, but it was quite cozy.

It was almost dusk by the time we completed the last step, which was placing a thick layer of dry grasses over the fir boughs on the floor. By then our hands and hatchets were sticky with sap from the fir trees, but rubbing our hands and axe handles with bee's wax helped to remove most of the tacky substance. After we crawled through the low entrance, the grass wanted to stick to us as well. But there was nothing to do except to sit in the increasing darkness and try to find a spot where the fir boughs did not poke into us excessively from underneath. Our spears were too long to bring them completely indoors; thus, we laid them down between us, with the spearheads and a significant portion of the shafts sticking out beyond the doorway. High winds prevented us from starting a fire, and anyway, we were too weary to care. So, Black Wolf and I huddled under our cloaks and decided to have something to eat and drink before going to sleep.

"Tris, this brings back memories," Black Wolf said. "When your Puh and I were boys, never did I think that one day I would be doing this with his son."

He stopped to take a bite of dried meat and chewed for a bit. "Your Uncle Mror and I were the same age. Your Puh was younger and started out as sort of a tag-along with us." I was surprised to hear this. Because Black Wolf's hair was still as dark as a moonless night and his face was relatively unlined, I had thought that he was at least a few winters younger than Puh.

Black Wolf went on. "But as Mror grew older and spent more time away with your Aunt Vee's family to help them bring in meat—they had no surviving sons, remember, just Vee—your Puh and I grew to be pretty thick. Even though your Puh was busy starting his family long before I was, we still managed to maintain ties. He paired very young, you know. That is, very young for those of us of The People. You Old Ones achieve your full size and adulthood quite a few years before we do. But he had not yet even reached fifteen winters. These days you might not think so, seeing his scarred and weathered face, but your Puh once had a countenance as fair as yours. And your Muh was considered to be a great beauty. They were an uncommonly handsome couple and they so doted on one another that no one could bear to refuse them the right to pair in spite of their youth. Also, it bolstered their cause that by then your Puh had already been functioning as the head of the household for some while after Mror left to pair with Vee. He may not have attained fifteen winters and official manhood yet, but he had certainly been carrying the load of a mature man."

I smiled. I always enjoyed hearing about what Muh and Puh were like when they were young. At the same time, I could not help feeling envious of their evident freedom from complications that would have prevented them from sharing their love for one another.

"And besides," Black Wolf continued, "it was strongly suspected that they were already lying together. You were proof of that. You followed not too many moons after the pairing ceremony and then your brother Dak came the year after that. He and your Muh were already working on their third baby by the time Little Fawn and I were expecting Morning Star. But unlike Mror, who out of necessity became more and more entangled in his mate's family affairs, Tor and I grew to be closer than ever. Especially after most of my family picked up and moved some distance to the northwest to find open land and escape from the spreading influence of that pestilence of a village. At that point, Tor became the only other man with whom I had contact on a regular basis. He is like a brother to me. I *know* we will find him and your Uncle Mror. I just know it."

"How do you know?" I asked.

I wondered at his rock-solid faith in a positive outcome. I wished I would have a Dream that Puh and Uncle Mror were happily sitting around a campfire, stuffing themselves with freshly roasted meat, talking over the details of the day's hunt, and laughing at Uncle Mror's tales.

Black Wolf took another bite and chewed as he considered his reply. Little sighs of wind whispered between the tiny gaps in the pine bough walls. A fox cried out eerily somewhere in the distance as I awaited his response. He shook his head.

"Because I just cannot bear to think of any other outcome," Black Wolf began. "Your Puh and Uncle Mror and I grew up together. Tor and I have raised our families together. They are the only real friends that I have ever had."

Chapter Five

The vultures linger nearby. A lone lion circles round and round. The vultures will not stay away nor will they come close enough to allow me to catch them. Wolves come and stare with their yellow eyes, trying to decide if they can get to me. Ripples of color fill the skies. I am so cold. The ground crumbles more and more.

The waning moon was fading in the early morning sky. Although I was unnerved by the Dream, I felt reassured by the thought that we would find Puh and Uncle Mror today. Black Wolf and I moved quietly around our camp, getting ready to hit the trail once more. I thought it seemed that Black Wolf's persistent optimism was beginning to crack. He looked serious and haggard. I was oddly cheered. I could sense that Puh close at hand.

The sun would be nearly half way up by the time we entered the grasslands. It was good to walk and loosen up all those joints and muscles that had been kept nearly immobile as we slept in our little shelter, too crowded to even turn over or change position. Black Wolf and I ate our breakfast of dried meat as we walked along, now and then absently brushing at the dried grass bedding that stuck to us from head to foot.

When we finally came to the edge of the forest, I drew in my breath at the grandeur of the panoramic vista that unfolded before us. The tall grasses were sadly yellowed and somewhat flattened after a long winter under the snow, but waves of colorful spring flowers rippled in the unceasing winds. Far across the great expanse, the distant trees and rugged snow-veined mountainsides provided a stunning backdrop under a procession of startlingly white peaks. I had been here many times before, but this sight and that of the immense blue skies with their ever-changing clouds never failed to inspire awe in me.

We scanned the scene for any signs of human activity. We saw a long-stripped horse carcass that had been torn apart and spread out over a large area. It looked as though it might have been a lion or wolf kill as the tracks of both animals filled the site. We noted that there were no indications of tool marks on the bones, or signs of a methodical butchering that would show it might originally have been the work of men. However, it was hard to tell for sure after the predators and various scavengers had finished with it.

Over to the west and looking tiny in the great distance, a small herd of mammoths stood bunched together near a swampy pond, drinking and looking for aquatic plants on which to graze. To the east of us, but again, a long way away, was a mixed gathering of horses and a few ibex bucks. And farther still, were many deer and a lone elk who were attempting to gain fodder by nibbling on new shoots of grass or the leaf buds on the brush at the edge of the tree line. A little closer, wisents could be heard snorting, grunting, and stamping their feet at us. They had nothing to fear. We would keep well away. They looked shaggy and were shedding great patches of their woolly winter coats. Many of the cows appeared as though they would be ripe to give birth soon. Several calves were already present, sometimes bawling to their mothers and scampering after them in an effort to keep up. I instinctively looked for any scavengers that might be feeding on a recent kill. This would likely lead us to our first clues as to where we might find Puh and

Uncle Mror, since they would be attracted to carcasses left behind by successful hunters.

The trail continued through the plains but it was not as easy to follow here. The resilient grass was prone to reestablishing itself quickly and we had just the barest notion of where to go to follow it. Out in the open where we had no protection from the tree cover, the hot sun soon warmed the air and aggravated the fading burns on my exposed skin. Insects swarmed freely. The worst were the merciless gnats and tiny black flies. I lost count of how many times I was bitten.

We kept watch for lions. They were the most dangerous predators we might meet in this place. They were stealthy and powerful, and blended with the dead grass remarkably well. Black Wolf and I each kept a spear in one hand and a hatchet in the other. Lions often hunted in cooperation with one another, so it was helpful to have more than one weapon at hand in order to fend off multiple animals at once.

To my astonishment, Black Wolf suddenly started singing. Loudly. He saw my wonder and said quickly, "It scares most of the predators away!" He continued to belt out his song in a booming bass:

The mighty hunter is bold and brave
The mighty hunter does not mind a cave

The mighty hunter does not easily scare
Not even if it is a big old bear…

His repertoire included songs of long-lost ancestors, songs of love, songs of animals, and songs of celebration. He must have been right because we did not see any predators. What wildlife we did see—other than the persistent biting insects—promptly ran or flew away. He was also correct to be apprehensive. Since there were only two of us, predators that might seek to avoid a larger group of men would be considerably less hesitant to attack just two or three.

At last, we saw the vultures. They were circling over an area by the canyon recently made so notorious by the infamous bear. Black Wolf elbowed me.

"Let us go and see what those vultures are watching," he pointed up at the large avian forms as they soared overhead in the bright skies. After a pause, he continued, "I know that is near the cave bear's valley, but I am more concerned about the possibility of lions being over there than just one lone bear. Those birds may be waiting for lions to quit a kill so they can move in for their share."

I nodded. We left the path and began to cut across through the clumps of grasses, low shrubs, and the undulating ocean of flowers. I constantly scanned the scenery for the slightest hint of movement that would betray the presence of lions.

Then something else occurred to me. Snakes.

"We will have to watch for vipers and asps that might be sunning themselves on the rocks, too," I said.

"Yes. It is good that you remembered them," agreed Black Wolf. "I had completely forgotten that the snakes would be emerging now that the weather has warmed. Although they still may be groggy, I would not care to test their sense of humor."

"I do not think that they have a sense of humor at any time of year."

All at once, I heard a voice that almost seemed to originate in my head.

"Black Wolf, I think I hear someone."

Black Wolf had resumed his song but he abruptly stopped singing. We both listened. Black Wolf looked at me questioningly. Then I heard a whistle, long and wavering, as though the note was struggling to get out. But I knew that whistle!

"It sounds like Puh! That way!" I pointed toward the entrance of the canyon.

Burdened as we were with our packs, cloaks, hatchets, and spears, we quickened our pace to a lumbering run in that direction.

The canyon was situated between the rocky slopes of two mountains. It was one of the many passes that gave access to the larger plains on the other side of the range, but it was actively avoided by most men. The terrain was treacherous and it was almost devoid of life. It had been called the Canyon of the Cave Bear because the loose, rocky soil provided easy digging for bears, which in turn allowed them to create their dens. This was an important feature in a land where, even on the warmest days, permafrost existed once you dug down more than a few feet into the loam. Sometimes lions were seen in this area, too, as they were apt to take over any old lairs that had been vacated by the bears. This fact did not improve the canyon's reputation.

There were no more whistles and Puh's voice had been so faint that I had to stop periodically to renew my bearings.

"Puh! Puh! Where are you? Puh!" I called out to him.

"Why, Tris! You do have quite a set of lungs on you!" Black Wolf said to me with a smile. "Your spoken words are so quiet that I never realized you do have quite a voice when you choose to throw it." Then he turned his attention to our mission, cupping his hands to his mouth and shouting, "Tor! Tor!"

We were getting closer. Now I could hear Puh's words, but they did not make any sense.

"Come to the tree. You will see it. It is the only tree inside the entrance to this canyon! But when you get to the tree, stop. Be sure to stop. Do not come any nearer." Puh sounded very hoarse. Had he been shouting and whistling for a long time?

"All right, Puh. We are coming." I called to him so he would know I understood.

Black Wolf could not yet hear Puh.

"What is he saying?" Black Wolf inquired, wearing an anxious expression on his face.

"He says go to a tree and stop there."

"What tree?" Black Wolf asked.

"I do not know. But I hear running water so it may be there is life in that canyon after all."

Then we saw it: a trampled spot in the grass. We ran to the scene. Puh and Uncle Mror's travois sled had been ripped apart and flattened. The skeletal remains of a wisent calf were strewn all over the place. Faint watery blood-splashes stained the grass but they could have been from the calf.

We followed drag marks so well etched into the earth that even the rains had not washed them away. We were being lead toward the opening of the canyon.

Again, Black Wolf and I broke into a run until we had to start climbing up and over scattered boulders and rocks to continue. While looking out for snakes I noted up-turned tufts of grass and rocks, and saw that more blood had congealed in those sheltered areas.

"Look at this," Black Wolf said, stooping to pick up something. It was a knife. He passed it to me so I could examine it. "This is not your Puh's?"

"No," I confirmed. "This is not Puh's. Perhaps it belongs to Uncle Mror?"

It was similar to Puh's in that the handle was made from an antler, but it was a slightly darker color and the blade was formed somewhat differently. It showed signs of recent use. I tucked it into my pack and we resumed our scramble up the steep canyon entrance, leaving the plains behind.

As we came to a place where the canyon yawned to expose a small valley, the tree came into view. It was a large black alder, looking lifeless in its leafless state. There, a tiny trickling spring bounced down the surface of the stone face behind the tree, creating a place where there was a little grass, a few alder saplings, and sparse bushes.

"Puh, we are here. Where are you?"

We stopped at the tree trunk, as instructed, but Puh was nowhere to be seen.

"Tor?" Black Wolf shouted once more.

Black Wolf and I scrutinized the slopes that surrounded the apparently empty area before us. No breath of wind stirred the little foliage that kept a tenuous hold in that unforgiving soil. Except for the soft burble of the spring, everything was still and the air temperatures within the confines of the canyon walls were well on their way to becoming decidedly hot.

"Tris!" Puh's voice rasped out. "Black Wolf! Stay by the tree! Do not move."

It was then that I noticed the broken soil, scattered sticks, and mangled clumps of grass not far from the base of the alder. I nudged Black Wolf and pointed to the disturbed patch of earth. Nearby, and almost indiscernible from the rest of the confused landscape, was an enormous mound of earth that appeared to have been excavated from the canyon floor some time ago.

"There is a trap," said Puh, as he struggled to be heard from the depths of the hole. "The ground is very fragile. You could fall in."

"It will be all right," I assured him, wondering how long he had been imprisoned down there. I looked for the safest way to approach the trap, but what I found was Puh's spear lying on the ground near the brush. The shaft was so deeply cracked that it was almost fractured into two pieces. I picked it up and turned it over in my hands, and then saw that the side which had not been exposed to rain was still coated with dried blood. I showed it to Black Wolf.

"Tor's spear," he said, "it has been well used."

I decided that the only way to get to Puh was to shed all my gear to remove any excess weight. I also stripped off my bulky tunic because I was now sweltering in the day's heat after that race across the prairie and climb up the sheer slope. I wiped away the beads of sweat that had formed on my forehead, and then went down on all fours and began to crawl toward the opening in the ground.

"Get ready to grab my ankles if the rest of the trap gives way," I said to Black Wolf.

"Tris, stay back!" Puh demanded in a voice that must have been so ravaged with thirst that by now he could barely project audible words. "Do you understand me? Stay away!"

As I moved forward, I could feel the remains of the trap's camouflaged covering flex beneath me and I flattened myself, inching carefully ahead. I could hear Black Wolf lower himself to the ground as well, but he stayed near my feet. He understood that he would be my anchor if the remaining top structure of the trap or the crumbling ground beneath its edges began to disintegrate. As I neared the pit's ledge I could discern the fetid odor of decaying flesh.

Finally, I reached the splintered rim of the fissure and found myself peering down at Puh. He shaded his eyes and squinted to look up into the glare of day. Despite his warnings to keep back, he grinned at the sight of me, his smile deepening the creases that lined his face.

I was relieved to see him standing there in a beam of sunlight, but dismayed to see his condition. He was covered with dust and dirt. His eyes and cheeks were hollow and his lips were cracked. He had huge gashes across his chest, and his blood had soaked the front of his clothing.

I extended an arm to reach toward him, using my other arm to help distribute my body weight over the fragile surface, but he was much too far down to come anywhere near touching him. As my eyes adjusted to the pit's shadows, I saw the source of that unmistakable reek of corruption. I was stunned to see a huge bear lying lifeless at the bottom, its fur looking scruffy as it was molting its undercoat. Then my heart sank to see what appeared to be Uncle Mror, pinned almost completely under the bear. Dead. Puh could see that I had grasped the situation. We looked at one another wordlessly, my arm still dangling over the edge of the pit. Tears for Puh's suffering and poor Uncle Mror's demise came to my eyes but I forced myself to concentrate on rescuing Puh. First of all, Puh needed water. I did not want to ask any questions of him or give him any reason to talk until he had a chance to take in fluids.

"Black Wolf," I said, "would you hand to me one of the water bags? Carefully. The ground here is just a frail platform suspended over a pit and it could collapse at any moment."

"Is your Puh all right?" Black Wolf asked, placing one of our partially filled water bags into my waiting hand. "Here, give this to him."

"Yes, I think so," I replied. Moving as smoothly as possible, I brought my encumbered hand to the edge of the pit. "Puh, can you catch this?"

Puh nodded so I gently lobbed the water bag at him. Puh caught it, fumbled with the ties to open it and eagerly took his first sips. He cautiously let the water swirl around in his mouth before he swallowed, but he choked and gasped on the liquid as it went down. The next sips went down a little easier.

I watched Puh drink and drink, letting the water wet the inside of his mouth each time before swallowing. Finally, he cleared his throat, drank, coughed, and cleared his throat again.

"Many thanks," he said. "I am so very glad to see you." His voice sounded low and husky, but it was stronger already. "I have been down here for six days and five nights. This bear..." Puh motioned to the dead bear "...attacked poor Mror and me when we were just getting ready to butcher a wisent calf. Brave Mror, he tried to shield me but it grabbed him and began to drag him off. I pursued and repeatedly lanced the bear with my spear, but it just turned to swipe at me and kept going as though it had not felt a thing. I followed, with Mror still struggling to escape its jaws. I hoped to get an opportunity to take a lethal jab at the bear. I tried to position myself where I could do the most damage, and then, just as I was lunging to drive in my spear, the ground gave way beneath us." Puh paused, brought the water bag to his lips, and drank once more. He shook his head at the horrible memory. Puh's voice was calm, but his eyes betrayed much sorrow and said much more than his words conveyed. "You cannot see them because the bear takes up most of the bottom of the pit, but it was full of standing spikes. I landed on top of the bear so I was not injured, but Mror and the bear were impaled on the spikes when they fell."

My mind reeled. I could hear Black Wolf moan quietly in his grief for Uncle Mror.

Puh cleared his throat several times before he could continue to speak.

"I have had plenty of time to think of a way out while I have been stuck down here. The edge of the pit is too soft to stand on it and pull me out, but if you and Black Wolf made a rope and slung it over that tree limb, you could hoist me out while standing at a safe distance. I am sure that the men who dug this trap must have used the same branch to lower and raise themselves, and remove the soil from the depths of this hole. It must have been a very tedious process."

"Yes," I said. "That would work. You must be hungry."

Black Wolf was already passing to me various food items, probably the first things he laid his hands on: a very tired-looking apple, a small bag of nuts, and another containing dried meat. I dropped these down to Puh.

"Many thanks," he said again.

"Tris, do not move," Black Wolf spoke. "I think our tunic material is sturdy enough to make a reasonably strong rope. I can whip it up by cutting apart our tunics and working in any of the long strips of leather we have with us."

I took in his point right away. Ordinarily, we made rope from any number of plants or by slicing thin strips of bark off bushes, but that process was too time-consuming for this application.

Luckily, our clothing would provide a much faster option. Our leggings and loincloths were made from very light flexible skins so that we could wear them and move about in comfort, but our tunics were made of thick heavy elk hides that we hoped would hold up the weight of a full grown man. That said, we could—all three of us—give up the rest of our clothing, too, if it was needed to get Puh out of there, but we would try the tunics first. I could hear Black Wolf beginning to slice the garments apart and into strips.

Puh pulled his tunic over his head, balled it up, and tossed it to me.

"You will need more than just two tunics. Take mine, too," he said.

I nodded and, shifting only the arm I had used to catch it, passed the tunic back to Black Wolf. My initial thought had been that I would help Black Wolf assemble the rope, but then I realized that any movement on my part might make the side of the pit fall in on Puh, and take me with it, since Black Wolf was no longer hovering by my feet.

Puh was eating and still drinking, slowly but determinedly. He started on the old apple, and then, after he consumed a handful of roasted nuts, took small bites of the dried meat, closing his eyes as he chewed and taking frequent sips of water. In between mouthfuls, he resumed his story.

"If you had not come today," he began "I do not know how much longer I would have survived. If I had any tools with me, I could have eaten the bear as a last resort but I had only my spear and I lost that as we fell. I was using my knife to begin work on the calf when the bear found us. It must be somewhere on the ground back by the sled. If there had been any workable stone that I could knap into a tool, I might have made a blade, but this pit is just lined with dirt and gravel. I expected to die here since no one thought that I would be home for some days yet, and would not begin to look for me until the time of the new moon. How did you come to find me?"

"Puh, I Dreamt…I Dreamt of the bear…of Uncle Mror. I could not see you in my dreams but I could feel you."

"You are a Dreamer." Puh smiled with comprehension. "That is good. Gran always said that you were different, that you had the qualities of a Dreamer in you." He tiptoed up and reached futilely for my hand and I again tried to touch him, but when ledges of soil started to drop I froze in place. Puh took another drink of water, ate another bite of meat. He seemed to be regaining more vigor with every moment. "Your mother and siblings were well when you left them?"

"Yes, they are well," I answered. "They are eager for you to come home again."

"It is ready," Black Wolf announced. "I am going to toss one end of the rope over the tree branch, pull it down and then, using a stick, I will push the rope down the limb toward you, Tris. You guide it down to your Puh and I will hoist him up."

"Yes," I replied, and waited for the rope to make its way down to me. I felt the rope hit the center of my back.

"That is as far as I can push it to you," said Black Wolf, "unless I can find a longer stick. There are lots of dead branches on the ground over here but none of them are very big. Can you get at it? It is right at the middle of your back."

"I think I can touch it." I slowly rotated my arm at the shoulder until I could put my hand on the end of the rope, and then gently pulled it forward along the length of the branch until I could ease it down over the pit. "Puh, can you reach it?"

Puh stretched up and grasped the rope.

"I have got it! I am holding on! I am ready, Black Wolf!"

As Black Wolf began to heave on the rope, my back and head were pelted with bits of the alder's bark, catkins, and a few old cones. The branch creaked under the strain.

Puh was climbing the rope as fast as Black Wolf was hoisting him. Dirt and dust came off him in little clouds with every move. I was thrilled to see Puh finally emerging from the depths of the trap.

"Tor, you are almost there!" said Black Wolf when Puh was clear of it. "Take my hand and I will pull you away from the pit. After you are on the ground I will haul Tris back by his feet." Black Wolf stepped closer to the trap in order to help Puh to safety.

"Many thanks, old friend," Puh spoke a moment later. "Many thanks, Tris."

"Rest Tor, now that you are above ground again. And eat and drink some more. We can refill the water bags from that little spring before we go."

I was still as I waited for Black Wolf to grab my feet. More tree litter fell on me as he experimentally jerked the rope ends as they hung from the tree branch.

"This is a nice strong rope! Our womenfolk will be annoyed to see what we have done to our tunics, but we can tell them that not only did these tunics help to save a good man, but now we can use it on our next hunt to hang up and bleed our kills!" Black Wolf said, giddy with the success of Puh's rescue. "I could hang up a sizable buck with this rig!"

There was more yanking on the rope, more falling litter and then Puh suddenly cried out.

"Black Wolf!"

I felt the small outer limbs of the tree branch come down on my back, just as I had a glimpse of Black Wolf as he tumbled headfirst past me. My arm shot out for him and I felt more dirt crumble into the pit from under my chest.

Puh quickly pushed the broken sections of branch aside and instantly took hold of my ankles with a painfully strong grip. I had Black Wolf by the wrist and I was looking down into his terrified face. For the first time, Black Wolf had seen Uncle Mror and the dead bear, and the sight testified to the ugly fate that potentially awaited anyone unfortunate enough to fall into the trap.

"I have you," I said. I started to extend my other hand, but stopped as the edge of the pit gave away a little more.

"The branch broke!" Black Wolf gasped.

"But I have got you. Puh has a hold on my feet. Can you pull yourself up?"

It was very difficult for Black Wolf to climb up my extended arm, hand over hand. He was struggling to get a good grasp but even Black Wolf's enormous hands could not encircle my thick arm. Plus, his sweaty hands and my perspiring arm did nothing to help the situation..

Black Wolf kept slipping back down and each time I had to re-clasp him by the wrist to stop him from falling to the bottom of the trap. I tried to assist him by pulling back on my arm to shorten the length of his climb, but it was very awkward to heft Black Wolf's full weight in that way. It seemed as though there ought to be something more I could do other than just lay there, unable to do anything but keep him from dropping into the pit.

It was becoming increasingly apparent that Black Wolf was a heavy man and that neither of us would be able to hold on indefinitely. The brittle trap cover under my body was showing signs of breaking apart and the earth at my end of the pit was now sifting away faster than ever. If we did not move quickly, I guessed that both Black Wolf and I would be swept into the trap within a very short time. But after a moment's inspiration, I thought I had come up with a likely solution.

"Black Wolf, grab hold of my braid and pull yourself up." I instructed.

"What?" Black Wolf looked startled.

The sweat on my forehead was now starting to drip off the end of my nose and the drops landed on Black Wolf's face with fairly regular splats. He blinked.

"Grab my braid," I repeated. "I will raise you up higher so you can get a good grip on my braid. Then you can pull yourself up and climb over me."

Puh was now sitting on my lower legs, holding on to the backs of my knees.

"Yes, once you get up over the ledge, then I can help you the rest of the way," he added.

Black Wolf did not need to be told a third time. I drew him up as high as I could and he shifted his grip from my arm to my braid, which was hanging down my shoulder past the level of Black Wolf's face.

I felt the shock of his weight suspended from my hair, but it was a minor consideration at the time. Grunting with effort, he swiftly climbed up and I first put an arm around his torso, then braced his knee and, in turn, his foot, each time pushing to heave him up towards Puh. Next, I felt Puh lean to reach for Black Wolf and yank him forward. I winced as one of Black Wolf's boney knees was planted into my back. Both Puh and Black Wolf were partially on top of me for a moment before they rolled off and onto the dirt. I was very glad to be free of their weight and also, the discomfort of their hard knees and elbows jabbing into my flesh.

Then, I heard the whoosh of falling soil and felt the rush of wind that was being blown up into my face as the trap's earthen ledge displaced the cool air at the bottom of the pit.

Puh and Black Wolf each clasped onto one of my ankles and quickly tugged me clear of the side of the trap. There, the three of us lay on the ground where we came to rest, with Puh and Black Wolf still at my feet, too spent to move.

"That hair! I will never look at it the same again!" Black Wolf panted. "It makes a fine rope, even better than the one I had made. Tris, I am so grateful for what you have done." Black Wolf paused and looked at me for a moment. "I owe you my life."

"And I owe both of you mine," said Puh.

Black Wolf turned to Puh and waved his remark aside.

"You owe me nothing," Black Wolf said to Puh. "You have repaid that debt just now. But Tris? I owe him my life many times over. If Tris had not caught me as I fell, had not continued to catch me each time I slipped, how would you two have gotten me out of that trap? If I was not first buried alive, I would have starved to death before that tree grew another branch that was big enough to pull me out or Tris's hair grew long enough to reach me at the bottom of the pit.

Hang a buck?! Bah! I should hang myself next time and make a proper job of it."

"Well, you know what that means, Black Wolf!" Puh chuckled soundlessly. "You weigh more than a buck!"

"Come to think of it, I am sure I do." Black Wolf nodded. "Maybe not as much as red deer buck, but certainly more than a fallow or roe. I wear their hides and I have eaten enough venison that I am probably more deer than man. But I do owe you, Tris. What can I give you?"

Black Wolf looked me in the eye knowingly. I knew what he meant. He knew what I wanted more than anything and I desperately yearned to tell him *Yes! I want Morning Star!*

But it was not right. Black Wolf was speaking in the excitement of the moment and I could not let him make a promise that he might later regret, not even to gain the woman I loved.

I held his gaze firmly as I reluctantly made up my mind.

"You are too generous. I cannot." I told him.

"But I am offering. I insist. I want you to tell me what you wish for. If it is in my power to grant it, I will."

"I would feel as though I were taking unfair advantage. But think on it until the coming of the new moon and then, if you still insist, ask me again."

"All right," said Black Wolf. "Agreed. But in the meantime, I *will* insist on giving you a puppy. Little Fawn was speaking about doing just that before we left the village. We can discuss the rest with the coming of the new moon."

Puh was hanging on our words. He knew exactly what we were talking about.

Chapter Six

The three of us were now covered with dirt and bits of detritus. My overtaxed arm and upper body muscles trembled from the strenuous exertion I had expended as I attempted to extricate Black Wolf from his predicament. We lay on the ground under the tree as we recovered our breath and rubbed our aching limbs. I noticed that Puh was gently probing the slashes on his chest. I moved closer to him.

"Are you badly hurt?" I asked.

"I had hoped to be able to see the wounds more clearly now that I am up where the sun is shining," Puh replied. "I do not think I am seriously injured. But you are a little scraped-up."

Puh motioned toward my chest and stomach. I looked down and saw that I had numerous shallow scratches which were weeping blood after being dragged across the ground over sharp pebbles and sticks.

Puh stood up and walked to where the water trickled down the rock and began to cleanse the blood off his chest and lean belly. When I joined him to wash the dirt out of my small cuts I could see that the slashes on Puh's torso looked clean and had already begun to heal. I also noted that there was a lot of dried blood on the front of Puh's leggings and booted feet.

"I cannot be like this," he muttered. "Every predator within a day's hike will come looking for me."

Puh took off his boots and untied his leggings so that he was stripped down to his loin cloth. His pale freckled flesh looked startlingly white compared to the weathered skin on this face and hands.

Puh began to scrub the blood from one of his leggings under the running water, occasionally stopping to mix in sand to provide abrasion. It was a laborious process.

"I will help. Give me one of your leggings," I said.

"I will take the boots," Black Wolf offered. "This is not the first time I have had to wash blood off clothing and it will not be the last. But you are right. This is prime lion country. It is no place to be walking around leaving a scent trail that smells like dinner."

"I saw a lion yesterday," Puh began. "At least I think it was yesterday. All of the days rather blended in together. Yes…it was yesterday and she was a lioness. She stalked round and round the pit, looking at me every moment, trying to figure out if she could get me out. They are such great jumpers that I have no doubt she could have leapt down, killed me as easily as a rabbit trapped in a hole and, even with my weight and bulk in her jaws, would probably have been able to leap back up to the ledge. But her problem was that the fragile overhang would have prevented her from getting out again. After a while, she gave it up as a bad idea. Then last night, a pack of wolves came sniffing about. They too eventually decided that I was not worth the risk and they left, but not before causing a small landslide on one side of the trap."

"That does not sound restful," Black Wolf said.

"Those must have been sleepless nights," I agreed, again noting Puh's reddened, fatigued eyes.

"Yes, mostly. I did not get much sleep while I was trapped because there was nowhere to lie down. What little rest I did get was while sitting on the bear's flank with my head on my knees. And anyway, I was afraid to sleep lest I was caught unawares and entombed by an avalanche of earth. But I did not want to sleep. I thought it was my final night in this life. I watched the moon and the stars make their journeys across the sky. I saw the Northern Lights…or maybe I only dreamt of them…I may have been hallucinating at times." Puh paused. "And, as I watched the night grow old and the birth of a new dawn, I reflected on all the days I have lived, all those whom I love so dearly and would leave behind...my beloved Awna…all my children. I cannot tell you how thankful I am to be delivered from that trap."

I stopped scouring Puh's legging long enough to touch his shoulder.

"I am glad as well, Puh," I said.

Puh gave me a weary smile and patted my hand.

"I am a lucky man to have a son such as I have in you and a friend as I have in Black Wolf." Puh turned to grin at Black Wolf.

"I would say that we are all lucky men this day," Black Wolf agreed, smiling back at Puh.

We arranged Puh's leggings and boots on bush limbs where they could soak up the rays of the sun. We would need to occasionally take the leggings down and roll them in different directions to keep the leather soft and pliable. While we waited for his damp clothing and footwear to dry we brushed ourselves off, washed the grit from our faces, and then sat down to eat and drink. Puh looked pensively toward the pit.

"I am very glad to be out of there. Besides the obvious reasons, a bear dead six days does not smell like a blossom in spring," he mused.

Black Wolf sniffed at the air toward Puh and wrinkled his nose.

"Just now, neither do you," Black Wolf stated.

"If it had not been so cold at the bottom of that pit, the odor would have been much worse." Puh continued as though Black Wolf had not spoken. "Intolerable, as a matter of fact; it was bad enough as it was." Puh was silent; he seemed to be thinking for a moment. He soon resumed, "That trap is a hazard for anyone who comes through here. You cannot see it until you are right upon it, even now that it has been sprung. Before we leave, I would like for us to go up there," Puh pointed up the steep embankment on the other side of the pit, "and push at some of the boulders until they start to roll down the hill. I think they will hit more boulders and lumps of earth on the way down. With luck, we will loosen enough rock and dirt to fill in most of the hole. And it will give poor Mror a burial. When I first fell into the trap and hoped I could find a way out, I had planned to also remove Mror so that he could be brought home and properly buried. I tried to get him out from under the bear, but the spikes that impaled them made it impossible to separate the two. Besides, the more I moved around in the pit, the more the walls collapsed in on me. But this way, even if we cannot bring him home, we can at least protect him from the scavenging vultures. For all the lioness and the wolves made the hairs stand up on the back of my neck, those vultures were the worst thing I had to deal with down there. They were not after me—at least not yet—but they were very eager to…to try…" Puh stopped in mid sentence but then went on. "All the same, if any vultures had actually come down into the pit, I would have done my best to catch them. They would have at least provided some sustenance."

I shuddered inwardly at the thought of tearing apart a vulture and eating it raw. I had sampled vulture once and even cooked, the flavor was underwhelming.

"Do not think on it, Tor." Black Wolf clapped a massive hand on Puh's shoulder. "Yes, that is what we will do; we will knock down some rocks and earth, and be done with it. Then we will go back to your sled and see what we can salvage. The wisent calf is long gone and digested, and probably any food you may have packed for the trip as well. But your cloak, your tools, and other gear should all be there somewhere."

* * *

When Puh's things were mostly dry, he donned them again. His movements were still stiff and a bit shaky but his expression was grim and determined. Black Wolf picked up Puh's broken spear and gave it to him.

"Do you want to keep the spear's blade and haft it to a new shaft?" Black Wolf asked.

"No." Puh shook his head. "This is an unlucky spearhead. It could not help me to save my brother. I will leave it in the trap with the bear where it belongs."

And with that, Puh tossed the spear into the pit.

Black Wolf, Puh, and I set about packing our gear and carefully skirted the sides of the pit to the lower slope where we began to ascend the steep canyon walls.

We moved slowly and carefully, staying on solid rock surfaces as much as possible and testing every step before we put our weight on each foot. By the time we reached the plateau, we were winded.

It seemed odd to look down on the trap from this perspective. The pit looked so tiny and harmless from up there, no more than just a dark hole in the ground. We surveyed the boulders to find those that might best suit our purposes and came to an agreement on which ones to roll down onto the canyon floor.

Some of the boulders we tried to dislodge would not budge. They were too deeply embedded in the soil. We had nothing sturdy enough to pry them into motion, so we had no choice but to push and shove with our bodies.

We were successful in rolling nine large boulders and many smaller ones, as well. After each one trundled and bounced with an accompanying rumble down the canyon wall and the dust finally settled, we saw that the landslides not only filled the trap, but also covered the roots of the alder tree and partially buried the bushes.

We gazed down upon the results of our work.

"He was a good brother," Puh remarked quietly. "He was a good man."

I tried to expel from my mind those last images of Uncle Mror as he lay pinned beneath the dead bear and attempted to remember him as he was in life: a vibrant, robust, and powerful man. He was of medium height much the same as Puh, but he had a solid roundish build without actually seeming fat, with muscular arms and legs as thick as tree trunks.

However, despite his daunting physical appearance, Uncle Mror had a perpetual glint in his eye and a jovial demeanor. As a Keeper of Stories he was a famously consummate storyteller, too. And, as he had so doubtlessly proved in the end, he had both courage and heart. It did not seem possible that a spirit so full of vitality should be gone from this earth.

We stood in place, lost in thought for a few moments. Then, we each in turn picked up our belongings and began the treacherous descent back down to the grasslands.

* * *

The air was rapidly cooling and the sun was well into its decline by the time we reached Puh's sled. As Black Wolf had guessed, anything edible was gone, but under the demolished sled were almost all of Puh and Uncle Mror's belongings. Puh's and Uncle Mror's packs were both damaged as the scavengers had torn into them to get at the food, but using the tip of his knife blade as an awl and cured gut to sew the holes,

Puh managed to restore his pack sufficiently enough to make it usable.

"I will save these things for Mror's sons so that they will have something tangible with which to remember their father," Puh said as he stowed Uncle Mror's things. This reminded me that I still had Uncle Mror's knife in my pack. I retrieved it and placed it in Puh's hands.

"Black Wolf found this," I said. "I think it is Uncle Mror's."

A series of emotions played across Puh's face as he looked at this oft used tool.

"Yes. It is Mror's," he spoke soberly. "Many thanks."

"What about your sled?" Black Wolf asked. "Do you want to salvage the reindeer skin covers? Or the remnants of the poles?"

"We may as well take away whatever we can," Puh sighed. "If nothing else, we can always burn the broken poles for firewood."

"Well, we will have to find somewhere to spend the night," Black Wolf remarked. "We can head back to the little birch and fir tree shelter Tris and I built yesterday, but we will have to hurry to get there before dark. Can you make it all right?" he asked.

Puh nodded.

"I will make it." He paused. "I am grateful for your tremendous, resounding voice, Black Wolf. Had I not heard your singing, I would not have known to call out and whistle for you and Tris."

"I am glad for that," Black Wolf laughed. "I will remind you of it next time you roll your eyes at me when I start to sing."

"Are you going to start singing right now?" Puh asked with a grin.

"Yes," Black Wolf replied.

Oh, there was a big old wolf, his color it was black
And there was no animal in the forest that he could not track...

* * *

It was nearly dark by the time we reached the little shelter where Black Wolf and I had spent the previous night. Even before we arrived, I knew that it would be much too small for the three of us. Working quickly and easily together, we took down the original hut, selected a small clearing within the birch grove, and then constructed another, larger sanctuary from the same elements.

There was little wind that night, so we had no misgivings about building a fire. We harvested flaky strips of birch bark from some of the larger birch trees for tinder. The oily bark had many uses. If the weather conditions had been wet, it would have made a good roofing material for our shelter. The bark was easily made into baskets and trays, too. Sometimes we distilled the bark to make birch tar for waterproofing things, such as the soles of our boots.

We also produced birch oil, which was another fine agent to make things moisture-repellent, as well as a good topical ointment for wounds, burns, and insect bites. Birch oil was good for preserving the wooden handles of our tools and spears, and it had many other practical applications as well.

But tonight, the thin, slightly scraped and pulverized slices of birch bark simply provided us with a tinder that enabled us to quickly start a fire. We were weary and more than ready to sit in comfortable warmth as we drank water and ate our evening meal.

"There goes the last of my sled poles," Puh said, putting the rest of the broken sled frame on the fire. Although the poles were a complete loss, we did find that the reindeer skins that made up the floor, sides, and top of the sled could be used to cover all the fir bough mats which would keep us off the damp ground as we slept. It was would be a tremendous improvement over the grasses that Black Wolf and I had used.

"We will need to hunt soon," Black Wolf pointed out. "We still have some dried meat and fish, and a few roasted nuts, but I do not want to let our supplies dwindle too much more before we go after a fresh meal."

Puh and I nodded in agreement with Black Wolf.

"Tomorrow," Puh said, "we will go after the first creature we find that does not eat us first."

We were very hungry. The nutrient-dense foods we had carried on the trail had sustained us, but they were never enough to fill our stomachs. Puh and Uncle Mror had likely planned to gorge on meat the day they had killed the young wisent in order to make up for several days' diet of trail food. Then Puh had gone without eating for at least five days while he was in the pit, so he must have been feeling even more in need of food than either Black Wolf or I. Puh had been alternating between nibbling at food and drinking water all day, almost since the moment we had found him, which further depleted our stores. Fortunately, there was much game in this area and there was plenty of clean water nearby.

"After we fill our bellies a few times, then what?" Black Wolf asked. "Tris, Little Fawn, and the children, and I were planning to go up to see my cousin Gray Elk to look at his pups and breeding stock. I had hoped to maybe bring back a male pup or two, but that was before we heard about the bear. Then Tris and I left Little Fawn and the children at the village to visit with Eagle Owl and set out by ourselves."

"You heard about the bear? I wish I had," Puh stated, shaking his head.

"I guess you had not been up this way since last spring," Black Wolf speculated.

"I had not. As you know, sometimes I return with my family to hunt sheep, goats, deer, elk, ibex, and the occasional wisent or aurochs, but last summer we stayed at the coast longer than usual. There were a lot of easy pickings: fish, seals, shellfish, eggs from sea birds, fruit, berries, whalebone, shells. We even dug up some clay where the surf had bared a wide gray layer of it in a dune and we made oil lamp pots. But this vein of clay had too much sand mixed in. Some pots broke on the way home because the clay was too fragile, even after baking it. The old clay and shell lamps that we already had were better. At least my little girls Saree and Twie had fun playing with it and Awna used the clay to encase fish before baking them on hot coals." Puh paused as he added more wood to the fire, carefully placing each piece in a way that would allow the fire to breathe. "Anyway, we had brought down three elk, maybe twenty deer, and lots of small game, too, all close to home. We had no need to venture all the way to the prairie and would not have come this time, either, except that Mror and I were itching to get out on a trek after a long winter of hibernating. Plus we were hungry for wisent calf."

"Wisent calf meat would be very good right now," Black Wolf agreed. "I did not hear about the bear either until we arrived at the village. They said that bear had made a reputation for himself the previous fall and they claimed they had set traps for it."

"Well, they caught it, all right." Puh looked perplexed. "I have never heard of a cave bear that behaved as did this one. They usually eat plants, nuts, and berries. It completely ignored the dead calf, although it would have been more typical for a bear to take over another's kill and scavenge anything it could get off it. Cave bears have never bothered us before, unless it was a sow with little ones in tow. And even then, she will just stand her ground and huff at you. Maybe feign a charge to scare you off. You just do not hear about them being so aggressive. But I suppose that animals, much the same as men, can go mad."

"You have had a bad time of it, Puh," I said. "We should rest here for a few days until you are ready to travel."

There was a mumble of assent from Puh and Black Wolf. We had been conversing while lying in semi-prone positions and now we were teetering on the brink of consciousness. I did not think I could keep my eyes open for much longer. That night I was relieved to sleep a dreamless slumber.

Chapter Seven

I awoke at dawn to the sound of rustling outside our shelter. Dim light filtered through numerous tiny gaps in the walls. Black Wolf and Puh were still dozing. I peered into Puh's face. Puh was breathing deeply and easily and his lined visage looked thoroughly at peace. Although Puh's cheekbones were still quite prominent, he appeared less drawn and his complexion seemed to have a somewhat better color than it had the previous day.

Moving silently, I sat up and leaned toward the opening of the shelter. I could see that something was ambling through the dried leaves in the shadows under the trees. After a few moments its rodent face poked into a pale sunbeam and I recognized the quills on the top of its head and shoulders. I slowly reached for my spear. The plodding porcupine was still unaware of my presence. I waited until it had wandered into the clearing in front of our shelter and had nearly completed its crossing before I darted out with my spear, stabbing it in the body behind the right foreleg. It squealed sharply, but only for an instant. The spear had gone right through its chest and come out the other side.

The porcupine's cry startled Puh and Black Wolf into wakefulness. It would be a more than sufficient breakfast and they were well pleased. Puh and Black Wolf began to build up a large blaze in fire pit.

Using my knife and Puh's skinning blade, I worked to carefully prepare the porcupine carcass to be roasted on a spit. I removed the spiny skin that was surprisingly fragile, considering how intimidating the long quills seemed on the outside, and gutted the creature. Then I lopped off the head, paws, and tail. Black Wolf immediately took the liver from me.

"I am going to cook this for your Puh right away." He then presented to me a newly-made spit. "I have arranged the spit's frame over the fire pit, so it is all ready for the carcass. I have also peeled some slender branches for these." Black Wolf picked up the small heart and kidneys, which he impaled on the sticks and took them to be cooked over the red coals.

Puh wanted to share the liver with us but Black Wolf and I refused his offer. I am not as enthusiastic about porcupine meat as I am about some other kinds, both because of the taste and, like most small game, it lacks the level of body fat that we usually strive to attain to meet our own energy needs. But this large rodent would help fuel our efforts to bring down something more substantial.

When the meat was ready, we ate eagerly until the bones were picked clean. I carried the carcass and the other porcupine remains some distance from our shelter so that the scavengers and predators would be less apt to be attracted to our camp. Then we sat down to discuss our plans for the day.

"I am already anticipating our next meal and this is the perfect time to go looking for it." Puh grinned.

I grinned as well; I was so glad to see that the spark had returned to his eyes.

* * *

We decided to comb an area within a relatively short walk from our shelter. We would hunt until the sun had begun its trip across the western sky and then we would turn around and head back from wherever we were at that time. We did not bring much with us. We left even our cloaks at the shelter so we would not have to carry their bulk. Puh, Black Wolf, and I were bare-chested in the bracingly cool morning air, but the day's warmth would soon catch up with us. In the meantime, I was shivering, and for once I was envious of Black Wolf's preponderance of body hair. We each carried our spears, a sheathed knife, and empty sacks for transporting meat. We also stuck hatchets into the ties that secured our loincloths around our hips. We walked slowly, stepping carefully and quietly. We did not speak. We communicated with one another only through looks and motions. Our eyes constantly canvassed the woodlands for signs of any animals that might be using the area.

The skies were bright and a breeze shook the newly emerging spring foliage. Many birds warbled and chirped from the waving branches of trailside brush and the trees overhead. The ground was too littered with dead leaves and pine needles to see much in the way of tracks, but we did see a few tufts of winter wool caught in a bush and we came across a shed deer antler that looked as though it had been lost last season.

A little later, we saw deer in a single-file procession, threading its way between the trees, but they were too far away to pursue. They bounded off as soon as they noticed us, but we were not disappointed since deer were not our preferred quarry today. At this time of year, deer hunting required a lot of waiting by a game trail from a perch in a tree, and it was usually an uncomfortable perch at that. Puh and I would usually pick trees on either side of a trail so that the deer would have to walk between us and then we would each launch our spears into the unsuspecting victim. Deadly force and accuracy were needed or you could end up chasing a wounded animal for quite a long distance. Some natural law seemed to dictate that they never, *ever* ran toward our dwelling. Thus, it was always a very tiresome journey to bring home the eventually dispatched animal. And if luck was not with you, you could wait all day and still return with no meat.

* * *

Eventually, I heard soft snorting and shuffling sounds. I looked at Puh and Black Wolf. Puh had stopped and was looking back at me. He held up a hand to indicate to Black Wolf that he should stop too.

We stood there, listening and sniffing the air. I pointed at some plowed up patches of earth and dead leaves. Puh and Black Wolf nodded to show that they understood. Boars. More than one. Many more than one.

This was probably a large sounder, that is: a group of farrowing sows nesting nearby with their offspring, and it was likely that they had been disturbed from their daily snooze by our approach. Boars have poor eyesight, but they have exceptionally keen hearing and sense of smell. I suspected that the sows may have become conscious of our proximity and were snorting to show their agitation.

We started moving ahead again at the same slow, stealthy pace, our spears at the ready. The snorts grew more audible but we still could not see them. I was fully expecting that one or more of the sows might charge out of the brush at any moment in an attempt to drive us away from their nests.

"I will pick one," Black Wolf whispered. "Nothing too big, that is for sure. I will stay at its head and keep it busy. I will leave the rest up to you two." He paused. "I would give anything to have a couple of my dogs with us right now."

We nodded in agreement. Ordinarily, Black Wolf's dogs would keep the boar or sow distracted until one or two of us could get behind it and grab its hind legs and then flip it over on its back while another would put his spear though its heart. But this time Black Wolf would take the place of the dogs.

Our plans were shattered when all of a sudden a veritable herd of large dark hairy shambling bodies burst out of the undergrowth uttering wild piercing cries.

Black Wolf, Puh, and I each scrambled up the nearest tree and climbed to safety as the sounder continued their rampage through the clearing. They were impressive animals that ranged in size from littlest striped youngsters to that of a moderate bear. Their bulky physiques looked oddly out of place on top of those skinny legs and dainty hooves. With us out of sight, they seemed to forget the cause of their initial panic and they soon began foraging in the ground cover, digging with their tusks to find food. Although boars are primarily nocturnal, this sounder must have decided to feed for a period before returning to their nests. We watched them until they had moved off, keeping track of which ones had ventured away from the main body of the herd.

"That one," Puh whispered to us.

Puh indicated a lone black sow whose shoulder would have been about thigh height on me. An ideal choice would have been a smaller animal, but she was the only one that had fallen significantly behind the rest of the sounder. Plus, as a sow, she at least would not have the huge tusks or gaminess of the males, although her incisors would still be formidable.

We climbed down from our roosts in the trees and began to stalk her, taking care to stay downwind and stepping in the newly churned soft earth that was noiseless beneath our feet. Black Wolf moved to walk in between Puh and me.

She did not realize that we were in pursuit until we were almost upon her and then she wheeled to face us. As Black Wolf had said, he met her head-on, driving the spear into her upper snout. The tip of his spear plowed a furrow into the flesh along the hard bone and as he kept pushing forward the spear entered into the corner of her left eye socket.

In the meantime, Puh and I rushed in from the sides. She was too big to easily flip over and her sharp flailing hooves would have posed serious hazards, so instead we drove our spears into the vulnerable areas just behind her forelegs.

I felt the shaft of my spear flex as she struggled violently and I shifted my grips closer to her body to lessen the strain, just hoping that my spear would not break before she finally passed from life.

She screamed and squalled as we kept her pinned by our weapons. She repeatedly lurched backwards as she tried to escape, but we stayed with her.

At last, the sow's legs collapsed underneath her and after a few death throes, she lay still and silent. Puh, Black Wolf, and I stood there panting, momentarily afraid to ease our grips on our spears. It seemed ironic that an animal that had been so vigorous only moments ago was now so completely inert.

"Sows are good eating," Black Wolf said between gasps for breath, "but I do not like to kill them. The noise always gets to me…the insides of my ears feel as though they might burst. Why do they have to scream like that?"

"Well," Puh turned to Black Wolf, "she sees a huge creature with even more black fur than she has, so of course she is going to scream."

Black Wolf laughed heartily, in spite of himself.

"Much to my chagrin, I often have that effect on women." Black Wolf said ruefully.

"No, my old friend," Puh grinned and elbowed him, "those women scream with delight because they see a big strong maker-of-babies."

We butchered the sow on the spot, placing the haunches, shoulders, back meat, heart, liver, and kidneys in sacks. We suspended the sacks from a long section of sturdy deadwood, which Puh and I shouldered between us on the hike home, to keep the blood from dripping all over us during the trek. We regretted that we had to leave much of the meat on the carcass, but it was only practical to take what we could use. If we had been hunting close to home, we would have returned with the whole gutted carcass, but this time we took what we could eat in one sitting. The rest would feed the woodland scavengers. Nothing goes to waste in nature.

Our reverse trip back to the shelter was much faster, since we made no attempts at stealth. We moved at a quick steady pace, buoyed by the thought of tonight's feast. After enlarging the fire pit, we reused the same spit that had roasted the porcupine and began to cook the organ meats. Then we added additional spits so that all the meat was roasting at once. The dripping fat produced bursts of savory scents with each hissing plop that fell onto the hot coals. The smaller organ meats cooked quickly and were greedily devoured. After the organ meats were gone, we were still so hungry and so tantalized by the aroma of the cooking meats that we lost patience and sliced off the crispy parts on the outside of the roasts and ate them, even though we burned our fingers and the insides of our mouths in the process. All was consumed by the time we went to sleep. We were happy and our stomachs were completely engorged.

* * *

We decided to stay at this camp for one more day to rest, digest, and make plans. Puh looked well except for the healing slash marks on his chest, although he still seemed perhaps a bit more gaunt than usual.

By now Puh had heard the whole story regarding my first dream. I also divulged my conversation with Muh about making the trip with Black Wolf and his family to go to Gray Elk's so as to not injure his pride. Puh chuckled at our concern for his dignity.

"I do not have the Dreams, but Gran does, and they are not to be taken lightly," he said. "If you have seen something in a vision, Tris, that is all the explanation I need."

"Now I feel a little silly," Black Wolf admitted. "I should have known better than to think we needed a story to come out on this mission. But I still wish to go up to Gray Elk's if you are up for it, Tor. Or do you want to start for home?"

Puh ruminated on this question for several moments.

"Poor old Rooph will be lucky to make it through another winter or two," he broke off and put a hand on my knee. "I am sorry, Tris. I know you love him, but a dog's life is only too brief and Rooph has already had a long one." Turning back to Black Wolf Puh went on. "So we could use another dog if Gray Elk has any young pups we might like."

"I would be surprised if he does not. And remember, I have promised to give Tris a puppy. You might even like to select several pups that will one day help to pull your sleds."

"No," said Puh. "Just one. What with two sons and four daughters at home we do not have room for any more than one or two dogs."

"Ack," Black Wolf grinned, "where is your sense of adventure?"

* * *

We had little sense of adventure that day. We were almost too full to move. We lazed around the camp, looking over our gear and assessing how much longer our water and dried food supplies would hold out. We could renew our water bags tomorrow on our way to the mountains since we would encounter numerous streams, but we would need to hunt again before we reached Gray Elk's.

As we lay out our various pieces of equipment, we saw that almost everything was still in good shape. The exception was Black Wolf's spear. An inspection showed that he had broken off the tip of the blade when he had struck the sow. If there had been no other alternative, he could have reworked the tip and knapped a new point, but that would have taken much of the length off the spear head.

Since there were plenty of fir and pine trees in the area from which we could harvest pitch, we used some of our time to cook a batch of glue so we could haft fresh blades to our spears. It was instrumental that we found a slab of stone with a shallow concave surface that could be placed among the hot coals in the fire pit.

When the stone's mass had absorbed enough heat, gobs of sticky pitch and bee's wax were added, along with ash from the fireplace and pulverized dead grass. This made strong glue that helped keep the new spearheads securely attached to the shaft. Lastly, the heads were hafted in place with strips of cured gut. We saved the leftover glue by twirling a small stick in it, building up layers until the stick had a glob of dried resin at one end that could be heated and reused. We then touched up the blades of our knives and hatchets to complete our hunting preparations.

* * *

I awoke the next morning fortified with a distinct feeling of well-being. Weak sunlight was just beginning to penetrate through the shadows of the trees. I heard soft footpads outside the shelter. Without moving, I shifted my eyes so I could look out the opening and saw a fox sniffing at our fireplace, probably hoping to find some remnants of our last meal. I smiled and almost felt a kinship to this animal, since my hair had been compared to the color of fox fur for as long as I could remember. He seemed to sense my nearness. The fox met my eyes with a keen but lingering glance and then he turned and ran away with light bouncing steps.

Puh and Black Wolf were awakened by the sounds of the fox dashing through the crunchy leaves. We did not bother to make a fire; we just sipped a little water and then gathered our belongings under the slowly brightening skies. Black Wolf, Puh, and I then hit the trail, soon veering off on a path that would take us toward the distant mountains.

My sunburned peeling skin now itched where my pack rode on my back. I squelched the urge to rear up against a tree like a bear and scratch the bothersome area, but the thought was very tempting.

We would have to re-cross the prairie at its western edge to avoid the swampy lands where Black Wolf and I had seen mammoths a few days earlier. Gray Elk lived still farther to the west.

I had never been there before, but Puh had traveled to Gray Elk's with Black Wolf many times over the years, so I had heard the descriptions of Gray Elk's cavernous mountainside home. It was a grand place consisting of many large rooms that were decorated with elk and giant deer skulls, each sporting an enormous spread of antlers. The stone walls, which Nature had carved out of the mountain itself, were softened with hides and lustrous pelts.

Gray Elk's family was famous for the excellence of their dogs. They had been breeding and trading them for generations and they knew more about canines than anyone. Unlike wolves, Gray Elk's dogs were bred to be gentle toward their human families. They were slightly smaller and lighter in build than their wild relatives. The dogs' snouts were blunt and their ears sometimes flopped over instead of standing up straight, giving them a deceptively daft appearance. But they were smart, loyal, and protective of their homes and those they loved. Rooph had begun life at Gray Elk's mountain aerie, coming home in Puh's arms as a small pup when I was just a young boy.

As we skirted the bogs we observed a small herd of mammoths as they slowly lumbered along, feeding almost constantly.

"Many an Old One has lost his life to those beasts," Puh spoke gravely.

"Many men of The People, too," said Black Wolf. "I have not heard of men embarking on any mammoth hunts in many years since. To kill such an animal, it takes a large group of very strong men. They must be skilled hunters and they must formulate an intelligent plan. There just are not enough people in this region to bring them down any more. Even if a hunter was lucky enough to survive the slaughter of a targeted mammoth, you still had to worry about the rest of the herd. Those brutes stick together. The bulls are usually solitary animals, of course, but they are also the largest and the strongest of the species and therefore, to be avoided."

"It was such a waste of life." Puh shook his head. "In years past, the taking of a mammoth was a part of achieving manhood and young men eagerly awaited the chance to prove themselves. The resulting feasts and celebrations were something to behold. But the last mammoth my family brought down killed my oldest brother Bror when he was just Tris's age. I lost my taste for mammoth meat after that."

"It used to be the same with The People," Black Wolf said. "I remember hearing about that tragic hunt. I was just fifteen winters at that time and I had been so anxious to go mammoth hunting with my father, brothers, and our male kin. But once I heard about how Bror had died, that squashed any excitement I felt for the pursuit of that particular creature." Black Wolf looked quickly at my father. *Squashed* was an unfortunate choice of words. He hastily went on. "Bror was so young and strong. He was the epitome of a fearless hunter. I guess that was his downfall. Was Mror's first born son named in honor of Bror?"

"Yes, he was. Bror's death was a terrible loss to the family." Puh noted. "Normally, the mammoth's meat, hide, and tusks would have been highly prized, but my parents could not bear to keep them. They gave it all away to another branch of our clan who were struggling to survive after injuries kept them from providing adequately for themselves. There was none of the usual celebrating and we never spoke of mammoths again…at least not until now. It was heartbreaking, but it impressed upon me that a hunter's most important tenet is to come home alive. No daring deeds or unnecessary risks. Just stay alive so you can hunt again and provide for your loved ones. A man is no good to his family if he is dead."

I was in complete agreement with Puh and I was glad that killing a mammoth was no longer part of achieving manhood. It was one thing to bring in food to feed the clan. It was quite another to be foolhardy.

One of the few situations in which we might consider going after a mammoth would be if it were so mired in swampy muck that it was more or less immobile, utterly exhausted from struggling to free itself, and if it had been abandoned by the fellow members of its herd. Other than that, we might pursue a very old, very young, or ailing animal, but again, it must be alone or you risked being attacked by its enraged companions. And even at that, except for the youngest mammoths, the process of taking one of these elderly or sick giants was still fraught with extreme peril.

We left the mammoths behind us, regaining the trees once more near the foot of the mountains. We stopped to refill our water bags at a swift-running stream and resumed our trek, keeping an eye out for a place to camp for the night before the sun set.

* * *

I had been listening to clicks, popping sounds, and squirrel-like cries for some time. I could see by Puh's facial expression that he heard them too. He looked alert and he had been picking up palm-sized stones as we walked. Gradually, Black Wolf heard them as well. We did not speak, but automatically slowed our pace as the sounds grew louder.

Puh held up his hand and we each stopped in place. Silently, he set down his cloak and his gear. Then, keeping his hand up to indicate that we should stay still, Puh crept forward with a stone at the ready in one hand; his other holding several more.

Ahead, in the low undergrowth just off the path, was a handsome wood grouse cock in full mating display, his black and white tail feathers fanned and neck arched. His pale beak faced skyward as he emitted his series of clicks, pops, and chatters. He was looking away from us, obviously wooing a hen somewhere nearby and singing his courtship song to her with all his heart.

A moment later, the cock was distracted by an unwelcome interloper, also in full exhibition and song for the elusive hen. The fowl rushed one another with explosive wing slaps, making audible cracks that resembled the crash of two pieces of timber being struck together. Their brilliant red brows gave them a maniacal appearance as they battled. Their attention was so engrossed that they were completely oblivious to us.

Puh let the stone fly with a forceful swing and the wood grouse fell away from one another; one made an escape, the other lay on the ground in a feathery heap.

Puh held up the limp grouse in triumph and we joined him. We set up camp on the spot, first building a fire pit and then erecting a lean-to with some fallen branches and the sled-cover hides.

The grouse made a fine meal for the three of us. Later, we were quite content to curl up in our cloaks and sleep with a blaze still crackling cheerfully at the opening to our shelter.

* * *

The fire had gone out by morning. Once again, we packed our belongings and set out down the trail. The mountains were looming over us now: dark, forbidding, and still topped with snow that blew downwind from the peaks like the tail of an icy earthbound comet. We soon reached the steep slopes. As flatlanders, our legs were not used to this kind of hiking, so we had to stop periodically and rest, kneading the muscles on the backs of our legs to ease the pain.

When the sun had climbed halfway up the sky, we spotted a band of Old Ones in the distance. They were making a descent through a layer of clouds that hugged the mountainside, carefully maneuvering their sleds along the arduous and rocky pathway. We soon recognized two of the men as Uncle Mror's oldest and youngest sons, Bror and Lor.

Bror had been born a few years before me, making him about nineteen winters old. He and I had always been close; we were more like brothers than cousins. Bror was stout, even compared to most of the Old Ones and his physique was already nearly as brawny as Uncle Mror's had been. In contrast, Bror's brother Lor, at fifteen winters, had just attained manhood this year but he was still somewhat slender in build.

Their companions were young men from other clans who were about the same ages as Bror and Lor. They were pulling sleds laden with reindeer hides and an assortment of dried, smoked, and fresh meat. They had been hunting in a valley on the other side of mountain range where the seasonal reindeer migration was still going strong. They were in good spirits and looking forward to returning home again after being away for more than a moon.

I could see that Puh was trying to decide out how to break in on the conversation to tell Bror and Lor about their father. Before he could find an opening, they took note of his anxiety.

"How did all three of you come to lose your tunics?" asked Lor. "And Uncle Tor, what has happened to you?" He pointed to the fresh scars on Puh's torso.

Puh appeared stricken. He swallowed and almost seemed to be choking on words unspoken. Moments passed before he could bring himself to reply.

"I am glad that your journey has been fruitful, but I must tell you terrible news." He looked from Bror to Lor and then began to explain about Uncle Mror and the bear. "Your father and I left for the grasslands with the new moon and we had just brought down a wisent calf when we were set upon by a large cave bear. We had seen the bear rambling around but paid no mind since they have never bothered us before, but this one suddenly came straight at us and lunged for me. It was then that your brave father stepped between the bear and me, stabbing it with the blade he had been using to cut up the calf. The bear took him instead of me and turned to leave. I followed, sinking my spearhead into the bear as well and as often as I could, but then the ground collapsed beneath us and we, all three, were swept into a deep spiked pit. A trap. Your poor father was killed instantly."

Bror and Lor were struck speechless. Their eyes teared, but otherwise they stoically endured the story, nodding at certain points to show that they understood.

"How did you get out?" Bror finally asked.

"I was rescued by Tris and Black Wolf." Puh motioned to Black Wolf and me. "They found me and pulled me out of the trap. We then initiated a rockslide to fill the pit, so that your father is now properly buried. If you should wish to go there to honor the place, it is located east of here, not far inside the Canyon of the Cave Bear. You will know it when you see an alder tree and a small spring cascading down the face of the rock." Puh removed his pack and he began to dig out Uncle Mror's belongings, and then handed the bundle to Bror. "Here. Take this home with you. These items belonged to your father. If you do not mind, I would like to keep his spear for a while, at least until I get home or until I can make another one. My spear was damaged."

Bror and Lor nodded.

"Of course," Bror said. "Keep it for as long as you have need. Many thanks for our father's things. We are sorry for your suffering but glad that you were rescued." He paused to put a comforting arm around his younger brother who had begun to silently sob. "And we offer you many thanks for telling us what happened to our father. We will stop in to see Aunt

Awna on our way home and let her know that you and Tris are well."

"Many thanks," said Puh. "Will you also tell Awna that now we go to Gray Elk to see if he has any new litters? If he does, Black Wolf may choose some pups and Tris may pick one too."

"Yes, Uncle Tor, I will." Bror nodded. "We made a side trip to Gray Elk's yesterday and traded some meat and hides for a few of the new season's pups. We will be back for them later this coming summer when we and our sleds are not laden with all of this paraphernalia and game."

"Did Gray Elk have many young dogs on hand?" Black Wolf inquired.

"I do not know." Bror shook his head. "I did not ask to see them, since we were not taking any at that time and would not for some moons. We just wanted to make our deals while we were in the area and had goods to trade." Bror was answering questions in a quiet monotone, but he appeared to be under some stress and his eyes were wet with unshed tears. No one spoke for a moment. Then Bror went on. "Well, we had best keep moving. We are eager to end this excursion and our families will be happy to dine on some fresh meat for a change. So, I will leave you now and wish you all a good journey."

"Many thanks. Good journey to you, as well," Puh replied.

"Good journey." Black Wolf and I echoed.

"I am so sorry about Uncle Mror," I added. My cousins just nodded; they seemed too numb to articulate a response.

Puh and I then embraced Bror and Lor, and Black Wolf touched their shoulders, offering his sympathy, too. We parted to continue our separate errands.

I was cognizant of the great pain that accompanied Bror and Lor as they left us. I turned to gaze after them for a moment and watched the group of men make their way down the slopes, Bror's arm still around Lor. I could not fathom the depth of their anguish. I felt a particular empathy with them since it was only due to incredibly lucky circumstances that I was not also grieving for a father found dead in the same pit.

There was no imagining the utter desolation I would feel if I lost Puh. Not only had he sired me, but he was the person with whom I had spent most of my waking hours since I was a young boy. He had been my mentor, my partner, and my confidant. We knew one another's thoughts even without speaking.

Was that why he entered my dreams? To call me to him when he needed me?

Chapter Eight

Gray Elk's dogs alerted him to our coming long before our arrival, so he was ready for us when we stood inside the cave's entryway, calling out our greetings amidst the tail-wagging wriggling panting barking throng. Gray Elk waded through them, ordering the dogs to get out of his way.

"Back! Back! Get back, you great furry beasts!" He good-naturedly pushed his way toward us. "Ah, Black Wolf! Welcome!" Gray Elk grasped Black Wolf by the forearms, grinning broadly. "This is a pleasant surprise! How good to see you!"

Gray Elk, as might be expected, had hair the color of a dark storm cloud. It was worn in three long braids, one at each ear and a thicker one that went down the length of his spine. His beard was long, but neatly trimmed, and his mustache ended in two plaits that extended downward from the corners of his mouth. He looked well fed without seeming corpulent. He was richly dressed in deerskin clothing and a bearskin cloak that looked becoming and well groomed compared to our worn and shaggy wisent cloaks.

"Do you remember Tor? And this is his son, Tris." Black Wolf indicated Puh and me.

"Ah, yes! Of course I remember you, Tor!" said Gray Elk, "one of the *Or*-men: Bror, Mror, Tor, Kror, Zor…a fine group of brothers! And I remember Orr, your father, another good man as well." He took Puh and me by the arms just as he had with Black Wolf and we nodded and smiled our acknowledgement to him. "Come in! Come in!"

Grey Elk waved for us to follow as he led the way into the cavern. Despite the great height of the ceiling and the many lighted oil lamps, I had a sense of the walls closing in around me. I had never seen so many oil lamps in all my life, and they were each aflame! I could not imagine how they could procure so much oil. I sniffed at the air in an attempt to guess the source of the fat that fueled the lamps, but came to no sure conclusion. That led me to believe that they were probably burning oils which were rendered from many different types of animals. It was lucky for Gray Elk that his domicile had such immensely tall ceilings, as had they been low, they would have been blackened with soot and the air would have been fuggy with lamp smoke.

The floor sloped downward precipitously as Gray Elk took us to yet another long passageway, and finally bringing us to a massive chamber with a roaring fire at its center that provided light and heat to the huge dwelling. I noted that the fire's smoke was escaping through a gaping hole in the ceiling of the cave. Up by the chimney hole, Grey Elk was preserving numerous large chunks of meat, keeping them suspended in the smoke over the fire. Some of it, no doubt, was fresh meat newly acquired from Bror.

The walls had many ledges and all were adorned with elk and giant deer skulls and antlers. A myriad of rooms apparently branched off the main room, but most of them appeared to be dark.

A woman emerged from one of the lighted rooms. She seemed to be about Gray Elk's age. She was tall and held herself very erect. She was a handsome woman with dark hair that was lightly sprinkled with silvery stands.

As much as Muh prided herself on creating clothing for her family that was artfully constructed, this woman wore a garment that would have made Muh stare. It was a long gown that came down to her ankles and both it and her short little boots were trimmed with the fur of many minks. As beautiful as it was, all I could think was that she would never be able to get through deep snow while wearing such articles. She wore a necklace of polished deer teeth and curiously, she had a hole in each of her earlobes from which a dainty sea shell dangled on a fine cord.

Puh seemed to know her; he nodded and smiled at the woman. Gray Elk introduced her to me as his mate, Buttercup.

"Welcome!" she said. "How very nice it is to have you in our home!" Then she turned to Black Wolf and embraced him; she had to tip-toe and pull him down to her height to kiss his cheek. "Welcome, dear Black Wolf! How is Little Fawn and how are all your children? Come and sit. You must tell me about them! I have just sent the girls to get water and something for us to eat while we wait for our evening meal. You men must be very hungry."

After we were all seated on mats around the fireplace, The Girls, five women who appeared to be Gray Elk's and Buttercup's daughters or possibly their sons' mates, soon appeared. They were attractive women and like Gray Elk and Buttercup, well dressed. One was obviously heavy with child and another, less so. They smilingly offered us cups of water and invited us to take handfuls of shelled nuts and dried fruits. Gray Elk apologized for the paltry snack, saying that although they had plenty of stores, there was not much of an assortment from which to choose after a long winter of eating out of their food caches. But it was not as though anyone else could have possibly offered us anything more exotic. At this time of year, the variety of food supplies was necessarily limited no matter how well-off you were.

"All the same, you are very good to make us welcome and share your food with us," said Puh.

"You are very kind to say so," Buttercup remarked graciously to Puh. "I think we still have some of the honey and rosehips that you so thoughtfully brought to us last spring. We will have some rosehip and honey tea with our meal this evening."

Buttercup left us temporarily, but returned with The Girls to help place spits over a section of the fireplace where the coals had been heaped for cooking.

After a trail diet of dried foods and meat roasted over a campfire, it was exquisitely delicious to eat a home-cooked meal of roast reindeer meat, quail stuffed with onions, dried mushrooms and herbs; seasoned and marinated roasted tubers and root vegetables that were steamed in tightly woven baskets, which were hung over the coals and continually wetted to keep the steaming process going; roasted apples stuffed with grains, pieces of nuts and minced dried fruits, and many more delicacies.

Buttercup, The Girls, and a few small children dined with us, but they retired from the room as soon as the meal was consumed. The sounds of readying and putting children to bed explained their departure.

"Where are all your young men?" Black Wolf asked after Gray Elk and Buttercup's family.

"Our sons left us a few days ago to deliver a couple of male pups to our cousin Spotted Horse," Gray Elk replied. "But they have no plan to hurry back. They hope to travel out to the White River when the salmon run at the beginning of summer in order to catch and dry a load of fish before they come home to us."

"Those salmon will not run for at least another moon," observed Black Wolf, "they will be gone for quite some time. I was hoping to visit with your sons while we were here."

"Yes," nodded Gray Elk, "but they are bored with tending and breeding dogs, chopping and hauling wood up the mountainside, and the constant hunting that are required to sustain the household. I think that if it were up to them, my line of dogs might well die out with me. Sky Fire and Running Buck want to spend more time at the coast where they say it is warmer and life is easier. I would not be surprised if they set out on their own someday. After this last winter, I cannot say as I blame them. I am always hearing about how The People are straying farther and farther north and west. There is new land to open up and the younger generation cannot wait to do it. Luckily for me, my daughters' mates are more eager to learn about dogs—which ones to keep for breeding stock and which ones to take in to add to the bloodlines. They are due to return from a reindeer hunt at almost any time now. Perhaps you will have an opportunity to visit with them, instead."

"Speaking of reindeer hunts, on our way here we ran into some of Tor's nephews who had just come from hunting reindeer," Black Wolf stated. "They had a hefty load of hides and meat on their sleds and they mentioned that the reindeer were still moving well. They said that they had stopped in here to make trades for pups. I suppose your dogs will eat most of the reindeer meat that they brought in."

"Indeed, they will." Gray Elk laughed. "I have never seen any one of my dogs turn down a meal yet! That fresh meat was most welcome! Those two pups I sent to Spotted Horse are some of the largest pups I have bred up until now. They will put a sizable dent in his food cache, that is for sure, but at this time of year better his than mine. However, that is what he wanted. Spotted Horse asked me to wait until I had some pups that were half-grown in order to see which ones were going to be the biggest. He hopes that these dogs will help to discourage some of the predators that meander through the territory where he has resettled his family. It is very good land with lots of game, but there is also a lot of competition from those predators."

"So you do have some pups on hand?" Black Wolf asked. "I only saw the dogs that greeted us at your entryway."

"Yes. But the dogs you saw earlier are all I have left. They include two rangy youngsters about six moons old whom I would be glad to get out from underfoot. They are one male and one bitch, littermates to the two that are on their way to Spotted Horse. These pups will not be quite as big, I think. But they do want to chew on everything in sight and they romp all day long. You know that age. If you would prefer little ones, I will have plenty on hand in a few moons or so, when I hope some of my bitches will whelp later this spring. But that is for you to decide."

"Will you trade for them?" asked Black Wolf. "I might like to take both pups."

"Of course," Gray Elk nodded.

"May we look at them?" Black Wolf requested.

Gray Elk indicated with a gesture that we were to follow him back to the entryway, where the dogs were all curled up a-snooze, except for the two smaller dogs that were laying together face-to-face, playing a tugging game with a scrap of leather.

A few of the adult dogs briefly wagged their tails and raised their heads to look at us, but they soon returned to their naps. Gray Elk's dogs varied in color from pure black to all white, but these two pups were almost identical in appearance. They had white and black markings mottled in with their long, pale grayish fur and although the male was slightly larger, they were similar in size.

The young dogs stopped their game and approached us, willingly submitting to the subsequent inspections and the caresses that we lavished upon them.

Black Wolf encouraged me to select a dog. They were both fine animals. My decision was made for me when the little bitch lay at my feet and turned belly-up, begging for a rub.

"Well, Tris," Black Wolf nudged me. "I think she has picked you. Do you like her? Or would you rather wait and pick out a new pup?"

"Yes, I do like her," I nodded.

"She is yours, then." Black Wolf smiled and patted my shoulder thumpingly with his weighty hand.

"Many thanks, Black Wolf," I nodded again. "Many thanks."

The pup and her brother followed us back into the main room, hoping for more attention. The bitch sat with me, intently gazing into my face and occasionally trying to lick it. It was not long before she was belly-up once more, looking almost impossibly appealing as she lay there with her paws and ears flopped over. In the meantime, Black Wolf's new pup was trying to crawl into Black Wolf's lap and chew on his hands, which made his negotiations with Gray Elk a little more lengthy and a lot less serious. They finally agreed that Black Wolf would return with his family in the summer to see any new pups that might be available and then settle up for all the dogs at that time.

Then Gray Elk turned his attention to us.

"So," he began, "I can see that you must have had some adventures on your journey here. You have lost your tunics somewhere along the way. Did you meet up with some forward women who would not let you leave without leaving certain favors—and maybe certain clothing—behind?"

"No, but Mror and I garnered some unwanted attention from a bear," Puh answered.

Once again, the story was told about Puh and Uncle Mror, and how our tunics were sacrificed to make an impromptu rope.

"Cheerful, pleasant Mror has passed from life?" Gray Elk shook his head over Uncle Mror. "I am so very sorry to hear of it. I will miss him and his hearthside stories. Mror was a good man. It is a hard life sometimes." He paused and then added: "Who will be the Keeper of Stories, now? Will it be his eldest son, Bror? I was very impressed with Bror while he was here yesterday. He seems to be an exceptional young man: smart, steady, conscientious. He certainly resembles his father physically. He is built like a stump-puller. Bror is not as loquacious as was Mror, but he must know all of his father's tales by rote, both the traditional stories of the Old Ones and all the anecdotes that Mror used to entertain us with."

"I do not know if Bror will want to be a Keeper of Stories," Puh replied. "But it is true that he is a fine man. Mror was very proud of him."

Gray Elk nodded. Then a thought seemed to cross his mind.

"Can I give you each a gift of tunics to wear on the trek home?" he offered.

"Many thanks, but for me, no," said Puh. "I have my cloak, so I will be warm enough. Again, many thanks for your consideration."

"For me as well," I seconded. "But many thanks for your generosity."

"Thank you, cousin," Black Wolf spoke with a grin, "but I guess I cannot accept either, especially since I am always wearing my own coat whether I am clothed or not."

Black Wolf was too tactful to mention that it was unlikely Gray Elk would have a tunic that was large enough to fit him, in any case.

"Yes, Black Wolf, it is true that you wear your own woolly covering at all times," Gray Elk laughed. "It must be a delightful convenience to have in cold weather, but you must heartily regret being so furry each summer."

"Either way, I do not have much choice in the

matter." Black Wolf noted with a rueful smile.

"I suppose not," Gray Elk agreed. "And you do not even have the advantage of shedding your winter coat to be more comfortable in hot weather like many animals do."

* * *

Later, Gray Elk had left us to go to sleep and we made our beds around the hearth.

"What will you call her?" Black Wolf said to me, indicating the pup as she dozed at my side.

"Raena," I answered. "Again, many thanks for her, Black Wolf. You did not have to do this. But I am grateful and I do like her."

"She is a beauty and she seems very sweet tempered," Puh remarked.

"Her brother is a fine dog as well," Black Wolf nodded. "Too many of the dogs I have at home are becoming old. Others are not ancient, but the signs are there that old age is not too far away. If I can get one or two more this summer that will set us up in the future to have plenty of dogs for hunting and to protect the homestead." Black Wolf was silent a moment, but then he looked at me. "I have not forgotten my words, Tris."

 **Chapter Nine** 

Morning Star is weeping in the darkness, weeping as though her heart will break. There is no comfort for her.

I awoke with a start, and in my confusion could not remember where I was. I was afraid for Morning Star. What could have happened to her? Had it happened yet? Could we get back to the village in time to help her? There was almost no light. Something was licking my face. Then I felt Raena's fuzzy body lying up against me and I realized that she was that *something*.

I sat up and remembered that I was in Gray Elk's dwelling. The fire had burned down to embers. I stirred the coals, bringing a few small flames to life. Afterward, I made my way through the semi-darkness to the woodpile at the end of the room to collect fuel with which to build up the fire. Raena followed my every step and I had to dodge her once or twice to avoid stepping on her.

When the fire had caught, I placed larger pieces of wood onto the flames. Next, I took Raena through the passageways until we were outside again, where we both found a place to relieve ourselves, just as I had done with Rooph when we were at home. Only this time we were accompanied by Gray Elk's full complement of breeding-stock dogs. It was a little unnerving to see them milling around outdoors in the semi-darkness, where they might have been mistaken for wolves if you did not look closely.

I was eager to leave and find out whether Morning Star was all right. I wanted to tell Puh and Black Wolf about my dream, but did not want to say anything that might dampen our visit until after we had left Gray Elk's. The packing and good-byes seemed endless but, in reality, they were very brief and we departed before the sun had gained a foothold in the sky.

Our legs were still stiff from the previous day's climb up but, thankfully, the climb down stressed different muscles. Soon, however, an entirely new set complained and required us to make occasional halts to rest. At each of these stops, I debated whether or not to tell Puh and Black Wolf about my Dream. But since they both seemed inclined to forge ahead without any unnecessary delays, I could not see what good it would do to worry them, especially if nothing had happened yet. I decided to keep the Dream to myself for the time being.

The two curious young dogs seemed not to mind leaving their former home. They seemed to sense that we were their new family. The few times they looked back, we called them to us and distracted them with cuddles and food before moving on once again.

Raena and her brother were no help at bringing down the small game we hunted on the five-day journey back to the village, but they did relish the fresh meat that resulted. Their antics were amusing and they were good company. Sometimes I could almost forget about my continuing Dreams of Morning Star.

* * *

Each night as the moon waned, I waited to see if Black Wolf would ask me again: *What can I give you?* I wanted to allow him time to think about it and all it would mean for our families. I knew that Black Wolf wished the best for his children, especially his most cherished Morning Star. More than once, he had spoken of the men in the village with disdain as unambitious, slovenly creatures. He had said he would speak to the village elders about finding good matches for his daughter, but he did not seek the actual candidates there.

If Black Wolf was rejecting some members of his

own people, after consideration, how he would feel about me? And more to the point, how would Morning Star feel about me? Did my Dreams represent her reaction to the news that she was to be paired with me?

I wanted her more than anything I had ever wanted in all my life, but *only* if she wanted me, too. Because we had been happy companions thus far, it was my hope that she felt enough affection for me, and had ample faith in my capabilities as a provider, that she would willingly accept me as her mate. Or that at least she would not hate the idea.

* * *

On the night of the new moon, we sat around our campfire with the two pups and quietly ate a meal of dried meat. The pups had already wolfed down their food and were snoozing after a day of wild activity during which they had capered up and down the trail almost continuously.

As I listened to the deep hoots of nearby owls calling to one another, I looked up into the star-filled firmament to be sure that the moon was indeed hidden from view and wondered when Black Wolf would choose to speak.

Our food supplies were nearly exhausted. The rabbits we had attempted to stone during the day had escaped, pursued by two silly young dogs who had spurred them on to runaway all the faster.

However, we knew we were close to the village and that once we reached it, we would have all the food we could want. In fact, we hoped to arrive at the village the next day. We were tired and eager to finish this journey. Puh had been away from home almost a whole moon cycle now, and Black Wolf and I had been away since the full moon.

As we labored to chew the hard slabs of meat and stared dully into the dancing flames, Black Wolf cleared his throat.

"So, Tris," he started, "I meant what I said. What can I grant you?"

"You are very good to ask me again," I responded without hesitation. "I will answer this time. I wish to have your consent to give…um…my attentions to Morning Star."

"*Give your attentions to her?*" Black Wolf choked a little on his dried meat. "Would you not like to be paired with her?"

"Yes, if she will have me."

"She will have you if I tell her to. And I *will* tell her to."

"Many thanks, Black Wolf, but I hope it will not come to that. I want it to be her choice."

Puh wore an amused expression. I am sure he was thinking of himself and Muh, since they had coupled by choice for love, despite generations of tradition in both The People and the Old Ones.

"Tris is right, Black Wolf," Puh spoke up. "If a man wants a happy life, he must find a loving woman. Without that, a pairing can be very troublesome. Many thanks for your willingness to pair your daughter with my son. We will welcome Morning Star into our family, as you have always welcomed Tris into yours."

Puh and Black Wolf seemed very pleased with the arrangement. I was thrilled, ecstatic, and overjoyed, especially after years of thinking that I would pine for her forever.

But I still harbored a stubborn underlying fear that she would reject me. I tried to push the thought from my mind and in my excitement I managed to sleep only after absolute exhaustion overtook me.

* * *

The only sound in the shadows is that of her weeping. She could not do this thing. Why could they not just leave her alone?

The new day brought a cold drizzling rain. Puh, Black Wolf, and I were sodden, as were all our clothing and gear. But, at least the last of the puddles of snow had finally melted away into the muddy landscape.

We began to shiver whenever we stopped moving, so we trudged forward, barely talking, although Puh and Black Wolf sometimes smiled at me. I smiled back. I hoped for luck and for Morning

Star's acceptance. I would know soon enough.

The log walls of the village were a welcome, if ugly sight, and the smell of the perpetually burning refuse hung over the area like an evil omen. As we approached, we were met by the grinning faces of two men.

"Why, there he is! Congratulations, Black Wolf," one of the men gushed with enthusiasm as he spoke, "We hear that your eldest daughter has been promised."

"Why, she is," Black Wolf was flustered for a moment, "but I do not know how the news could have traveled here before us."

"You sly dog," another of the men replied with a laugh. "Do not play with us after landing the village's best hunter for your daughter! Such luck! What a happy arrangement!"

"I think you are misinformed," Black Wolf's demeanor darkened forbiddingly, and he walked on without further comment.

Puh and I were struck mute.

"Do not worry," Black Wolf told us. "Whatever has happened, I will fix it."

As we walked toward Eagle Owl's abode, various people greeted and congratulated Black Wolf but he ignored them.

When Black Wolf ducked his great height through Eagle Owl's doorway, the family sprung up to receive us with smiling faces. The smiles quickly faded to attitudes of apprehension. Eagle Owl scurried for food and water, but Black Wolf acknowledged him only with a curt nod. He then gave the children and dogs a few pats on the head without differentiating between dog and child. There was a pregnant pause, during which Black Wolf glowered angrily at Little Fawn.

"I must talk with my mate. May we use your sleeping chamber?" Black Wolf finally spoke to Eagle Owl.

Eagle Owl was taken aback by Black Wolf's apparent outrage. He nodded with a widened eye. Black Wolf took Little Fawn by the arm. She had been standing there looking so pleased but now she wore an expression of alarm. My eyes sought out Morning Star from amongst the people in the crowded space. She looked weary, but she smiled at me. She brought gourd cups full of water to Puh and me.

"I am so glad that you have safely arrived," she said quietly to us. "Come and stand by the fire. You must be so cold and uncomfortably wet."

We were indeed chilled and soaked to the skin, but as Puh and I moved to stand closer to the fire we all heard Black Wolf's raised voice.

"But I have promised her to Tris!" he roared.

"You were not here," Little Fawn said indignantly. "It was a good offer. We will never get another chance like this."

At that moment Morning Star's demure eyes fluttered wide open. She abruptly left us, storming into Eagle Owl's bed chamber and confronting her parents.

"Why do I not get a say in this?" she shouted, "It is my life! He will never touch me!"

"You!" Black Wolf sputtered furiously, "You will do as you are told!"

"I cannot hear this," I whispered to Puh. I rushed out the door into the gloomy rainy afternoon. Puh and Raena followed me. Her words echoed in my ears. *He will never touch me.* Tears stung my eyes. I had expected a possible rebuff, but nothing this blatant.

"Where are you going?" Puh asked. "Black Wolf will fix this."

"You heard her. She said *he will never touch me.*" I muttered despondently, continuing down the path.

"They all say that at first. She is at that age when she likes to flirt and know she is admired and appreciated by men, but she does not want to actually be taken. This is especially true of first daughters like Morning Star who are shy after witnessing the births of all their younger siblings. But she will grow out of it." Puh looked into my miserable tear-streaked visage. "Come, let us get out of the rain."

Puh tugged at my arm and pulled me toward an abandoned stick and mud house. Two of the walls were almost completely gone and the roof leaked badly in spots, but at least we would have a dry place in which to talk. We each found a seat on some of the lumpy piles of debris. Raena looked at us, wagging her tail a bit. She whined and licked my wet face. Poor Raena was clearly upset, too.

"Good girl, Raena," I said, burying my face in the thick fur at the back of her head. Her thumping tail raised the dust where she sat on a dry section of the dirt floor.

I was desperately trying not to think of Morning Star's cutting words, but I could not get them out of my head. They echoed again and again. *He will never touch me. He will never touch me.*

"So," Puh began, speaking to me as my face remained hidden in Raena's ruff. Puh placed one leathery hand on my head and another on my shoulder. "Take a moment. Then we will go back to Eagle Owl's and settle this. It is going to be all right. I am sure of it. Black Wolf is a man of his word. Morning Star will accept you. She has known you all her life. I know that she must care for you."

I shook my head. I did not think that it was going to be all right or that she would accept me. Her words had been vehement. I had known her to be spirited and to speak impulsively but I had never heard her talk that way before. Caring for me as a longtime friend and agreeing to be paired with me were two entirely different things. Morning Star was a beautiful young woman. She could have any man she desired.

"It will. It will." Puh assured me. Raena's tail thumped again.

A short while later, Raena's brother trotted into our enclosure and excitedly greeted his sister. Black Wolf was on his heels, toting the same impedimenta that he had carried on our long trek together.

"Let us camp here," he said, stashing his belongings in a dry corner.

Puh and I were bewildered.

"What are you doing?" Puh asked.

"I am preparing to build a fire," Black Wolf said as he removed chunks of the shattered wall from what had once been a fireplace.

"Yes, but what are you *doing?*" Puh repeated.

"Ack," Black Wolf replied with disgust. "That foolish woman of mine. Some acquaintance of Eagle Owl's—Snow Leopard—flattered and finagled his way into an agreement for Morning Star. *Without my consent!* She spouted off some sort of nonsense that he was an excellent match and I was away from home all the time and she had to make decisions for the family *every* day. I told her that I would speak to Snow Leopard and tell him that he cannot make arrangements such as these with my woman and my cousin. And then I left. Let them stew a while. But in the meantime I have to find this Snow Leopard. Eagle Owl says that he will try to arrange a meeting."

"You do not know him?" Puh asked.

"I know *of* him, but that is all. He has a home at the far end of the village but is seldom there. He was paired, but his mate died in childbirth last winter. He has several small children who are now in the care of his family. I am sorry for those children and I am sure he wants a mother for them, but it is not going to be my daughter! He did not make any deals with me!" Black Wolf finished by muttering: "Morning Star! Just turned fifteen winters old and she thinks she knows everything! We should have named her *Shooting Star*!"

Black Wolf began to savagely pull down a section of broken wall so he could use the pieces of wood to add to the flames.

Black Wolf continued to build up the fire, and he was still grumbling to himself when Eagle Owl arrived. Eagle Owl looked somewhat sheepish, but appeared determined to help however he could.

"Well?" Black Wolf demanded impatiently.

"I came to find you. I followed your footprints in the mud to this…um…place, and now, if you are ready to go, I will take you to Snow Leopard. He does not stay in the village long, so if we are going to talk to him, we will have to do it soon."

Black Wolf stood and handed the stick he had used to poke the fire to Puh.

"All right. Let us get this over with, Eagle Owl." He turned to Puh and me and added, "I will not be away for too long."

We nodded our response to him. We did not envy Snow Leopard, whoever he was. Black Wolf was in a ferocious mood and at that moment, had the appearance of a man who could tackle a rampaging lion and win.

* * *

But Black Wolf returned wearing a somber expression. He removed his dripping cloak and hung it on a cracked wooden frame that poked crookedly out of the dilapidated wall. Emitting a long sigh, Black Wolf sat down and wiped his rain-soaked face with his hands, his drooping braids looking as dejected as he did.

Eagle Owl stood there awkwardly, as though he was not quite sure what to do.

I could not take the suspense any longer.

"Did you find Snow Leopard? What did he say?" I asked anxiously.

"Oh, we found him," began Black Wolf. "He let us in. He was very polite, but very firm. He said that his agreement with Little Fawn and Eagle Owl, who was the male representative of the family, is binding as far as he is concerned. He will not release us from the agreement. Not even after I told him that Morning Star is promised to someone else. Snow Leopard said that the only way he will bow out is if his competitor meets him in the Challenge Circle and manages to defeat him."

"*The Challenge Circle?*" Puh leapt to his feet. "I have heard of the Challenge Circle. That is where the men of The People go to resolve issues of honor?"

Black Wolf hesitated before answering.

"Yes," he began, "it is one of the traditions of The People. When there is a serious disagreement between two men—including disputes regarding who has the right to be paired with a certain woman—the men must do battle in the Challenge Circle. Barehanded. And to win, a man must kill or disable his opponent, or batter him until he renounces his claim."

"I must warn you, Tris," Eagle Owl said, "Snow Leopard is older than you by many years, but he is experienced at this sort of thing and he is smart and crafty. But you have your youth and powerful physique in your favor. Do you know how to fight a man barehanded?"

"Only what Puh has taught me and from tussling for sport with my brothers and cousins," I responded.

"In the way of the Old Ones?" Eagle Owl asked.

"Yes," I replied with a nod. That meant wrestling with brute strength and using your hard points: head, elbows, and knees, to smash soft points: noses, throats, stomachs, and groins.

Puh, Black Wolf, and Eagle Owl exchanged glances and then glanced at me.

"You will need to learn how The People fight if you want to go through with this. Snow Leopard will use closed fists to land his blows. If you cannot learn to throw your fists, you will at least have to learn how to block his," Eagle Owl informed me.

"This has to be up to you," Puh said, looking at me soberly.

Black Wolf and Eagle Owl stared at me as well. I realized that this was not only about Morning Star and me; there was also Black Wolf to consider and his desire to save his daughter from a pairing with a villager, an arrangement he detested and had long sought to avoid.

"I will meet him wherever and whenever he likes." I stated.

"I will take the message to him," Eagle Owl nodded. "And Tris, I am so sorry for my part in this. I had no idea that…that you might…it never occurred to me… "

"Many thanks for your concern," I told him. "And many thanks for taking the message to Snow Leopard."

With that, Eagle Owl left us once more.

* * *

The rain stopped and the sun was low in the sky. The fire had dried us and most of our belongings, all but our heavy cloaks. Puh, Black Wolf, and I considered the situation.

"Well, Tris," said Black Wolf, "we will have to take you out and see if we can give you a quick lesson in throttling snow leopards—the two-legged kind. But for now, I am hungry. Let us fill our stomachs."

Black Wolf removed a bag of dried meat out of his pack and handed each of us one of the hard slabs.

"Many thanks," Puh and I said in unison.

The dogs were close at our elbows, straining forward to get a look at the meat. Black Wolf's hand went back into the bag and he retrieved two more chunks for the pups, which then set about happily gnawing on their prizes.

"Ack. More dried meat," Black Wolf lamented as he contemplated our uninspiring dinner. "I was hoping for a meal of fresh meat tonight. And maybe some roasted tubers and leeks. I am aggrieved every time I think of all the meat we had to leave behind when we killed that sow. That feast was so delicious! Oh well. When we leave the village tomorrow to find a good place to train Tris, perhaps we can hunt up some small game."

"Yes," Puh agreed. "We will kill two birds with one stone."

"Now that would be a trick!" Black Wolf grinned, regaining some of his humor. "I would like to see that the next time you are stalking wood grouse. Maybe you could kill both the cocks or even the cocks *and* the hen, too!"

"Is there more meat?" Puh asked. I searched my pack for the food bag and passed it to him. Puh explored the contents. "Oh, look! Dried fish! I thought it was all gone. Who wants dried fish?"

Eagle Owl returned as we were still eating.

"Snow Leopard says he will meet his rival in the Challenge Circle in two days, just after the sun rises," he announced. Then Eagle Owl sniffed. "What is that smell?"

"Fish," Puh answered.

"Fish? What kind?"

Puh looked at the slab in his hand, turning it this way and that.

"I do not know for certain," he admitted. "But it looks as though it could be some of the cod we caught last summer. Or maybe the summer before…"

"Do you mean that it is fish from the ocean?" Eagle Owl looked intrigued. "I have never had any fish taken from the ocean. Let me try some."

Puh handed one of the tough slices of fish to Eagle Owl. At first, it presented him with some difficulty, but finally, after several attempts to make an impression on the well-dried fillet, he managed to break off a mouthful.

"My teeth are not what they used to be," he conceded. "Usually, I have to soften my dried meat in water before I try to consume it, but this is quite good. Bring some the next time you want to trade for spearheads or cutting tools." Eagle Owl squatted in front of the fire and held his hands to the flames.

"What is the plan for tomorrow? It will be Tris's only day to prepare for the fight. I know of a good place to spar, outside the east gates."

"We were just discussing that," Puh said. "And we will need to hunt, as well. We have precious little food left."

"I will be here at sunup and I will bring food and water," Eagle Owl volunteered. "It is the least I can do after behaving like such an old imbecile. I so enjoyed having Little Fawn and your children with me, Black Wolf, it felt as though I had family of my own at last. And I thought you would be pleased. I cannot tell you how sorry I am that I stepped in where I did not belong. And now, look what I have done to Tris."

"I am not afraid," I assured Eagle Owl.

Actually, this was not merely a statement of bravado. I truly was not frightened or even much concerned for my own well-being. If Morning Star did not want me, I honestly did not care what became of me. My thought was that, at best, neither Snow Leopard nor I would have Morning Star. But, for Black Wolf's sake, I could win her freedom from a pairing with Snow Leopard.

The only thing that made me uneasy was whether Morning Star *wanted* to pair with him. However, as well as I knew her, I could not imagine that she would want to be attached to a much older man who lived so far from the home she loved.

The only other person Morning Star would know in the village would be Eagle Owl, and even though he was a doting relative, he would not be much of a companion for a young woman left alone for long periods of time while her man was away. Grimly, I accepted the fact that although I could not hope to have Morning Star, I could perhaps give her a chance to find someone she could love, someone closer to her own age who would not take her from her cherished life in the forest.

* * *

We were ready for Eagle Owl when he arrived the next morning. True to his word, he brought several bags of food, which were gratefully welcomed by Puh and Black Wolf. I ate mechanically, knowing that I needed to fuel my strength, but I had no appreciable appetite.

The sun was burning off the morning haze as we set out for the village gates. Eagle Owl chatted pleasantly about where we might find game and where we could fill our water bags at a nearby creek.

When we saw that Eagle Owl was panting with effort in order to keep up with us, we adjusted our gait to accommodate his slower pace, since Eagle Owl was no longer used to walking long distances. Raena and her brother were still with us, but even though Eagle Owl held them back when we sighted potential game, we came up empty-handed. Our close proximity to the village meant that all animals were habitually wary of humans, and although we tried, we were unable to close in on any prey.

We soon made up our minds not to waste any more time at that futile task and Eagle Owl led us to the clearing he had referred to as a *good sparring place*. This ground did indeed look far superior to any of the rough terrain that I had noted in the village. We lay down our spears and packs and Eagle Owl found himself a comfortable seat on an old log.

"Stand here, Tris," Black Wolf instructed. "Both you and Snow Leopard will be symbolically bare-chested to show that you carry no weapons." I shrugged. I had no tunic to wear, anyway. "You must stay within the Circle at all times. But that is not a problem because if you get anywhere near the edge, the crowd will push you back in."

"There will be a crowd?" I asked. I had not anticipated an audience.

"I would be surprised if there was not," Eagle Owl answered. "It is customary for everyone in the village to attend."

"When the men of The People fight hand-to-hand," Black Wolf said, "they close their fists like *this*." He demonstrated with his big, raw-boned paw. "And most men take swings," he continued, swinging his arm wide. "Those wallops can stun you, knock you down, and even cut your flesh. But you can see them pull their arms back and then try to avoid the blow. Since I have long arms, I have learned to sneak in quick jabs with my fists because the typical man with shorter arms than me has to come in closer to make contact. Then, my arms do not have room to extend so I just poke out like *this,* and it often causes some dismay because there is no wind-up to give it away before the fist lands."

"That would cause certain vexation in most men," Puh agreed.

"First of all, you will need to learn how to block his swings before he can strike you." Black Wolf's right fist shot out but I brought up my left arm to knock aside the blow. He grinned. "That is it! You are quick! But Snow Leopard will keep striking at you, so you have to be ready to do this over and over. And, you have to get in your own hits. We will try it again but when I poke at you, try to hit me back. Just a little jab, mind you. Save your real hits for Snow Leopard."

Puh and Black Wolf took turns showing me how to handle myself during the skirmish as Eagle Owl looked on, keeping a hold on the dogs and adding helpful suggestions now and then.

When the sun was midway through its decline in the sky, we realized that we had best return to the village before darkness set in.

"There is only one more thing," Puh said. "We need to make Tris look like a champion. We have been on the trail for many a day and we were caught in a rainstorm yesterday. We need to spruce him up. And a bath would be good." He looked at Black Wolf. "Come to think of it, you and I could use a wash, too."

"I know just the spot." Eagle Owl said as he rose to his feet. "Follow me."

It was only a short distance to a pretty little stream that rambled between stands of catkin willows. The creek was shallow but the fast-flowing current provided plenty of clean, if rather cold water. We stripped and scrubbed until our skin glowed.

"It feels so good to at last wash all the bear-trap sand from my scalp," Puh noted as he wrung out his wet hair. "I think I am finally free of the scent of dead bear, too."

"It is just as well," Black Wolf nodded. "Your Awna will be more apt to enthusiastically embrace a mate who does not attract flies."

"That is likely true." Puh paused. "Although she probably endures worse when we are at the coast. Slaughtering seals and cutting up fish in mid-summer heat does nothing to enhance one's personal aroma. Never mind flies, Awna always says that the odor is enough to attract every seagull that nests within a day's flight. You get used to the stench, but I could still smell it for days after we arrived at home again."

"But the resulting meat is tasty!" Eagle Owl grinned appreciatively.

When our ablutions were completed, we then dressed. Next Puh and I labored to twist each other's damp hair into the traditional cords of the Old Ones. Muh was the one who usually took care of that chore, so it required a little trial and error to get it right. I was surprised to see that when Puh's curls were wet and straightened out, they were far longer than mine, easily long enough for him to sit on.

Black Wolf's braids were apparently seldom renewed. Occasional grease kept them neat and stiff but other than that, I never saw him pay any attention to them.

Despite our ragged clothes, we felt much more presentable as we strode back to the village. Before leaving us Eagle Owl again insisted that he would bring food to us that evening. However, it was Little Fawn who delivered it.

Black Wolf frowned with an utterly dark expression when he saw her. Wearing a nervous smile, she set down the birch bark tray piled with baskets of food and nodded her greeting to Puh and me.

"Many thanks, Little Fawn," Puh said gently, returning her nod.

"Yes, many thanks," I repeated.

Black Wolf had not yet spoken to Little Fawn and he looked so irate that she seemed to take a moment to gather her courage to address him.

"May I see you?" she asked Black Wolf.

He stood abruptly and wordlessly led her a little way from our decrepit hovel.

"Why are you staying in this place?" Little Fawn questioned, "You could be at Cousin Eagle Owl's with us. *With your family.*"

They probably thought they were whispering. Puh and I looked at one another. The only way to avoid hearing the conversation was to get away and go for a walk. Puh motioned toward the wide opening in the broken walls and taking the two dogs with us, we quietly made our escape. But as we departed, we could still hear Black Wolf's words.

"You *know* why I am not there."

"What have you gotten Tris into? This should never have happened! He is a dear sweet young man but he would never be an appropriate mate for our daughter…"

Puh and I started to walk faster to distance ourselves from their discussion.

We walked to the farthest set of gates, found them closed, and turned and took another well-worn path through the seemingly deserted village. Most of the village's inhabitants were indoors, probably eating their nightly sup. The few people we saw studiously avoided looking our way, nor did they say anything to us.

It was almost dark when we returned to the broken-down dwelling where we were camped. Black Wolf was alone and, apparently, he was still seething. He was visibly struggling to control his emotions. For the first time he seemed to realize that we had overheard a conversation presumed to be private.

"I am sorry you had to hear that," Black Wolf said. "Confounded woman! She is standing her ground like a mama bear over her cub! I do not know what I am going to do with her. And Eagle Owl, too, that old fool! I know he meant well, but…" he sighed heavily, "oh, but never mind. Come and eat while the food is still warm."

I joined Puh and Black Wolf for our evening meal, but my mind was divided between my thoughts of Morning Star and tomorrow's contest with Snow Leopard. I felt pathetically under-prepared. I had never before struck anyone or anything in anger. I had killed many animals, fish, and fowl—hundreds and hundreds of them, actually—but they were killed out of necessity. To eat or to avoid being eaten.

The idea of fighting someone I had never met to achieve my own aims was foreign to me. I finally rationalized that it would be akin to two stags battling over mating rights to the does in a harem: the cagey veteran buck versus the young untested challenger.

I was not sure if I was physically or mentally ready to metaphorically lock antlers with this man, but that was beside the point. The fact remained that events had been set in motion that would only be decided on the morrow.

 **Chapter Ten** 

It was a restless night for all of us. Even the dogs seemed uneasy. When the gray morning came I felt as though I had not slept at all. I was still haunted by my persistent Dreams of Morning Star as she broken-heartedly shed tears.

As planned, Eagle Owl met us outside the rickety building where we were camped. He then escorted us to the Challenge Circle. When we arrived, the villagers were already starting to assemble, despite the fact that the sun had not yet cleared the horizon. They were eagerly sharing gossip and gabbing about the coming event.

The Challenge Circle was constructed of huge mammoth tusks, stacked and overlapped end-to-end to form a jagged ring on the ground, perhaps nine or ten paces across. The inside of the Circle contained the same kind of mud and uneven patchy grass that made up most of the village's landscape. It did not look like a promising surface on which to fight, but I still did not care much about the actual process aside from the fact that I was determined to win, no matter what it took to succeed.

More and more villagers were arriving by the moment; including, to my surprise, Little Fawn and the children.

I could see that Morning Star was searching the crowd. When she spied my face, she squeezed her way through the mob.

"I would like to speak with you," Morning Star said as she reached my side.

I nodded. She took my hand and pulled me away from the throng. Her mother, being distracted with keeping her youngest children from wandering off, had not yet noticed that Morning Star was missing. However, Puh and Black Wolf had witnessed her approach and observed our sudden departure and they stared after us with open curiosity.

"Oh, Tris," she began. "I am so sorry for this! Parents! Why can they not leave us alone?"

My chest ached with sadness at the sight of her, now that I knew she did not want me. I just gazed at her forlornly, unsure of what to say.

"You have been my friend since I was a baby," she continued. "I would give anything so that you would not have to fight this man."

"Do you want him? To be paired with him?" I asked.

"What?" Morning Star looked at me as though I had asked her to pull a venomous snake out of her ear. "No! Ack! He is almost as old as Da. And he is a conceited boor, besides."

I was relieved to have my instincts so unequivocally confirmed.

"I have cried every night since my mother and Cousin Eagle Owl promised me to him," she added.

I was startled.

"What is it, Tris?"

"For the last many nights I have Dreamt that you are weeping."

Puh then called out to me; apparently, Snow Leopard had arrived.

"I would give anything to keep you from fighting this man." Morning Star repeated.

"I have to go now," I stated, reluctant to leave her. "But if any man *has* to fight to win me, I would want him to be you." She suddenly tiptoed and gently kissed my lips. It was the first time either of us had ever kissed a would-be lover. It happened so quickly that I almost wondered whether I had imagined it. At my look of surprise, she added softly: "Did you not know? There was never going to be anyone but you."

At that point, Puh came and grabbed me by the arm just as I was reaching for Morning Star, stunned and incapable of speech. At last I understood! *"He will never touch me!"* She had been speaking of Snow Leopard! *Not me!*

"Come on, Tris." Puh said as he pulled me away.

We returned to the outer edge of the Challenge Circle just as a brilliant orange sun broke over the tree line.

Now, the fight took on real meaning. Now, I cared about what happened. Puh and I rejoined Black Wolf, Eagle Owl, and Snow Leopard, identifiable by his snow leopard fur head covering and cloak. A stranger also stood by. I guessed this man to be a friend who was there in support of my competitor.

Snow Leopard was probably less than thirty winters old. I supposed that he might have been considered a handsome man, but for the cold and haughty air about him. He had black hair that hung down to the middle of his back in four braids and his beard was trimmed short. At a glance, the trimmed whiskers gave Snow Leopard the appearance of being younger than his peers, who typically wore their beards long in order to sport elaborate plaits.

Snow Leopard was tall, a little taller than I; but I was the heavier of the two of us. He looked fit and smug. He either did not know or did not care that Morning Star did not wish to be paired with him.

I, on the other hand, I was still giddy; Morning Star's kiss had given me the feeling of invincibility.

"So, who is my rival?" Snow Leopard asked as he removed his magnificent head covering and cloak, and passed both to his comrade.

Snow Leopard then slipped strings of eagle talons and bear claws from around his neck, carelessly placing them on top of the furs piled in his friend's arms. Finally, he pulled his tunic over his head and haphazardly threw it on top of everything, leaving his ally to hold his belongings until the Challenge was over.

"My good friend Tris is your rival," Black Wolf was stiff with formality as he presented me. "Snow Leopard, this is Tris. And this is his father, Tor."

I started to open my mouth to greet Snow Leopard, but stopped when he flinched as though stung.

"Is this a joke?" Snow Leopard was incredulous. "You have promised your daughter to a man of the Old Ones? If it is a joke, it is a very bad one. I will not fight him."

Black Wolf's polite façade disintegrated into a trembling rage and he stepped closer to Snow Leopard, towering over him.

"You will fight him, or you will fight *me!*" he said through clenched teeth. "Are you a coward? Or are you just an insufferable snob?"

"All right." Snow Leopard glowered at us but affected a bored tone. "Anyway, this will not take long." He took his place within the Circle.

I removed my cloak and gave it to Puh, who met my eyes with his own and he briefly laid his hand on my arm. We exchanged wordless but significant nods, and then I stepped over the tusks and into the ring. I stopped just out of Snow Leopard's reach and waited for him to make the first move. I did not know what else to do.

Snow Leopard looked me up and down, his mouth twisted into a sneer.

"Even if you beat me, you do not have the slightest chance of being paired with Morning Star," he whispered fiercely. "Black Wolf must be mad to even think of entering into an agreement with your family."

I did not respond.

"A beautiful woman of The People from the East would never demean herself by pairing with someone like you. You will never lay a hand on her."

I stared into his eyes, watching to see whether Snow Leopard would begin to lean one way or the other, like a wisent readying to charge. Despite the cool morning his forehead was beaded with sweat.

"Do you understand me?" he asked angrily. "Can you even speak?"

I remained silent, my deeply ingrained hunting skills busily at work. A predator does not make noise. A predator observes his prey and bides his time until it makes a faulty move.

Snow Leopard darted in for a quick blow, the

same kind of lightning jab that Black Wolf had demonstrated to me, but I knocked it away. In his frustration, Snow Leopard came at me again, but I grabbed his incoming arm and pulled him forward until he tumbled to the ground.

Snow Leopard rolled to his feet as gracefully as his namesake and upon becoming upright again, he seemed to take a moment to reassess the situation. In a flash, he was back on me with a series of quick blows. I warded some of them off with my right arm and took a stab at his jaw with my left which made his eyes roll up in his head for an instant, but he shook it off with no apparent lasting effect. I did not yet think that I was hurt. I did not feel any pain, only an acute awareness of my antagonist. Nothing else existed in that moment for me.

Snow Leopard and I slowly circled one another.

"*You!*" he hissed. "You are wasting my time! I should be preparing for another hunt instead of proving to everyone in this village that you are unworthy of a woman of The People. I *will* kill you!"

He flew in at me again. I lowered myself so that he came up over me and then I abruptly straightened, hitting the underside of his chin and his throat with the top of my head. I heard him gag for a moment and, when we separated, blood flowed from both sides of his mouth. It was not as effective as I had hoped, since I had planned on hitting him square in the throat, but he had bitten his tongue quite badly. At least there would be no more taunting from him. He was too preoccupied with spitting out mouthfuls of blood.

Snow Leopard was learning that I did not fight like one of The People. He was discovering that if he intended to win, he would have to change his strategy. Hatred shone from his eyes. He feinted in one direction and then darted in on my other side to land blows that hit my arms and chest as I tried to block him. Then Snow Leopard made contact through a good shot to my brow with his sharp fist.

Now both of us had red rivulets running freely down our faces. He sneaked in another jab to the left side of my head that caused an intense ringing in my ear. Snow Leopard continued to spit blood every few moments.

I had to find a way to stop those blows. By now, Snow Leopard had landed so many that the skin over his knuckles had split open. As I wiped at the streaming blood to keep it away from my eyes, I took advantage of the distracting movement to follow his example. I shifted my torso to the right and he turned to meet me but at the last moment, I dodged to the left and grappled Snow Leopard in a bear hug, pinning his arms to his sides. I squeezed hard, and heard Snow Leopard's breath leave him in a rush.

For a moment he struggled to release himself. When he seemed to faint, I dropped him to the ground.

But as he fell, his eyes popped open and I realized that going limp was just a ruse to escape my hold; to make me let go before I had inflicted too much damage.

Snow Leopard sprang up and flung himself at me, and we both hit the sodden ground with a distinctly wet thud. His quick jabs rained in on my ribs before I brought my arms in to protect my body. Ignoring his bony fists, I grabbed him by the skull and head-butted him. This made my eyebrow bleed more heavily but provided an opportunity to get back on my feet while he recovered his momentarily strayed wits.

I had barely made it to my feet when he launched himself at my legs and brought me down onto the muddy terrain once again. I drove my knee into his abdomen as he landed on top of me and at last, this was the end.

I had knocked the wind out of him. Snow Leopard lay there, gasping for air like a fish out of water. I scrambled to my feet, my chest heaving as I regained my breath.

I stood back and finally spoke to him.

"Do you withdraw your claim on Morning Star?"

Snow Leopard's face was a sickly gray color. He had no breath with which to speak. He nodded. He knew that if he did not relent, I would be upon him again before he could regain function and that this time, I would finish him.

Black Wolf and Puh joined us in the Circle.

"He was right," Black Wolf said cheerfully. "It truly did not take long!"

Puh took my arm and began to lead me away.

"You did well, Tris. Very well, in fact. But you are bleeding," he added, looking at me with deep concern.

"I think that some of that blood came from Snow Leopard," Black Wolf quipped.

It was only then that I noticed the general attitude of the crowd. No one looked very pleased.

"Congratulations on your victory, Tris," Eagle Owl said as he also scanned the faces, "but...and I mean this in the kindest way...I think you should leave. Leave the village at once."

I desperately wanted to see Morning Star, but I realized that he was right. The crowd was becoming increasingly menacing as the moments went by. Snow Leopard's friend was now in the Circle with him, helping him to sit up, but Snow Leopard had promptly rolled over and he was vomiting.

I studied the many faces but I saw neither Morning Star nor her family. Puh and Black Wolf positioned themselves on either side of me and escorted me away from the Circle, with Eagle Owl trailing behind.

We stopped at the broken-down hovel to collect our gear and then proceeded to Eagle Owl's house. Puh and Black Wolf attended to my wounds, which had stopped bleeding except for the trickle running down from the cut on my brow. Eagle Owl swiftly packed bags of food, both fresh and dried, and pushed them toward Puh and me.

"Go now. Go quickly! Go home while you still can." Eagle Owl stopped and stood before us with a look of affection and regret. "Safe journey," he continued. "I will come out and see you with Black Wolf in a few days."

"Many thanks to you, Eagle Owl," said Puh, grasping his forearm in farewell.

"Yes, many thanks," I repeated, also taking Eagle Owl's forearm in parting.

Black Wolf accompanied Puh and me to the doorway, where he put a brawny arm around each of us.

"I am going to stay here to await my family and take them home," Black Wolf said. "Be well. I will see you soon."

He was grinning broadly, still elated at the outcome of the Challenge.

"Safe journey," Puh nodded to Black Wolf. "And many thanks to you, my old friend."

"Safe journey, Black Wolf," I added. "Many thanks for standing by me. I will esteem you for it, always."

"Tris, it is I who must thank you," Black Wolf said as he looked at me kindly. "You were willing to put yourself in a very dangerous position for Morning

Star and you had the courage and the strength to triumph over some very serious odds. But then, that is why I put my faith in you as Morning Star's future mate. I know you will take good care of my daughter, that I will never have to worry for her nor any of the children you will have with her. When you become a father, you will realize just how much this means to me."

I was stunned and touched by Black Wolf's remarks. I probed my mind for something appropriate to say in response.

"I love her and I will always do my best by her." I vowed.

It seemed an inadequate statement to me, but as the multitude of thoughts swirled around inside my head, I found I was stricken speechless. I had wanted to ask so many questions: *When could I see Morning Star? How soon would they come to visit us?* And nothing had been said about when the pairing ceremony would take place. Would it be during the next moon? The next year?

I did not think that I could wait a year or anything like it. But still, the words did not come. My eyes searched Black Wolf's for any kind of comfort or information but he just looked at us with a gleeful smile.

"Go now," Black Wolf spoke at last. "We will talk soon."

With that, Puh and I departed. I had yet hoped to get a glimpse of Morning Star, if for nothing else, to get a sense of her feelings now that the Challenge had been completed. However, it was not to be. Was she really glad? I was eager for more of her kisses, to have her for my own.

***

"Well, Tris, you have done it." Puh smiled at me as we hiked steadily down the trail. "You have won what you have always wanted."

"Yes," I smiled a little bashfully, "what do you think Muh will say?"

"Your Muh will be happy for you. She will be upset when she sees your face because it will be swollen and bruised by the time we arrive in a few days. But, after all, it was for a good cause."

"I hope Muh agrees with you."

"She will," Puh assured me. We walked a few more steps before Puh went on: "Your Muh will most definitely appreciate what it means to you." He sighed. "I can hardly wait to see your Muh and your siblings again. I have been away from them far longer than I have ever been gone before."

The words were unspoken, but I knew that he was also contemplating the sobering reality that this time, he was extraordinarily lucky to be coming home to his family.

* * *

We heard Rooph's excited barking before we saw our home. Rooph and the younger children ran out to welcome us, followed by my older siblings and Muh, carrying Baby Mi. Ru took Mi from her mother's arms so that she could greet us. Muh clung to Puh, joyfully receiving and returning his fervent kisses. Muh then sorrowfully inspected the healing claw marks on his chest and next, she questioningly looked into my cheerful face, now puffy and discolored in spots, just as Puh had predicted.

When we entered our dwelling and I removed my cloak, Muh winced and shook her head as she saw the additional bruises on my torso.

My brother and sisters were full of questions about the new dog and our journey. Puh was eager to answer their queries and embrace and kiss each one. In fact, three winters old Saree complained at his exuberance.

"Ooh! Puh-Puh!" she squealed. "You are squeezing me too tight!"

A remorseful look passed over Puh's face and he eased his grasp on the squirming child.

"I am sorry, Little One," he said to her, gently setting her down with a final kiss on the top of her head. Undeterred, Saree clung to his leg, and the others also vied to be close to their father. Puh was well pleased to be back within the bosom of his family, but Muh frowned. She shushed them and sent them all outside.

"Do not annoy your Puh and brother with so much talk. They have been away for a long time and they must be tired and hungry. I am sure we will soon hear all about it." Once the room was quieted Muh turned to us. "I am so very glad that you are both home again."

Muh began to gather food and drink to serve us, but Puh pulled her into his lap and held her tightly, kissing her long and lovingly.

"Do not bother with the food just now. Just let me hold you." He rocked her in his arms for a moment, kissed Muh once again, and then began to speak: "Bror and Lor stopped in?"

"Yes." Muh sighed and it bespoke much worry and grief. She hugged Puh tighter. "They told me what happened. I was so terribly sorry to hear about Mror, but so relieved that you and Tris were all right. They said that you might bring home a dog. I see that Rooph and Raena are already good friends. She is very pretty."

"We also brought home the promise of a pairing for Tris," Puh said lightly.

Muh gaped at Puh, and then turned to look at me. I just grinned a sappy grin. Muh turned to Puh once more.

"Oh, how wonderful! Who is the family? Who is the girl?" Muh asked.

"It is a family we know well. And a very nice girl. I think she will keep Tris on his toes."

"Oh, do not tease me with suspense!" Muh laughed. "Who is it?"

"She is Black Wolf and Little Fawn's eldest daughter, Morning Star." Puh told her.

Muh looked at Puh and me in mute surprise, seemingly torn between happiness for me and her dismay at all the possible difficulties that could result from a pairing between a man of the Old Ones and a woman of The People. Then she must have decided that this was indeed happy news because she smiled broadly and wriggled to escape Puh's hold.

"Let me up, let me up." Muh said to Puh. She stood and warmly clasped me to her. "Oh, Tris, I know this is what you have always wanted. I am so pleased for you. Morning Star will make a lovely mate and I know she is very fond of you." She did not ask about the bruises and cuts on my face. Somehow, she knew. "Is there an agreement on when the pairing will take place?"

"Not yet," I finally found my tongue.

"Black Wolf will soon come to see us and then we will make plans," Puh said. "We had no opportunity to make them at that time. We were at the village and we had to leave in a bit of a hurry."

Muh gave us a somber but knowing glance, but soon brightened as a thought seemed to come to her.

"Spring is a beautiful time for a pairing celebration. Especially if we can add fresh greens to the feast. There will be lots of fresh spring greens ready by the full moon," Muh hinted. The full moon would soon be upon us and Muh well knew how long I had waited to be joined with Morning Star. I thought to myself: *Yes, that would be a good time to begin our lives together.*

* * *

The days passed peacefully as we awaited Black Wolf's arrival. After Puh's long absence, Puh and Muh enjoyed something of a honeymoon; not only lying together at night but sometimes they disappeared, returning later in the day, holding hands and smiling at one another.

Puh was right. If you want a happy life, find a loving mate. I hoped to have that with Morning Star.

Puh, my brother Ty, and I began work on constructing a new travois sled frame. We searched out supple saplings from which to make the sled and cut them down with our stone axes. Using bone chisels we shaped the ends and notched the places where the frames would join, held in place with glue and leather thongs that had been soaked in water before they were lashed around the joints. Ty, although he was still just barely on the threshold of adulthood, was a far better woodworker than I. He handled the tools with a deft touch and worked with complete concentration, frequently looking to Puh for confirmation of his technique or for his approval.

Puh, with endless patience, provided what little guidance Ty needed to accomplish his tasks. He always gave Ty plenty of well-deserved praise when his consummately executed joinery fit together as though the branches had grown that way.

Dak's death had left a huge void in Ty's life and I realized that probably no other person would ever truly fill that gap. I had Puh for a constant companion; Dak had been Ty's. Therefore, I took pains to be an amiable older brother in order to ease his grief and provide the camaraderie that Ty was so desperately missing.

I was glad that this sled project gave us something to work on together. And, it gave Ty a somewhat rare opportunity to spend time with Puh, without the distraction of the littlest siblings' constant demands on his attention. It was gratifying to see Ty smile with pleasure at Puh's compliments on his fine work. The boy who had always been so shy was coming into his own, gradually taking the form of a man. He was nearly as tall as Puh now. His dark red hair and high cheek bones showed that, in some ways, he resembled Muh's kin, but his broadening chest and shoulders testified to the fact that he would take after Puh, too.

Sometimes Puh and I, and occasionally Ty, left the family compound for the day to go hunting. We did not always come home with game but it was good to get out and see the world come back to life as the sun grew stronger and the days lengthened.

Although the warmer temperatures meant that Puh and I did not need the heavy tunics that we wore during most of the year, Muh busied herself with cutting and sewing new tunics to replace the ones we had ruined. We both had older tunics that still had lots of wear left in them, but Muh wanted us to look our best for the pairing ceremony. I, too, felt that it was important to represent our family in the best light.

* * *

After we had been home for six days Black Wolf and Eagle Owl arrived with several dogs in tow, including Raena's brother. This visit was more formal than was usual, given that it was to make arrangements for my pairing with Morning Star.

As Muh fussed over them and their comfort, she took a moment to casually mention that she favored a ceremony on the full moon, which was now only four days away. I thoroughly approved of Muh's idea. Black Wolf and Puh agreed.

That night, as we all sat around our outdoor hearth, Black Wolf led off the conversation.

"Well, Tor," he said as he turned to Puh. "I am glad this is done. And Little Fawn has come around to the notion that Tris and Morning Star will be paired. I knew she would. She loves Tris like a member of the family and surely there was nothing so likely to win her over as seeing Tris in the Challenge Circle, even if she had never seen anyone fight quite like that before. Most importantly, I believe, is that it was the first time Little Fawn realized that Morning Star truly loves Tris. During the bout, she found Morning Star at the edge of the Circle, sitting in the mud and sobbing because her dear one was taking such blows on her behalf. Little Fawn had to bodily lift Morning Star to her feet and drag her away."

Muh gasped. This was the first she had heard about the Challenge Circle. She had not asked and she probably preferred not to know.

"Yes, Tris!" Black Wolf looked toward me and grinned. "You are a hero at my house, now! Morning Star and all the children cannot stop talking about you. The boys have been inspired to throw themselves into mock battles with one another. Hawk head-butted Swift River and almost managed to knock both of them senseless! We have to watch to make sure that they do not do themselves a serious harm. The story of Tris and Snow Leopard will be told for many years to come. Of course, Snow Leopard is whining that it was not a fair fight and that a man of the Old Ones should never have been admitted to the Challenge Circle because of their killing strength. And Tris, what with your inexp-

-ience, that is what saved you. You only hit him once with your fist during that whole bout—your left, at that—it was a miracle that you did not shatter his jaw. If you had had time to learn how to become adept at throwing your fists, you could have killed him with such a blow. Snow Leopard should be heartily grateful that you did not seek to do more than disable him." Black Wolf shook his head. "The People at the village might not be happy about the humiliation of their finest hunter, but if they are smart, they will learn from it. The People and the Old Ones are not as different as some would think."

"We all want the same things," Puh agreed. "We all want to find a mate and be able to provide for our families and to beget the next generation."

Black Wolf nodded.

"That is not as easy as it used to be." Black Wolf said. "The People at the village complain about a lack of nubile women and a lack of game; they have to journey farther and farther away to find both. This has made me think about how it has been for the Old Ones, too. Life has been very difficult for many of the Old One's clans for a very long time. You have a nice living here in your long-held family compound and a few forays to the grasslands and coast every year, but most are not so lucky. And, like The People, I have not noticed that the Old Ones have many young women who are available for pairing. Even if they find a mate, then there is still the problem of procuring enough food to feed the family. How many clans struggle to bring their offspring to adulthood? Some are lucky to have two or three. You and I, Tor, have been exceedingly fortunate with our broods. And with our mates."

"All true," said Puh. "It can be tough, especially for our women who must bear our children while carrying on with a lot of heavy daily work, and still eat enough to support themselves while nursing one or two little ones at a time."

"I think," Black Wolf went on, "that The People and the Old Ones would benefit from combining our peoples into one people."

Puh and Eagle Owl looked a little startled. In fact, Eagle Owl seemed downright perplexed at the thought.

"Well," Puh smiled wryly. "I do not know if I want to associate that closely with someone like you."

"The next time you are stuck in a hole in the ground, see if I help to pull you out again!" Black Wolf laughed. They both chuckled, but Black Wolf continued. "I am serious. We have all heard the stories about pairings between the Old Ones and The People, but where these things happened, I do not know because I personally am not aware of any. So, no one around here has seen that the cooperation and fellowship between two peoples can be a good thing. Do you understand what I am saying? It is much the same as my travels to see Gray Elk to get new dogs. I could just have two dogs and let them breed, but I would need to bring in new blood now and then. New bloodlines make the animals smarter, stronger, healthier. I think it is the same with us."

"Well, there you are, Tris," Puh said, patting my knee. "You and Morning Star and your children will beget a new and improved line of people."

I just nodded. I had not really heard any of the conversation. My mind was still stuck on Black Wolf's statements that Morning Star loved me and could not stop talking about me.

Puh, Black Wolf, and Eagle Owl went on to speak about making future trades, particularly for the new batch of dried fish that we would make this summer. We had always managed to make our own spearheads and cutting tools; actually, learning to knap stone was one of the first things that a boy learned at the hands of his father. But last year we traded with Eagle Owl for a few spearheads and skinning tools, and Puh was very pleased with their quality.

Eagle Owl had access to sources of excellent stone and he could turn out pieces that were not only very functional, but especially when compared to our utilitarian blades, were works of art. As a man who worked with stone every day, he was not only able to produce exceptional blades, he sometimes used his talents to knap out tools, ornaments, and animal shapes when the creative urge struck him. He gave some of these novelties to friends or traded them for food or other necessities.

"Tris." In the midst of all the amiable chatter, Eagle Owl changed subjects and suddenly addressed me. "I want to make something special for you and Morning Star in honor of your pairing. Can you think of anything you need or want that I might provide?"

I was surprised by his question. I shook my head with a shrug and a smile.

"Many thanks for your thoughtfulness, Eagle Owl," I told him. "You are very kind, but I honestly cannot think of a thing."

"I will come up with something." Eagle Owl was undeterred. "Something that will bring you both luck. Every freshly paired couple needs plenty of luck as they embark on their new lives together. It is the least I can do after so very nearly ruining your chances of being mates."

With this statement Puh and Black Wolf both looked up sharply at Eagle Owl, eager to allay his guilt.

"Do not think on it, Eagle Owl," I said. "I know that you always do what you think is right for all of us. I would never question your motives. And, besides, it has worked out for the best."

We smiled at one another. Then Eagle Owl again switched topics and began to tell us about some hunters who traveled farther afield and returned with tales about other peoples who used new hunting weapons. There was something called an atlatl that *threw* your spear faster and with more force than could be achieved by hand.

He demonstrated how the notched stick functioned, but I wondered if it would work well with our lengthy, heavy spears. A spear had to be longer than its owner was tall, so that if you tripped and fell you were less likely to be impaled on your own weapon, and it had to be sturdy enough to subdue a panicked and thrashing beast. Puh must have been thinking along the same lines.

"Our spears would be too long and much too heavy," he said. "Specialized projectiles would have to be created. Also, until you developed a great proficiency with the weapon, you would lose a lot of control as to where your spear made contact with the animal. Then too, it would be subject to the whims of the wind unless you were hurling your spear directly downwind. I could see that a hunter would end up chasing after a lot of poorly wounded prey."

"I am not that fond of running," Black Wolf said as he nodded in agreement. "I think I will stick with my spear." He paused and smiled. "Both literally and figuratively."

"Then there are stories about a flexible stick that launches little spears into the air," Eagle Owl continued. "I am not sure how tiny the spears are or how powerful they might be, but I think they might work well on small game."

It was pleasant talk. All at once, it occurred to me that this was the first time I had been included in this kind of post-evening meal discussion that had always been restricted to talk between Puh and the visiting men. I was one of them now, but yet for as little as my mind was present, I might as well have been a day's hike away. Although I was able to focus on bits and pieces of the conversation, I was more apt to be absorbed in my own thoughts as I stared into the fire's hypnotic flames.

Gradually, I became aware of a soft whistling-rushing noise in the air aloft. I looked up into the nighttime sky, where a slow procession of clouds gently drifted across the face of the swelling moon and the sparkling stars that twinkled in the crystalline firmament.

Sometimes the whistling-rushing sound was louder, sometimes it was barely perceptible.

"Ducks," said Puh.

It was only then that I noticed that Puh, Black Wolf, and Eagle Owl had fallen silent, listening to the flocks of migrating ducks as they passed overhead, invisible to our eyes, but their cooing and the muted feathery flapping of their wings revealed their presence to our ears. The men resumed their talk, but I continued to gaze up at the sky, listening to the fowl and willing the moon to wax fat and round so that my pairing day would arrive all the sooner. Quiet chuckles brought my attention back to my companions. I turned to look at them.

"Tris, you look lost to this world," Eagle Owl observed.

"Perhaps I am," I admitted with a smile.

"He may be lost to *this* world," said Puh, "but he is contemplating finding the world of the future."

Chapter Eleven

Black Wolf and Eagle Owl departed early the next morning to carry the details of the pairing ceremony back to their family. Since Eagle Owl had so enjoyed the dried fish, Muh gave him a gift of fish to take with him. They would all return in three days, to place Morning Star's hands in mine. Then we would have the ceremonial feast, during which I would feed Morning Star and she would feed me, to symbolize our soon-to-be realized lifetime of care and devotion.

I found myself to be suddenly forgetful and clumsy. It was as though my mind had gone off a-wandering without me.

But I was deliriously happy as I imagined our lives together and what it would be like to physically possess her. The one tantalizing kiss that was little more than a brief touch of lips was all I had ever had of her and I was almost frantic for more.

* * *

Great Gran came to see us. We sometimes carried supplies up to her home, but Great Gran did not visit often. She preferred her solitude with her furry pets. She had lost her parents, her siblings, her mate, and all her offspring. My Puh was one of her few surviving grandchildren. She had known a good deal of grief in her sixty-four winters and it was almost as though she was afraid to be close to anyone except her squirrels.

Sometime after Black Wolf and Eagle Owl had gone, Gran hobbled down from her little hillside home. She found me absentmindedly sharpening a stone awl. I needed the awl to finish the necklace I planned to give Morning Star as a pairing ceremony gift.

"Ah, Tris, you are just the one I am seeking," Gran said as she sat down beside me.

Great Gran was small, but still sturdy and healthy. Other than her white hair, a number of missing teeth, and a slight limp, she might have been a much younger woman. Her hair had been the color of snow for as long as I had known her and she wore it up, like Muh.

Great Gran was attired in the typical daily garb of adult female Old Ones: a simple knee-length deerskin gown which was layered under an older gown that had been cut and resewn into an apron to help prolong the life of the newer garment. On her feet, Gran wore the tall boots that most women donned to protect their knees and lower legs. A squirrel was perched on the top of her head and another sat on her shoulder. Rooph showed little interest in the squirrels because he was used to her pets after all these years, but Raena barked furiously at them. I shushed Raena.

"Hello, Gran. Is there something I can do for you?" I asked.

Great Gran always had an aura of an intense keenness about her. When she looked at me, I felt as though she read my thoughts and saw all that was contained in my very innermost being.

Gran studied my battered visage and torso. She put her hands on my face and turned it left and right, so she could see every mark.

"Hmmm!" she said. "I Dreamt that you did battle with a man of The People and you won. You won a mate. When is the pairing ceremony to take place?"

"Yes, I did. I won Morning Star." I replied. "I am so happy, Gran. We will be paired on the day of the full moon."

Gran gave me a gap-toothed grin and gently patted my cheek. Her touch was cool and dry. She gazed at me tenderly for a few moments.

"Ah, Tris. You look so much like your Puh when he was your age," she said. "You are taller, of course, thanks to your mother's people, but your face, your light red hair, and your eyes are just the same as Tor's. He is a good man to take after."

"Yes," I agreed, smiling at her. We had spoken these words many times before.

"Well," she continued, "I would like to talk to your Muh and Puh. Are they inside?"

"Yes," I said again, knowing that right at this moment Muh would be giving Puh the look that told him not to let Gran in with those squirrels still on her person. "Let me hold your little friends while you are visiting," I offered.

Great Gran stood up, leaned in to kiss my forehead, and placed both squirrels in my hands as casually as if she were giving me a couple of pine cones. I just hoped that I could juggle the squirrels without losing one before she came back. Raena began to bark again and I shushed her once more.

Gran did not stay long. She retrieved her squirrels but before she began her climb back up the hill, she gave me a smile, a caress along my bearded jaw line, and finally a wave of her hand. I had just resumed sharpening the stone awl when Puh and Muh called to me.

"Gran wants to give you her house," Muh announced. I was startled. I pictured the little dwelling that was built into the side of the slope and the squirrels that inhabited it with her.

"But where will Gran live?"

"She wants to come here," said Puh. "Gran wants you to have a home of your own, and besides, at her age she would be safer if she lived with us. We have talked about this event coming to pass for years. I think it would be easier for everyone if Gran was with us so we can care for her as she continues to age…not that she needs much care yet. And, after all, there was a time when this was her home."

Muh did not look entirely pleased. Puh squeezed her hand to comfort her.

"I will put my foot down. We will allow no squirrels in the house!" he insisted. "Besides, Gran is not one to sit idle. She will help you with the chores and the children."

"Just so long as those squirrels do not come with her." Muh smiled reluctantly. "It is bad enough that she lets them eat up half of her food stores, they do not need to start on ours! We have enough trouble just coping with mice! But really, she should not be alone all the time. Maybe if she had the children to take up her attention, she would not miss her squirrels too much."

Actually, I thought it was more likely that the squirrels would be running up the hill and attempting to get back into their old house again, but I shrugged off the idea. My mind could hardly concentrate on anything these days.

* * *

Great Gran's dwelling had very little in it: a fireplace for heat and cooking, a place to sleep, and a side room where she stored her winter's supply of food and some dry firewood. All showed evidence of the generations of squirrels who had lived there.

How could I bring Morning Star here? But then, neither could I insult Gran.

Gran moved in with us the next morning. For the rest of the day, Puh and I removed the few things she had left in the store room and placed them outdoors to be burned.

We then swept the house clean and cut pine boughs, which we placed in every nook and cranny, and scattered them over the floor to help sweeten the smell. I could only hope that it would be presentable by the time I was to bring Morning Star to our new home after the pairing ceremony celebration.

* * *

We all felt the weight of the coming event. I had to admit that I did not think there would have been anywhere near as many preparations if I was about to be paired with a woman of my own kind. This was a momentous occasion for our family and we were profoundly aware that Black Wolf had done us a great honor by making it possible. Every family member, from Great Gran to my youngest sibling, my baby sister Mi at only ten moon cycles of age, was scrubbed to perfection and dressed in our best clothing. Everyone's red curly locks were twisted and corded into submission, and Muh and Ru had decorated their hair with multitudes of colorful feathers. Both the indoor and outdoor components of our household were swept and decorated with spring flowers and boughs cut from fir trees. Muh, Gran, and Ru assembled the foods that would make up our meal while Puh and I tried to stay out of the way and not to dirty our clothes or ourselves. My brother Ty, bored and annoyed with all the commotion, had wisely escaped to some quiet locale earlier that morning.

Puh and I had to find something to do to pass the time—at least I did—or else the level of apprehension and anticipation that I felt would become unbearable.

Muh suggested we take the younger children for a walk to get them out of the way while she, Gran, and Ru worked to finish the last of the pairing day tasks.

Puh readily agreed, and he lifted Baby Mi from her mat on the ground and began to shepherd the children toward the path that led away from our home. Saree took his free hand and, as I walked beside him, Twie grasped one of mine. In my other hand, I carried a spear. We were always sure to never leave the family compound without carrying at least one weapon.

Both Rooph and Raena escorted us, Rooph with his panting plodding steps and Raena bounding up and down the trail with her endless energy and quick light tread.

Puh seemed thoughtful. I was rather lost in my own reflections, myself, but his softly pensive countenance made me curious.

"What is it, Puh?" I inquired.

Puh broke from his reverie with a sheepish smile.

"I was just thinking," he began, "that it did not seem that long ago when I was carrying you as I now carry your baby sister. It does not seem possible that so much time could have passed so quickly. These days, you are big enough to carry me! And it will not be long before it will be you who is toting around children of your own. I guess every parent must feel this way when their offspring first begin to leave home…I thought I would be ready for it when the day came." Puh blinked and hesitated before going on, "I just want you to know that I love you…and that I am *so* very proud of you."

Puh had never before said anything like this to me. I had always hoped that he was at least satisfied with me as a son. Never for a moment had I ever doubted his love for me, nor for any of the members of our family, but it was good to hear these sentiments.

I felt as though a huge lump had suddenly grown in my throat. I swallowed hard to force it down. I took a deep breath before responding.

"Puh, those words mean a lot to me." I replied. "I love you, too. You have made me into the man I am and, if I am a credit to you, it is because you labored to make me so."

Twie tugged at my hand.

"Tris, I love you, too!" she exclaimed. "Puh-Puh, I love you, as well!"

Saree, not to be outdone, chimed in with her clear sweet piping voice.

"Me too! Me too!" she said with soundless laugh, "Love Puh-Puh and Tris and Twie and Mi!"

Baby Mi squeaked cheerfully as if in agreement, but only uttered "Puh-Puh!"

Puh halted our walk to kneel down and gather his little girls to him. He gave them numerous hugs and kisses, stroking their curly heads and their delicately speckled faces, telling each one how much he adored them and how they made him a very happy Puh-Puh.

"Puh-Puh, your whiskers tickle me!" Twie said as she rubbed her plump cheeks. However, she giggled and snuggled up to his bearded face, just the same, "But it is good sort of tickle."

Rooph and Raena could not be left out. They also came close to receive their cuddles and words of praise. Never was there a more handsome or noble dog than Rooph, nor a more attractive or smart dog than Raena.

After we had all spoken of our mutual feelings of affection, I belatedly realized that we were, each of us, sitting on the dirt where countless footsteps had worn away the plant life to bare ground in the middle of the path. I quickly stood up and brushed off my knees. Puh followed my example, taking a moment to gently pat away the loose earth that clung to the little girls' clothing. It would not do to arrive back at the family compound in anything other than spotless condition.

We did not stay away for too long. I did not want to take any chances on being tardy for the event that would be the most important of my life to date. I wanted this day to be perfect.

I was not only on edge about the pairing ceremony, but I was actually more afraid that something would happen to prevent Black Wolf and his family from coming.

I also worried that the gift that I had made for Morning Star would seem frivolous to her. I had used all of my spare time during the last few days to finish the necklace of tiny shells and now it seemed like a poor offering to the woman I loved and with whom I would spend the rest of my life. As I waited for her arrival, I placed the necklace around my own neck and tucked it inside my tunic. I would give it to her when the time felt right.

* * *

At last, Rooph's and Raena's barks signaled their approach. Eagle Owl and Black Wolf's entire family trooped into our compound, with Black Wolf and Little Fawn on either side of Morning Star. They had obviously taken pains with their appearances, too.

Morning Star's hair was not braided as usual, but hung, smooth and loose past her hips. She wore a garment of deerskin, carefully fitted, and trimmed at the neckline with the dark brown fur of a marten.

Morning Star's eyes were lowered at first, but she was smiling. When she looked up to meet my gaze, her grin broadened and my heart leapt like a startled deer at the sight.

We were all in place now. Black Wolf and Little Fawn grasped Morning Star by the elbow and led her forward to where I stood with Muh and Puh. Black Wolf took Morning Star's hands and placed them in mine. Her hands seemed so small and fine as I enclosed them within my own.

"Tris, son of Tor," Black Wolf began, "I give you my daughter Morning Star. May she bring you much happiness and many children. And may you each bring to this pairing much love and contentedness."

"Many thanks, Black Wolf," I responded. "I gladly accept her with every fiber of my being."

Our families rushed forward to congratulate us and there was much celebratory hugging and kissing. When the tide of people receded, Morning Star turned to me and gently touched the remnants of the damage to my face. Her formerly beaming expression dimmed somewhat.

"Your poor face," Morning Star lamented. "It is still healing."

"It is all right," I assured her. And it *was* all right. Nothing could possibly bother me now. Not even Black Wolf's teasing remarks when he overheard Morning Star's words.

"Tris is just following in his father's footsteps," he said. "It will not be too many years before his face will bear as many marks as his Puh's!"

Morning Star ignored him as well.

"Did I ever tell you how much I love your eyes?" she murmured to me.

I shook my head and wondered whether I had ever spoken to her of how I had always admired her dark brown eyes.

"They are wonderful, you know," Morning Star went on, "I have always wanted to have the slightly larger eyes that you Old Ones have, and yearned to own eyes of such a shade of green. It is true that your kind look a little different from The People, but I have always liked that difference."

I was surprised but pleased to know that she approved of my appearance. All the same, I was appalled that she would want anything other than her own astonishingly beautiful eyes. In my opinion, our drab irises and pale eyelashes were uninspiring, to say the least, compared to hers, so dark and liquid and alluring.

"Please do not wish to look any other way," I said. "I have cherished you just as you are for as long as I can remember. And most especially, I have prized your lovely eyes."

"Oh, Tris, you are sweet to say that." Morning Star's bright smile returned. "But still, I hope our babies have your eyes." She squeezed my hands as she looked up into my face.

I sighed wistfully at the thought of having children with Morning Star. Or, to be honest, the thought of begetting babies with Morning Star.

"I do not care what color eyes our babies have," I said earnestly. "Or what color skin or hair. Just so long as we are together."

* * *

It was a perfect day for an outdoor ceremonial meal. The air was pleasantly warm and many of the new spring leaves and blossoms on the trees were just opening. We sat or reclined on the numerous hides spread on the ground and ate a multitude of foods including reindeer, roast stuffed ducks, roast tubers and onions, and fresh greens. Some greens were eaten cooked and others were consumed raw. There were also the sticky sweet honey seed cakes that we only produced for special occasions. It was a cheerful meal that included much talk and laughter.

Everyone wished us well over and over again. Morning Star and I were too tongue-tied to say much in return except my *many thanks* and Morning Star's *thank you.*

Although it was not usual to give gifts at a pairing ceremony, Eagle Owl, true to his word, presented to us his offerings: an axe head for me and a grinding pestle for Morning Star. The axe head was magnificent. It was flawless in shape and substantial enough to cut even the hardest timber.

I hefted it in the palm of my hand approvingly.

"Many thanks to you, Eagle Owl," I said. "This is extraordinary! I have never seen its equal!"

The pestle was of a fine, green stone and it was also very well done. Morning Star held it up for everyone to see and then inspected it admiringly.

"I, too, want to thank you for the pestle," Morning Star turned to Eagle Owl. "It is just what I will need in my new home!"

She touched Eagle Owl's hand and gave him a quick kiss on the cheek that had at first had surprised him, because she bussed his blind side so that he had not known it coming until he felt her lips on his face. He blushed but seemed very pleased as he somewhat bashfully waved aside our remarks.

"No thanks are needed," Eagle Owl said. "Just be happy together. I hope you will remember me kindly each time you chop wood or do any pulverizing."

While everyone was busy with their food and conversation, Morning Star and I were absorbed with shyly feeding one another. I was used to shoveling generous amounts of food into my own mouth and I had to remind myself not to give her more than she could easily chew. Morning Star, on the other hand, seemed concerned that she was not feeding me enough and pressed ever larger pieces of food at me.

When we finished, Morning Star thoughtfully turned toward me. She studied me for a moment before speaking.

"I have to ask something of you," she whispered. "Why did you not ask Da for me sooner? You have been a man for several years and I have been a woman for a while, as well. I knew that you loved me too. I waited and waited. Why did you not ask?"

I was taken aback by this question, but searched my heart for a reply.

"Because I did not think that you cared for me, that is, that you cared for me as a mate. And I did not think that your family would consider me to be worthy of you." I told her.

"Oh, how could you not know?" Morning Star's expression softened and she caressed my face. "Do you remember the day we set out to visit Gray Elk and I arranged your hair before we left? My mother had just given me a lecture about behaving myself and readying my mind to be paired, because she and Da were going to start making serious inquiries about finding a mate for me. That morning I was so desperate for you to act before they could promise me to anyone. I hinted to you, but you just stared at me."

I was supposed to know? I was flummoxed. I could not recollect anything that would have suggested that Morning Star had wanted me, too.

"The same as you are staring at me right now," she continued. "Oh, I am sorry, Tris. I guess it could not have been easy for you, either. But here we are, at last. We are paired now. It may have been a rather convoluted route, but we have arrived at the same happy destination."

We both smiled at the thought.

"Yes. It is indeed a favorable outcome. One that I have desired since I was a boy," I replied. The words seemed somehow understated. After all, I was ecstatic! Actually, I was beyond ecstatic! She was mine! She was *really* mine! Morning Star was *finally really* my own mate and we now had our whole lives to spend together!

I then recollected the shell necklace I had made and reached into my tunic to lift it from around my neck.

"I made this for you," I said, "it is but a poor token of what I feel…"

"Do not say that." Morning Star took it from me and dropped it over her head, then rearranged her hair so that it was no longer tangled in the necklace. "I love it, Tris! I have never seen so many shells! Thank you! It is a lovely gift! I am going to show it to my mother and my sisters."

Morning Star stood and left my side to display the necklace, turning back to look at me with a glowing smile. Great Gran, Muh, and my older sisters joined the group, *oohing* and *aahing* with gratifying admiration.

I stood up as well, letting sensation rush back down into my numb legs after a long period of sitting.

"Your present went over very well," Puh said as he approached me. "I hope she likes her new home just as much."

"I hope so, too." I had noticed a slight odor in the air during the last few moments.

I was suddenly afraid that there could be some lingering smell from the pile of trash we had burned outside of Gran's house, and that it might be drifting towards us.

"I think I will walk up the hill and make sure that everything is as it should be." I told Puh.

"You are going to your new house?" Black Wolf asked. "I would like to see it, too. Morning Star's bundle of belongings is over there. I will retrieve it and carry it up for her."

Puh, Black Wolf, and I trudged up the hill with Rooph and Raena at our heels. The smell actually seemed lesser up here. I was encouraged to see that the little dwelling was clean and well aired. Someone, probably Muh and Gran, had brought flowers and greens and had added more supplies to what little I had already placed in the storage area, which was now well stocked with stacks of firewood, an additional water bag, and a several new baskets containing various foods.

I was touched and grateful for their foresight. I had expected to amass all our household goods myself, diligently laboring to produce and carry all our necessities up the hill to our home as quickly as I could procure them. I arranged a sleeping platform by the wall opposite the hearth and stowed a few personal belongings, such as my few spare items of clothing, and some of the tools I had made, or was in the process of completing, and my collection of spears.

Black Wolf looked around the cozy chamber and set Morning Star's pack on the floor near the hearth. He seemed bigger than ever since he could not quite stand up straight in the small room, but he nodded with a grin.

"This is a good place," Black Wolf stated. "It will be a happy place to begin life as a newly paired couple. You will be able to add on more rooms later."

"There is good ventilation in the summer, but the protecting hillside keeps it warm in the winter," Puh said. "It would be easy to enlarge the dwelling by excavating further into the hillside." He indicated the wall where I had placed our bed. "And maybe Tris will want to raise the ceiling a bit, too." Puh glanced from me to Black Wolf. "This home was not built with the idea that it might one day be inhabited by tall people."

At that moment, we were startled by the sounds of shouts and screaming. We looked at one another in alarm. I grabbed my knife and best spear, and Puh and Black Wolf took up two of my spears as well. We ran out the doorway and down the hill, the dogs barking as they loped alongside us.

When we reached the main compound, our families were gathered, sobbing, around Eagle Owl as he lay bleeding from gaping wounds to his chest.

"They took her! *They took her!*" Little Fawn cried. Her knees buckled and she collapsed against Black Wolf.

It was then that I realized that my Morning Star was gone.

Great Gran and Muh were somberly trying to stanch the blood that flowed from Eagle Owl's body. Eagle Owl struggled for breath.

"Snow Leopard...I never thought he would do anything such as this...whatever scruples and honor he once had are gone!" he gasped.

Black Wolf seemed almost too beside himself for coherent thought. I forced my reeling mind to focus and knelt beside Eagle Owl.

"Do you have any idea where he might have taken her?" I asked.

"No..." Eagle Owl shook his head, "except to say that...he is not familiar with this area...so he will not stay here...he will go to a place he knows."

Eagle Owl panted. "He came with…a large group of men…I did not count…but there were…maybe twenty of them…I did my best…I tried…to protect Morning Star…"

"Many thanks, Eagle Owl," I said, looking deeply into his eyes to convey my sincerity and momentarily clasped his heavily callused hand.

I left Eagle Owl's side and quickly filled a small water bag. Puh and Black Wolf rushed to assemble their weapons and pack a small amount of food and water, but I did not wait for them.

I noted many footprints where the raid had taken place and saw the blood where Eagle Owl had made his valiant stand. Starting to run, I followed the tracks down the path that led away to the east.

I could hear that Puh and Black Wolf were somewhere behind me, trying to catch up.

"Tris, wait!" Puh called, "Stop! *Tris, stop!*"

I would not stop. I could not stop. I was desperate to reach Morning Star. But Puh's persistence finally made me relent. I slowed my pace just enough to allow them to catch up.

"Tris," Puh said, "they will expect to be pursued! You cannot go running ahead on your own. They will leave a group behind to lie in wait for us at some point and if you find them first, they will surely kill you."

"That is right," agreed Black Wolf. "It will take all of us to meet them. They are only men of the village.

We, as free peoples of the forest, will be tougher adversaries than they are used to, but they vastly outnumber us, so we must stay together."

"They may only be men of the village in your eyes," Puh said, "but I would not underestimate them. They live differently than we do, but they are more accustomed to fighting to gain their own way and to eliminate rivals."

"That is one of the many reasons why I have never wanted my offspring to be paired with any of them in the first place." Black Wolf shook his head ruefully. "How Eagle Owl has withstood village life, I will never understand. I guess that once he became physically impaired and had to give up hunting and find another way to make a living, he would have needed access to more people who would trade for his blades. It has given him independence and made him a man of substantial means, but at what cost? How I wish we had never gone to see him! The old fool. And now he has likely given his life in defense of my daughter."

We had not stopped moving, but we now picked up our pace once again, running down the trail, alert for any sign that they might have veered off into the forest or separated into two or more groups.

There were occasional splatters of blood amongst their tracks, so I gathered that Eagle Owl had managed to wound at least one of them. The intermittently broken ground also bore signs of occasional struggles as

Morning Star resisted her abductors. These indications showed that my beloved mate was sometimes carried, sometimes dragged, sometimes trotting with them.

Attired as we were in our pairing ceremony clothing, we were soon exceedingly hot as we ran in the mid-day sun. We halted long enough to remove our tunics and tucked the sleeves into the ties that held our loincloths and leggings around our hips. This, at least, allowed our upper bodies to release some of the pent-up heat.

I wanted to run faster, but I knew I had to pace myself if I was going to travel any distance. Although Puh and Black Wolf were a generation older than I, they ran almost as easily as I did. We were doggedly determined to run until our chests burst or until we caught up with Snow Leopard and his cronies.

* * *

We had continued down the trail long enough for the shadows to noticeably lengthen when I heard the caws from agitated crows. Something was upsetting them.

We slowed to a walk, cautious now. The crows' cries became louder and more raucous as we neared. We stopped. I listened. I heard breathing, lots heavy breathing. Puh and I exchanged glances. Puh had heard it as well, and he motioned to Black Wolf that there was someone up ahead and pantomimed a person who was exaggeratedly winded. Black Wolf nodded. Whoever they were, we could tell that they had not been there long since they were still collecting their breath and the crows had not yet settled down.

We left the trail and stealthily crept through the trees and brush toward the group. It was impossible to be totally silent, but I hoped that the noise from the crows and the men's panting breathes and pounding hearts would help to mask our footsteps in the softly crackling litter that covered the ground.

Suddenly, Black Wolf put out his arm to stop our progress. He pointed towards his eyes and then toward a hammock of bushes and small trees just to our left. Black Wolf's greater height allowed him to see the dark forms hiding there before Puh and I were able to glimpse them. Black Wolf held up fingers to indicate that there were nine of them.

We could not avoid this deadly predicament. If we did not dispatch this band of men, there was every chance that they might double back to our compound in search of us and massacre our families as they awaited our return. And, unlike the Challenge, this would not be a matter of simply seeking disabling my opponents, as during the bout with Snow Leopard. This time, I was required to kill them.

Puh took me by the shoulders and wordlessly pushed me to stand between himself and Black Wolf before we burst forth from our hiding place. While I was moved by this gesture, it struck me as ironic that someone smaller than I would try to protect me from possible harm.

Slowly, we made our way closer and then charged through the last layer of brush to come down on the would-be attackers. With the advantage of complete surprise, we were each able to immediately slay the first man with well-placed jabs of our spears. But afterwards, we had no choice but to stand back to back and parry thrusts with the remaining six members of the ambush party. There was no time for thought, only action and reaction. We were in a frenzy of wild-eyed grunting stabbing rage.

Due to Black Wolf's great size, I was not surprised to see him easily handle the man who came up against him but even as well as I knew Puh and had always admired his toughness and strength, I was awed to see his courage and killing proficiency. The men of The People seemed to target Puh, apparently assuming that he would be the least difficult to take down but, in fact, with an economy of his powerful movements he dispatched a total of three men with remarkable deftness.

When only two of Snow Leopard's followers were left, they broke away at a run and we had to chase them down. Black Wolf's long strides brought him to the lagging man first. He swatted the man's spear aside and grabbed him by the head and gave his skull a violent twist, breaking the man's neck. Black Wolf's unfortunate victim dropped like a stone.

The second rallied and turned toward Puh and me with his weapon at the ready. He seemed to be the leader of the group. He was tall and sharp-featured, dressed in apparel that was of a quality far above even our pairing ceremony clothing. He was panting for breath and nicked here and there with small wounds, but then we all were. His eyes flashed with anger and indignation.

"Where is Snow Leopard taking Morning Star?" I demanded as we held him at bay.

Black Wolf came up behind us.

"If you tell us where Snow Leopard is taking my daughter, we will spare you." Black Wolf said, in hopes that the man might take the bait.

"What?" He retorted, chest heaving, "so you can go after them, and try to retrieve her? So that she can be paired with this *thing*?" He indicated me. "This *red-haired* thing?"

"That is an altogether unsatisfactory answer," Black Wolf replied. And he swiftly launched his spear forward with a powerful lunge that affixed the man to the tree at his back. He had to pull hard to wrest his spear free. He checked the blade for chips or cracks, and then solemnly looked up at us. "I have never killed a man before today."

"Neither have I," said Puh, "but there will be many more men to face before this is over."

We took a few moments to inspect our weapons and our persons for damage. My knife had been dropped somewhere. I had to search the area before I found it where it had been kicked to the side, half obscured by sticks and dead leaves.

Luckily—very luckily—none of our lacerations were deep. Black Wolf had a sizable gash across the outside of the palm on his left hand as the result of deflecting that spear-thrust away, but it was the worst of our collective injuries. Normally, Black Wolf's extended reach meant that he was seldom wounded about the face and body by the animals that we hunted, but this time, fighting an enemy armed with spears led to his being struck as often as were Puh and I.

Our new pairing ceremony clothes were sadly slashed and stained with blood and sweat. Puh and I, whose coiled and corded hair was not tightly braided like Black Wolf's, found that our cords were in the process of escaping from their bindings. We all three each looked as desperate as we felt.

I tried to swallow some water, but felt nauseous and gagged on it. I could see that I was not the only one who was a bit shaky from our exertions and the shock of the terrible carnage that had occurred at our hands. But before long, we were finally able to gulp some water and we were ready to resume tracking Snow Leopard and his troop—and Morning Star.

We set off at a trot, anxious to make up the distance we had lost while we were diverted with the failed ambushers.

The setting sun burnished the landscape with warm golden hues. Under other circumstances, I would have marveled at the beauty of the colors. But just then I could only think about trying to anticipate Snow Leopard's possible plans and the various counter-strategies we could implement to rescue Morning Star.

As the moon rose, I welcomed the refreshing and invigoratingly chilly night air. With each expiration, our breath misted in the pale lunar light. The only good thing about all the tears and slices in my clothing was that they provided some ventilation to cool my body.

As the temperature continued to drop, we were forced to eventually pause just long enough to don our tunics once more. And then we ran on in the semi-darkness, our footfalls beating a steady rhythm on the murky moonlit trail.

 **Chapter Twelve** 

The forest, often a friendly and cheerful place by day, could seem ominously forbidding at night. Different animals roamed at large, looking for sustenance, a mate, hoping to avoid predators or to find prey. Even with the aid of the moon's gentle glow, the path was still treacherous in places, and we frequently stumbled over raised roots and other low-lying obstacles.

We stopped periodically to listen and sniff the air, but we only heard the sounds of the wind in the trees and the rustle of small animals moving in the brush. Sometimes we were startled by the crash of a heavy beast passing through the woods somewhere close by. Even a comparatively well-lit meadow concealed a momentarily disquieting surprise when we spooked several coveys of quail that then exploded into the air from the grass near our running feet. But we kept moving onward.

* * *

The night had half-exhausted itself when we came to a stream where we stopped long enough to drink and to wipe at the blood and perspiration on our faces. As I washed, the gritty feel of the water told of all the dirt which must have accumulated on my body as the dust from each of our strides was kicked up and adhered to our sweat-moistened skin.

Nevertheless, the cold water and a bit of dried meat helped to energize us. We set off once again, cautiously trotting across the darkened landscape.

There was nothing to mark the passage of time until the moon set and the sun began to brighten the sky. We were heading roughly east.

When we passed sections of bare earth on the trail, we could see that Snow Leopard and his party were still following the path. The length of their gaits was considerably shorter now and it looked as though Morning Star was being carried as often as she was running.

Every time I saw her smaller footprints, my chest ached as I thought of her fright and her exhaustion. I hoped that she was not hurt. I also hoped the fact that the group had to keep going meant they did not have time to abuse her. Even if they thought we were now ambushed and dead, they could not know for sure that others would not be sent after them in pursuit.

We stopped to drink and eat another piece of dried meat as the rising sun still hung low in the sky. Puh, Black Wolf, and I had fought, run, trotted, walked, and staggered since yesterday afternoon, but nevertheless, we were still eager to resume tracking Morning Star as soon as possible.

We were just starting to jog forward again when we noticed that the telltale signs of numerous men having passed this way just before us had come to an abrupt end. We looked around us.

"Here," said Puh, pointing to some trodden white flowers just off the path. "I think that they turned off here. Many big feet would crush the plants like this." He knelt down and inspected the flattened flowers. "There are shells," he added. Puh picked up a few tiny sea shells and held them out for Black Wolf and me to see. They were shells from the necklace I had made for Morning Star. She was leaving a trail for us.

"Clever!" Black Wolf smiled grimly.

* * *

Snow Leopard and his group were doubling back through the woods. We headed away from the rising sun and followed the path of disturbed ground litter, trampled plants, and little sea shells. Given that the signs seemed to indicate we were following a very tired group, I hoped we would begin to hear or smell them soon, since they were now upwind.

I caught a faint odor of burning refuse before I heard anything. It was the scent that accompanied the inhabitants of the village wherever they went.

"I think we are close to them," I whispered.

Puh and Black Wolf nodded. We slowed our pace and proceeded onward, watching and listening carefully. The sun was high in the sky. The trail of shells had stopped, but I could hear distant voices calling out to one another, although I could not make out any words.

We kept to the cover of the thick brush as we approached the sounds. At one point, it became apparent that the voices were echoing as though they were in a cave or a canyon. I did not think there were canyons in the middle of this forest, but it was possible the area might harbor a hidden cave. The echo made it difficult to distinguish words but I could tell that there were only voices of men. If Morning Star was amongst them, she was silent.

Finally, we were close enough to understand the conversation and see the tops of the men's heads as they squatted around a fire pit nestled between a series of large boulders. It appeared they had managed to bring down a deer, and two of the men were just beginning to butcher the young buck. One member of the group was creating a pile of dried grasses, sticks, and pine cones, and then another began to strike a flint to a piece of iron pyrite to light it.

The crack of the stone impacting one another still reverberated against the rock surfaces, but now that the men were speaking in normal tones instead of shouting, their voices no longer echoed.

"Ack," said one man. "I am so worn out I do not think I could have gone much farther."

"Yes," said another. "I am glad to be left behind to ensure that those louts did not get by Badger Boar and the others, although I cannot think that Snow Leopard's own brother would leave any of them alive. Our comrades should catch up with us before too long."

The news that one of the men in the ambush party was Snow Leopard's brother evoked the memory of the last man who was slain. He had borne a remarkable resemblance to Snow Leopard. He had been a masterful fighter and every bit as fierce as his apparent sibling.

"They should be here by midday if they did not sleep too late," a third voice spoke up. "I hope they bring some game. That half-starved little roe buck we just brought in is not going to feed all of us for long. I will wait until the next sunrise and then I am going home, whether they show or not."

There were mumbles and nods of general assent. I was surprised that these men would give up so easily.

"I wonder how far Snow Leopard has journeyed

by this time," the first man said. "He and the others will have had their fill of the trail and carrying and dragging that fiery little minx by now. She is a pretty little thing but much too much trouble. The first thing she did was slam the heel of her hand into Snow Leopard's nose…he bled all over the place."

"Good girl!" Black Wolf murmured.

I smiled in spite of myself and recalled the splashes of blood that I had seen on the trail. I had thought that Eagle Owl might have injured some of the raiders, but now it seemed it may well have been Morning Star who inflicted the damage.

"I think that Snow Leopard has taken on far more than he ever anticipated," an unseen voice remarked. "He saw a beautiful girl and he had to possess her. And then there was that ridiculous Challenge."

"Right," the first man responded. "That was a misadventure if ever I saw one. He thought he would be fighting some love-struck young man of The People and instead he turns out to be the biggest man of the Old Ones anyone has ever seen. Snow Leopard must have soiled his loincloth when that brute took off his cloak. It is no surprise that Snow Leopard has not been able to eat solid foods ever since that ill-fated bout."

Puh glanced over at me, a slight grin spreading across his face and he nudged me almost imperceptibly with his shoulder.

"Yes, that is what happens when you bite your tongue nearly in half and you have a bunch of cracked teeth. I predict that most, if not all of those teeth will eventually fall out," agreed yet another voice, "and speaking of brutes, I hear the girl's father is a monster, a man big and hairy who mates with bears. And her mother is a ferocious giantess and a cannibal."

Black Wolf's eyebrows shot way up high on his forehead. Then he frowned. He silently mouthed the word *cannibal* with a questioning look on his face.

"I have heard that, too. I would have picked a more docile mate from a more docile family. A more traditional family. Black Wolf and his kin have been closely aligned with the Old Ones for generations. That is not the kind of family to which I would want to be tied."

Black Wolf had been visibly tensing with anger. Puh touched his arm and emphatically shook his head. My mind was racing. I did not care one whit what they had to say about us. I was willing them to say something that would divulge where Snow Leopard was taking Morning Star.

"Bad family or not," the first man stated, "I would not have even bothered to leave home if I had known we were going to steal a girl away from her pairing ceremony. Did Snow Leopard tell any of you about that or am I the only one who was ignorant of our true errand?"

"I do not think any of us knew," another said. "He told me that a clan of Old Ones had cheated him out of his intended mate and the girl was being foisted off to this clan against her will. I thought we were rescuing her. However, she has made it all too plain that she wants to be returned to that huge red-haired oaf. I cannot fathom why, but it is none of my concern."

"This entire outing was a really terrible idea. When my brother was trying to win his mate, it seemed that she did not like him much and he had to take her by force. Later, the girl ran away and he wanted a bunch of us to accompany him and go after her."

"That happened to my uncle! Three times, before he just let her go."

We listened as they then began to speak of anticipating a hot meal and a good night's rest before we gave up on learning anything useful and quietly slipped away, lest we were discovered.

* * *

We eventually found the path of trod ground again. It was fainter this time, since fewer men were now in the group. The earth was completely covered with living plants or plant debris, so there were no footprints to be seen, and no more shells. Perhaps Morning Star had run out of shells with which to mark their trail. We moved at a fast walk so that we would not miss the signs should they suddenly change direction, but for the most part, we were heading for the slowly dipping sun.

Unbelievably, I was neither tired nor hungry. I drank water and ate a little when we made our brief stops, but I was still driven by an acute sense of urgency. Black Wolf and Puh appeared drawn and sunken-eyed, but they too kept moving without complaint.

We did not know where we were being led as we trekked through the woodland, but Puh thought that we should come out on the trail again fairly soon. As usual, he was right. We stopped at the edge of the well-worn foot path and found exactly what we hoped: footprints belonging to perhaps six or seven men and one young woman.

Their tracks were shuffling now and Morning Star was on foot at all times. We found the place where they stopped to rest and at least some of the group had sat down or reclined on the ground. Then the tracks led away, continuing ever westward, toward the setting sun.

* * *

The moon had risen again, still round and bright, providing just the right ambiance for the wolves to sing by. Their distant howls rent the air and made the hairs on my arms and the back of my neck stand up. The wind had come around to blow out of the south, bringing with it a warm moist air, but it was from the wrong direction to provide any telltale odors that would give an indication that we were drawing nearer to our quarry.

The gusting breezes shook the tree branches making it more difficult to distinguish sounds from one another. Still, there was nothing to do except to put one foot in front of the other and hope that we would not go from being the hunters to the hunted.

We were grateful for the night's deep shadows. Since we suspected we were quite close to Snow Leopard and his group, we evaded the moonlight, slipping from one puddle of darkness to the next.

As we came to an open spot in the path, we paused for a drink of water and to rest for a moment. We had not spoken or eaten in some time. Puh broke out his nearly empty food bag and gave Black Wolf and me a little dried meat and a few shelled nuts that he found rolling around at the bottom of the sack.

As I ate, I rubbed at my burning eyes; they ached from staring so hard at the darkness and from being awake for so long. But the salty sweat on my hands made my eyes burn even more.

"That was the last of the food I had brought with me," Puh said quietly, tucking the empty bag into his waistband.

"I still have some dried meat and a few honey seed cakes left," whispered Black Wolf. "It will be enough to last through tomorrow, but then my food bag will be empty, too."

I had not brought anything edible with me, only water.

"Well, that will be all the less to carry," said Puh. "Let us move on. If we stand still for too long it will be all the harder to get going again."

Then I heard little huffing woofs. And growls. Rapid footsteps. Then shouting.

"Wait," I said. "Listen."

"It comes from ahead of us," said Black Wolf, hearing the clamor.

We edged toward the spectacle of numerous wolves as they surrounded the group of humans, growling and lunging in with a quick snap of their jaws to test the circle of men. This action served to locate the most vulnerable areas and endeavored to create panic amongst the people in order to get them to either run, or to isolate one or two individuals.

There was an occasional high-pitched yip from a wolf when it met with the tip of a spear, but they kept trying, nonetheless. The cries of pain from the men plainly showed that the wolves were having some success at achieving a degree of retribution.

The wolves repeatedly darted in from the dark cover of the forest and sunk their teeth into an ankle, giving the leg a vicious jerk in an attempt to pull the intended victim off his feet.

"I cannot see Morning Star," I whispered. "Can you see Morning Star?"

"No," Black Wolf said, "but I do see Snow Leopard. I recognize him by his short beard. How I hope one of those wolves bites him next!"

I was of the same mind but I was a little startled when Black Wolf continued, "If the wolves fail to do the job, I may just bite him myself!"

"I suggest that we let the wolves do some of our work for us," Puh spoke up. "Let them keep those men distracted while we get into position."

The wolves did more than keep them distracted. The wolves managed to split the men into two unevenly sized groups, one group of three men who were scarcely able to keep the wolves at bay and another of four men, with Morning Star huddled between them. It was too dark to see the expression on her face, but I could hear her gasp at times as a wolf leapt in close.

We worked our way from the shadowy trail and into the woods, passing between the trees and brush as quietly as possible. It was not an easy task on a dark moonlight-dappled landscape that was thoroughly littered with fallen tree limbs, small sticks, and brittle old leaves. The loosened coils of my hair sometimes caught on the low branches and briars, but I pushed through without taking the time to disentangle them.

Neither the wolves nor the men had yet sensed our presence. They were much too intent on one another. We instinctively headed toward Snow Leopard's end of the group. We did not really care about the other two- and four-legged combatants, except that we meant to avoid being either injured or killed by any of them.

The wolves still paced and circled, weaving in and out of trees and thickets, growling and barking hoarsely.

It was then that I realized we would have to charge between the wolves' large furry bodies before we could make physical contact with Snow Leopard and his men. Puh, Black Wolf, and I paused long enough to exchange glances. They seemed to have reached the same conclusion.

"All together…we charge through the wolves together," I said, "and shout as loud as we can to startle them."

My companions nodded. We poised our spears at the ready, nodded again and lurched forward as one, roaring like enraged beasts, with Puh on my right and Black Wolf on my left.

I saw Snow Leopard's open-mouthed shock as we descended upon him. I thrust my spear deep into his chest, habitually twisting the shaft after burying the head. He staggered.

"*You!*" he said as he dropped to his knees.

But that was all. His lifeless form slumped to the ground. I jerked back on my spear to free it from his body.

It was then that I saw the length of rope that was tied around Snow Leopard's left wrist. The other end of the rope was fastened around Morning Star's neck.

In the confusion, the wolves had retreated, but we could still hear them nearby, itching to rejoin the fray, especially now that a victim was lying prone on the ground.

Morning Star wriggled from between the other men and started to run, but she was brought up short by the rope that kept her attached to Snow Leopard's corpse. Desperation plain on her face, Morning Star pulled against her restraints. I took my knife from its sheath and quickly stepped forward to release her. As I re-sheathed my knife, Morning Star threw her arms around my neck. But other than to put an arm around her waist and pull her in tight, there was no time to do anything else or for words. She clung to me as I had never been clasped before, as though no force would ever rip us apart.

Black Wolf came around to her other side. Morning Star was now sheltered between us. Puh moved to stand in front of us. He spoke to the group of wounded, exhausted, and terrified men.

"We do not want there to be any more killing. We only want to retrieve our woman."

They looked at one another and slowly lowered their weapons.

"Snow Leopard has taken his chances and lost," Black Wolf said. "You would be wise to let Snow Leopard's mission die with him. If you persist in carrying on his cause, we will continue to carry on with ours and speaking for myself, I will fight to the death."

One of the men looked at Snow Leopard as he lay in a heap on the blood-stained turf.

"I say we leave him where he lies and get out of here before the wolves regain their confidence and attack us again," he said. "They will move in on Snow Leopard as soon as we are gone."

We all nodded in agreement.

As we started to walk away, Morning Star cried out, "Wait!"

She suddenly stepped toward Snow Leopard's body and using her foot, she gave him a rough shove that rolled him onto his back. Morning Star quickly knelt and reached into Snow Leopard's bloodied tunic, drawing out the remains of her shell necklace. Clutching the necklace to her breast with both hands, she returned to us.

"He took it from me when he found that I was leaving a trail," she explained. "I am ready to go, now."

I placed a protective arm around her waist again as we set out down the trail. The wolves were quick to fill the little clearing as we moved away.

Black Wolf looked over his shoulder for a moment.

"Snow Leopard will give those wolves indigestion, for sure," he stated.

 **Chapter Thirteen** 

I cut away the remaining rope from Morning Star's neck and threw it into the woods. She had not yet let go of me. In fact, she clutched my arm with a strength that I did not know she possessed. We warily sent the men up the trail ahead of us where we could watch them, just in case they had a change of heart. But given their limping gaits thanks to the wolves' sharp teeth and being foot-sore from the long journey, and considering that their exhaustion was so extreme they could barely carry their spears, we found we had little to fear from the thoroughly dispirited group.

When we reached the point where they would veer off on a different path to return to the village, we let them go without a word. They did not look back.

We trudged along until sun-up, when we reached a creek where we stopped to drink and eat and examine our wounds in the first blush of a rose-colored dawn. We had not intended to sleep, but within minutes of sitting on the dewy ground by the bank of the creek, each one of us was dozing soundly.

* * *

I awoke to the babble of the brook in my ears and a piece of honey seed cake still in one hand. A curious mouse had come up to investigate and bravely nibble the cake, but the tiny rodent ran away as soon as I moved my fingers.

The inside of my mouth was very dry and I felt incredibly thirsty. However, I was too comfortable to want to arise and drink from the little stream. And, I was too charmed by Morning Star's presence to want to leave her as she lay fast asleep, curled up against me with her head on my shoulder.

Morning Star had re-knotted the severed cord of her necklace and she was now wearing what remained of it. I was grieved to see the obvious rope burns on her slender neck and the scuff marks and scrapes on her arms and legs. Her face was streaked with dirt and her hair disheveled, but it did not detract from her beauty.

I was afraid to touch her, afraid to indulge in even one kiss that might awaken an unstoppable frenzy of passion within me. So I just lay there and stared at her, reveling in the wonder of her closeness, taking in every detail: the blackness of her eyelashes against her dark skin, the soft curves of her cheekbones, and the sweet contented expression that she wore on her face.

Black Wolf was lying on his back on the other side of Morning Star, snoring mightily. Puh must have been lying on the ground behind me. I could not see him, but I could hear his slow deep breathing.

Gradually, the sounds and heat of the day stirred the others, one by one, into wakefulness, beginning with Morning Star.

I was pleased to see her smile when she opened her eyes. She touched my cheek.

"Is my face as dirty as yours?" Morning Star asked with a grin.

"Probably," I replied, "but your face is much prettier than mine, dirt and all."

Morning Star giggled at the cacophony of sounds emanating from her father.

"This would be a very romantic way to wake up, with you leaning over me like this and your hair shrouding us as though we were under a sunlit red-gold awning, but listen to Da! He needs to roll over onto his side. How my poor mother has withstood that horrible racket all these years, I will never know." She shifted slightly and reached out with her foot to jostle her father's calf. "Da! Roll over, Da!" Morning Star ordered.

Black Wolf mumbled in his sleep, but he obeyed. The snoring stopped. We continued to talk quietly.

"Do you snore?" Morning Star inquired with an impish grin that made her dimples deepen. Her smile always dazzled me, but I collected my wits to reply.

"I do not have the faintest notion," I admitted. "But if you did not hear anything during this last sleep that is a good sign, because I do not think I have ever been so tired."

"Well, if you do snore I will just have to find a way to make you stop."

"Oh?" I asked. "Will you prod me with your foot, too?"

Still grinning, Morning Star pondered the question for a moment.

"I do not know," she began, "I will have to think of something. My mother threatens to wreak her vengeance by blowing into an aurochs horn aimed into Da's ear at random times all night. Mama says after all, that is just about the same as what she must listen to. But I would not do that to you."

"It does not sound like a very restful way to spend the night," I remarked lightly.

"No, it does not. I might try kissing you. Would that stop the snoring?" Morning Star asked as she looked into my eyes, her own sparkling.

One of her hands played with loose strands of my hair. I thought on her idea and I was just about beside myself with my eagerness to make love to her. I earnestly wished that we were alone.

"That would definitely stop the snoring." I told her, reaching to stroke her face.

Morning Star closed her eyes and laid her head against my hand. It fit perfectly, as though I had always been meant to hold her this way.

We then became aware of Puh and Black Wolf's movements as they arose. We suddenly became self-conscious about being seen by our fathers in such an intimate position.

I helped Morning Star to her feet. She moved stiffly. I, too, had to hobble as my legs seemed to have turned to stone after so much use over the last few days.

Our long journey had also been hard on our footwear and had worn through the soles in several places. Thanks to the many layers that made up our boots, our bare feet were not actually in contact with the ground, but the holes had allowed dirt, small pebbles, and other bits of detritus to get inside. Each one of us had to doff our boots, take them apart, and shake them out. We left the various pieces out to air in the sun.

Black Wolf, Puh, and I removed our tunics before we made our way down to the edge of the stream to drink and splash water on our faces and torsos, scrubbing vigorously to scour away the accumulations of grime and dried blood. We were thoroughly cut and bruised from the hand-to-hand combat, and scratched from pushing through the underbrush, thorny vines, and low branches.

It was hard to tell which parts of our physiques had suffered the most, but it seemed to me that our forearms may have taken the worst punishment as they were nicked and sliced as though we had each been fending off a fair-sized lynx. Even though the cool water stung our many lacerations and abrasions, we felt much revived, despite the fact that by the light of day, we still looked rather gruesome.

Both Puh and I found that our hair had come completely unbound; even Black Wolf's multiple plaits had fallen apart. He pulled the bindings from his braids and bent to dunk his head in the water several times.

Puh and I looked at one another and smiled. It was the first time in my life I had ever seen Black Wolf with his hair down. Wet, it hung well below his shoulders. Somehow, he did not look quite right.

"What is the matter?" Black Wolf asked as he noticed our grins. "What is so humorous? Do you not think that I ever wash-out my hair? But I will need help to put it in order, again. I suppose that my beard is well on its way to becoming a bird's nest, too."

Morning Star had joined us at the brook to wash her face and limbs. She waded ankle-deep into the clear waters and made an attempt to rid herself of most of the dirt that tarnished her lovely complexion.

"Your beard is not too badly mussed," she said. "But do not fear, Da. I will set you to rights when your hair has dried a little and you will soon wear your spider hat once again."

Morning Star wore a mirthful expression. After all, Black Wolf's unique way of wearing his hair was thought to be unusual even amongst The People, especially by those who lived in the village. However, they had always considered Black Wolf to be something of an oddity. They shrugged it off as being a natural consequence of an eccentricity he must have acquired during a lifetime of living as a savage in the forest. But one also had to take into account that a man who was nearly tall enough to look a giant deer in the eye could wear his hair any way he liked.

"Making fun of your Da, are you?" Black Wolf playfully chided. "Well, unlike *some…*" he pointedly looked at Puh and me, whose hair hung down and obscured half of our faces. "I cannot stand to have my hair in my eyes and long ago I found which is the best way to keep mine in check."

After we left the side of the creek, we settled on the ground once more, each of us sitting on our tunics. I motioned to Morning Star that she could share mine. She willingly sat next to me and began to untangle and plait her tresses. I then realized that we would both need something to fasten our braids, so I pulled a length of sinew thread out of the side seam of one of our empty food bags and cut it into pieces. I handed some of them to Morning Star and then began to braid my own unruly mass of hair.

Puh observed what I was doing and when I was done, he too started to unravel a section from the same sack as well.

"Good idea, Tris." Puh said. When he finished, Puh began to weave his hair into one long queue.

As Morning Star tied the last of her braids, she turned to her father.

"All right, Da, let me fix you up, now." Morning Star said, moving to stand.

"No, you stay seated," Black Wolf instructed. "You must be exhausted. I will lie down here so that you can sit while you re-plait my hair."

Black Wolf gave her the bits of lashings that he had taken from his braids and then, groaning a little as he shifted his aching limbs, he stretched out his considerable length, lying down on his stomach so that his head was in front of Morning Star. She leaned over him and her nimble fingers worked the thick glossy hair that spread out in a fan across Black Wolf's fuzzy shoulders, swiftly producing the familiar spider legs.

"The trouble lies in figuring out where to stop," Puh spoke, smiling mischievously.

Black Wolf had been so still, it was almost as though he had been asleep.

"Oh, that is *very* funny," Black Wolf grumbled. "You are just envious because you Old Ones have bodies that are almost without fur. That is why you all grow your hair so long, to cover your nakedness."

"Well, not exactly," began Puh, still smiling. "We wear clothing to cover our nakedness. Or more to the point, to protect us from the elements. We believe that our hair is what helps us make an intuitive connection with the world around us and those who live in that world. To cut any great length of our hair would be to diminish that insight."

"I would not presume to contradict you," Black Wolf responded. "I believe myself to be as adept at making my way as a hunter as any man of The People, but I have always coveted the innate second sense of the Old Ones."

Morning Star had finished with his hair by now and Black Wolf sat up, turning to face us and sitting with his arms lying limply across his knees. He gazed fondly at his daughter.

"Thank you, Morning Star. Now I feel civilized once again."

Morning Star then saw the gash on her father's left hand, where it had been flayed open as he pushed aside the would-be ambusher's spear.

"Oh, Da! Your hand! Have you cleansed the wound?" She reached for his hand, but he, too, wanted to see it.

Black Wolf looked at his injured extremity as though it was the first time he had noticed it.

"Hmmm…" he started. "Well, it bled-out a lot. That is as good as a washing."

Morning Star shook her head at him.

"Oh, Da! Let me see it," she demanded. This time, Black Wolf gave her his hand and let her examine it. "I suppose it seems clean enough. But I have nothing with which to wrap it to keep out the dirt. We must bandage this after we return home." Morning Star sighed and then looked at each one of us in turn. "I am so humbled by what you all went through on my behalf. And I have not yet thanked each of you for coming after me and rescuing me from that wretched man and his so-called friends. I know that it took much courage…that it was an exceedingly difficult task…I do not have the words…" she stammered.

"*No words?*" Black Wolf laughed. "If that is true, then this is indeed a rare occasion, for it will be the first time that you have been without words since you learned to speak!"

"Da, you exaggerate! I know when to speak and when to be quiet," Morning Star said with good-humored exasperation, but then added with a wry smile, "Most of the time, that is."

She made to awkwardly stand up and I quickly got to my feet to help her once again. Puh and Black Wolf rose to their feet as well. Morning Star went to her father and she gave him a long hug and kissed his bearded cheek.

"Oh, Da!" she said. "You may be an old bear sometimes, but I could not want a more wonderful father. Thank you, Da." She grinned at him as he returned her kiss.

"*Old bear!*" he said with feigned indignation. "Well, this old bear would not let anyone steal his little cub."

"Well, Da, I am afraid that you would not be very proud of your little cub if you had seen me while I was held captive. I fear that I was not very well behaved. I tried to make myself as disagreeable as possible in hopes that Snow Leopard would change his mind and let me go. I yelled and kicked and hit and bit every chance I got. When they became bored with dragging me, they had to carry me. And what with my struggles as I was being slung over a shoulder, I quickly became a very tiresome burden. Eventually Snow Leopard fastened a rope around my neck and pulled me along so he and everyone else could stay out of my reach. I do not wonder that Snow Leopard's friends were so quick to release me to you. I believe that they were all thoroughly sick of me by that time. I think the only reason they did not cheerfully throw me off of a cliff was because Snow Leopard had forbidden anyone to harm me."

"I would have expected no less from a child of my loins." Black Wolf said as he cupped her chin in his hand. Morning Star placed a hand over his and gave it a squeeze, and then she turned to hug and kiss Puh.

"Thank you, Tor," she said to Puh. "You have been a true friend to my Da and a second father to me. I will never forget what you have done."

Puh gave her that rocking hug I had so often seen him to give Muh, his arms wrapped around her body and a huge hand cradling the back of her head. Puh smiled and kissed her forehead.

"Of course we came after you." Puh replied. "And now that you and Tris are paired, you are my daughter, too."

Morning Star touched his lean, scarred cheek as she returned his smile, and then she came to me. Her eyes searched mine as she took my hands and gazed into my battered visage.

Finally, Morning Star stretched up to put her arms around my shoulders and kissed me warmly on the lips.

"Thank you, Tris," she whispered. "Thank you. Thank you. Thank you."

I nestled my face into her warm neck, drinking in the scent of her.

"There was no question about whether or not to pursue you," I whispered back, "and there was no coming home without you." I drew away just far enough to peer into her face. "Never doubt that. Even if you were not my mate, I would always have come for you."

"I know you would," she said to me, looking steadily into my eyes and holding me tighter. Then Morning Star went on, "I am so sorry that I had to break your gift…but you found the shells?"

"Yes," I said, "we found them and we all thought you were very clever to leave a trail for us to follow once Snow Leopard had broken away from the path. Do not worry, I can repair this necklace or make another one for you after we return home."

"How far are we from home?" Morning Star asked.

"Do you speak of your home or mine?" Black Wolf responded with a twinkle in his eyes.

"Mine," answered Morning Star with a broad smile. "That is to say, my new home. I have not even seen it yet."

Black Wolf opened his food bag, rolling down the edges until the last small pieces of dried meat and the well-jostled, broken-up honey seed cakes were exposed.

"I would guess that if we start out soon we should be home before sunset—*your home*, Morning Star." Black Wolf answered. "That is where your mother and the rest of the family will be waiting, too, as Little Fawn had said she would stay with Awna until we reappeared." Black Wolf doled out the remaining food.

"Eat up, now.   Then we can refill our water bags and embark on the last leg of this long, long trip."

Even after all the food was consumed we were still very hungry, all the same, we were in high spirits as we walked down the path. Activity helped to loosen our stiff muscles and soon we were walking easily again. Black Wolf began to sing at the top of his voice as we trudged along, entertaining us with his songs, some of which I suspected he made up as he went.

We came upon several small birds that were happily chirping and bathing in a large puddle of standing water. Black Wolf was in mid-song and as loud as ever. The birds hastily took to a panicked flight at our approach.

"Da! You are scaring all the birds away!" Morning Star laughed.

"If they can sing as much as they want to, then so can I," retorted Black Wolf.

Oh, there was a big old wolf, his color it was black
And there was no animal in the forest that he could not track
He met up with a cunning cat, a leopard of the snow
And when the leopard wanted to steal his cub, he then became a foe
The black wolf and his friends, they went after that bad cat
They chased him 'round day and night, until they ran him down flat

Then that evil thieving leopard, he met his end at last
At the hands of those whose hearts were true and their legs
were fast
And the sweet cub, she was saved, as the leopard
received his knocks
And she was returned well and whole, to her beloved fox

Black Wolf's songs helped to make the time pass more quickly. Puh knew some of them from many years of hunting excursions with Black Wolf, and he joined in on the words he could remember, but for the most part Black Wolf sang by himself.

We passed through a peaceful landscape of freshly sprouted grasses, newly unfurled green leaves, and multitudes of flowers. The sun-warmed air meant that Puh, Black Wolf, and I had once again tucked our tunic sleeves into our loincloth ties as we traveled. Puh and I kept to the shady sides of the trail, as was our custom, to keep the strong sun off our pale skin in order to prevent sunburns. Black Wolf and Morning Star had no issue with being out in the sun. After many years of trekking with me and my family, they were well accustomed to our switching sides of the path to keep under the canopy of trees.

Morning Star held my hand as we hiked companionably along, occasionally exchanging significant glances and small smiles. I was still awed at the idea that she was really mine, now. I was filled with a determination that I would endeavor to do all I could to be worthy of her and never make Black Wolf regret his decision to allow me to have his daughter—indeed, his favorite child—as my mate.

* * *

As the day progressed, the sun climbed higher and higher in a cloudless blue sky. The trail seemed to stretch out interminably before us.

"My boots need to be emptied again." Black Wolf announced. "They are full of dirt and pebbles and my feet are paining me something fierce. Also, I have managed to drink all the water in my water bag and I am still incredibly dry."

Our long ramble through the countryside as we pursued Morning Star had left each of us dehydrated and it seemed as though we could not consume enough liquid to quench our thirsts.

"My boots could use a good shaking, as well," Puh agreed. "I know of a little spring not far from here. It will be nice and cool there. We can clean out our footwear, take in some more water, and rest a bit before we finish our journey home."

"I like that idea," Black Wolf nodded.

"So do I," I seconded.

"As do I," Morning Star concurred. "Maybe we will find some fresh greens at the spring. It would be wonderful if we could pick up a little something to eat."

"If you are that hungry, we could stop and hunt up some game," I offered. "And it is possible we may come across an animal that might wander near enough to strike. It will delay our arrival at home by a day, but it would provide us with a solid meal."

"Thank you, but no," Morning Star shook her head. "I want to get home. We can eat all we want once we are there."

So, we made our way to a small verdant glen where the water table percolated up through the low spot on the terrain and provided a pool of sweet clear water. The spring was no bigger across than I was tall. The aquifer apparently rose and dipped at various times, depending on the season and whether or not we were facing drought conditions.

A snowy winter and recent rain meant that the water level was relatively high just now. Nevertheless, at a glance I could see that we would have to lie on our stomachs and stretch down with our arms in order to reach the surface of the water.

"I will fill a water bag so that you do not have to get down on the ground to drink," I told Morning Star. I was not sure that her arms were long enough to touch the top of the spring, in any case.

"Thank you, Tris," she smiled at me. "I will look for some edible greens while you draw the water." Morning Star gave my hand a parting squeeze before she left my side.

Puh and Black Wolf sat down in the shade and removed their boots, breaking them down to their individual pieces and laying them out on the ground in a row under the full glare of the sun.

I immediately loosened the ties that sealed my water bag and got down on my hands and knees at the grassy bank of the spring. I peered down, fully expecting I might see a frog or two, but instead I recoiled in shock as I saw a strange man staring at me from the water's edge.

I cried out in surprise and fell back toward Puh and Black Wolf, who now wore expressions of alarm.

Morning Star, too, turned to me and asked, "What is it, Tris?"

I was speechless for a moment.

"It is a man! A man in the water!" I gasped.

"*A man?*" Black Wolf repeated. "What is he doing down there?"

"I do not know, but I think that he was as startled as I was," I replied.

Puh then started to laugh. We looked at him questioningly.

"I think I know who you saw," Puh said. "Come with me, Tris." He put an arm around my shoulders as he led me back to the side of the spring. He knelt down and motioned for me to do the same. "Come on, Tris. Look." Puh pointed at the surface of the water. Two men were there now. One had his arm around the other. I looked more closely. I turned my gaze back to Puh and then peered at the smooth surface of the water once again. "Do you see?" Puh asked. "You are looking at us. It is a reflection."

"The same as seeing the trees reflected on a lake?" I asked.

The concept was beginning to materialize in my mind. Our potable water had always been drawn from moving streams or rivers, as standing water is usually considered to be stagnant and therefore undrinkable. Moving water did not provide a reflective surface. Lakes and ponds reflected with a distortion. Several times I had seen wobbly and fragmented images of myself in those waters, but I found them to be rather disturbing so I did not linger to stare at them. This time, Puh and I could see ourselves as keenly as though we were standing opposite one another, albeit the fact that leaning down like this, our faces were in the shadows and we seemed somewhat darker in appearance.

"Yes, just the same as trees on a lake," Puh nodded. "I was frightened the first time I saw myself, too. When you suddenly see a person where you are not expecting to come upon one, it is almost like being ambushed by a stranger."

I stared at us. So this was what I looked like. My hair, although it was still braided, caught the sunlight and outlined my head in fringe of blazing orange. I could still see the nick in my left brow where the scar from Snow Leopard's blow remained. My eyes skimmed over the other more minor marks that my face had acquired over the last few days and moved on to take notice of my thick neck, heavily muscled shoulders, arms, and chest.

I was stunned. Although I knew that I had been an adult for a few years, until today I did not perceive that I was truly a grown man. And now that I saw Puh and me side-by-side, I could at last understand why I had always been told that I resembled my father. Although I was taller, we had the same strong build, the same bone structure in our faces, the same eyes, and the same shapes to our noses and mouths.

The only difference, other than those brought about by age and injury, was that Puh was leaner than I in both face and body. Nearly every bone, muscle, vein, and sinew under the surface of Puh's skin was clearly defined. It seemed not to matter how much Puh ate or Muh fussed over him—since she saw his lack of fat as a sign that she was neglecting him—he never managed to acquire any extraneous bulk.

Puh rose to his feet. He looked somewhat discouraged and shook his head.

"Well, I do not need to lay there and stare at my ugly mug," he said. "I do not see it for years at a time and each time I do, it does not improve."

Black Wolf had come up to take Puh's place. His huge form blotted out the reflection of the sun on the seemingly depthless surface of the water.

"I must say that I look pretty good!" Black Wolf grinned, pleased with his own appearance. "I have not seen myself in sometime either, but other than a few scratches and bumps from our adventure, I think I look rather handsome."

"Of course you do, Da!" Morning Star laughed. "You are always very handsome."

"Come here and view this!" I sat upright and called to Morning Star. "You will be amazed!" I motioned for her to join us.

Morning Star stooped to place a handful of greens near our pile of belongings and then paused to give Puh a quick hug.

"Never say that you are ugly, Tor," she smiled at him. "You are a very fine looking man to me." Puh seemed to be deeply touched by her remark.

"Only because you are good enough to look past my rough exterior," he responded. "Go now and see your own pretty face. Then you will observe what is fine looking."

Morning Star sat down on the cool grass between her father and me. I put my arm around her as I drew her closer.

"Do you see?" I asked, and pointed to the spring where my image pointed back at me.

Morning Star paused to look at me for a moment but then turned to gaze at her reflection.

"Oh!" she exclaimed. "It is us! And that is *me*! I am so little compared to you and Da!"

"And so beautiful," I told her.

"My nose is too big," Morning Star stated flatly, "but I will let you tell me that I am beautiful because I love you."

She had spoken these words to my reflection in the water, but my heart melted when I heard them. This was the first time she had ever uttered the long-awaited phrase *I love you*. As before, by the side of the little stream, I sorely wished that we were alone. I desperately wanted to kiss her, to take her in my arms and fully possess her as my mate, but this was not the time or place.

"I *adore* you." I leaned closer to Morning Star and spoke softly into her ear. "I do so *adore* you."

"Well," Black Wolf looked over at us and cleared his throat. "Let us drink our fill, eat those greens, and resume our hike. We will want to get back to Tor's compound before dark."

I had not even shaken out my boots yet. I hurriedly removed my boots to take care of that chore and by the time I had consumed a quick handful of Morning Star's raw bitter greens and downed a mouthful of water, we were ready to hit the trail once again. But the magic of seeing our mirrored images stayed with me as we walked along.

Later, the setting sun and cool evening breezes reminded us to dress in our tunics once more. Familiar landmarks were all around us now. We were almost home.

Chapter Fourteen

We were still a long ways off when I heard Rooph and Raena's frantic barking as they perceived our approach. Black Wolf's family, Muh, Gran, and my siblings met us as we came up the path; Little Fawn and Muh sobbing with relief. Little Fawn embraced Black Wolf and Morning Star, and likewise, Muh pulled Puh and me to her as tears rolled down her cheeks.

"Do not cry," said Puh, kissing her, "We are here now. We are well and Snow Leopard has been slain. Do not cry so, my dear Awna."

"It is just that it was such a big group of men," Muh spoke as she wiped at her tears with the flat of her hand. "They killed Eagle Owl. I was so terribly afraid that I would never see either one of you again." Speaking the words seemed to renew her sense of grief. "And look at you two...and Black Wolf...your clothes...*oh*!"

I had never seen Muh, who was normally so stoic, so overwrought. Not even when Dak was killed. Then it dawned on me that not only was Muh traumatized by the anguish of potentially losing her mate and her eldest son, but also by the specter of the slow demise of her entire family.

Puh and I supplied nearly all the food for our immediate clan; without us, they would survive for a little while but eventually when the stores gave out and all they had to live on was what they could scavenge, it would mean starvation and death.

In a flash, the horror of the littlest one, Baby Mi, succumbing came to me, as she would suffer first when Muh's milk dried up. And then, one by one, the others would follow.

I felt intensely ashamed that I had been so absorbed in my own obsession to bring back Morning Star that I had never considered the awful plight that might have awaited my loved ones had we not succeeded. If Little Fawn was left in the same position, it would have been the same for Black Wolf's family.

Clans were heavily dependent on the hunters who brought home large game, enough to feed the whole family and to put sufficient amounts of dried meat away to get through the winter. These same men also procured the animal hides that clothed everyone, and hewed the great quantities of firewood needed to maintain cooking fires and bring warmth to the household.

Muh and my siblings, Little Fawn and her children—two women and ten children under the age of thirteen—would have been left alone at our family compound. The nearest help would have been my Aunt Vee and cousins Bror, Kror, and Lor, who were at least a day's hike away. Probably more than a day's hike when one considers that they would be moving at the pace of the younger children.

If they did choose to embark on such a trip in order to gain assistance, the chances were good that predators would be attracted to the procession and that few, and possibly none, would survive the trek. Even if they had been successful, it would have put a tremendous strain on Aunt Vee's family to have so many more dependents who would need to be fed, housed, and clothed.

Puh held Muh close, kissing her and murmuring gentle words into her ear at length until she at last regained her composure. Muh gave Puh a wan smile.

"You all must be half-starved by now," she said. "Rest for a bit…I will put together something for us all to eat."

While the food was being prepared, Little Fawn led us past an ancient grove of enormous pine trees to the meadow where Eagle Owl had been buried alongside Muh and Puh's lost babies, my brother Dak, and many past generations of our kin.

A stack of leftover firewood attested to the fact that they had had to thaw the permafrost in the earth in order to dig out the hole to the necessary depth.

Every burial site had a pile of stones on it, one rock to represent each winter the occupant had lived. Infants were given one stone, whether or not they had actually survived that harsh season. Some of the cairns were nearly obscured by grasses and other low-lying plants, but Muh and Puh's babies' single stone markers has been kept clear of weeds and they were still conspicuous amongst the many graves in the field.

Eagle Owl's resting place was graced with many stones. As we stood at the gravesite, Morning Star seemed to slowly wilt and she placed her forehead upon my shoulder. For the first time since the ordeal had begun, she wept.

I took her in my arms and stroked her hair. Her sorrow affected me much more than I would have thought possible. My own eyes began to flow freely at the sight of her tears. I wondered what Puh had said to Muh that so eased her heart.

I wished I could think of something appropriate to say that would solace Morning Star, but my mind was not up to the task. I held her tightly and kissed the top of her head.

"Oh, my sweet!" I finally whispered to her. "My sweet Morning Star, I am so sorry you are sad! My sweet, sweet Morning Star!"

The words did not make much sense and nor did they specifically address her despair, but she soon ceased weeping and wiped my cheeks dry. She did not speak but continued to nestle against me as we gazed down at the peaceful patch of earth that now held Eagle Owl.

"Eagle Owl was a fine man." Black Wolf choked on his sadness, struggling to articulate his pain. "I may have called him a fool on occasion, but those were words spoken in the heat of passion. When I was a boy, he was an older cousin whom I very much admired. He was the great hunter I so wished to emulate. And then, after he was mauled by the lioness, he never felt sorry for himself, he never wanted anyone's charity or pity. He was a loving, brave, and uncommonly generous man."

"Yes, my dear one," Little Fawn took one of Black Wolf's massive hands in hers. "Eagle Owl was indeed a very fine man. He would have been very pleased and honored to hear your speech. He was undoubtedly generous. He gave his very life's blood in his attempt to save another. Before we buried him, we painted his face with the marks of a fallen hunter so that when he meets with his ancestors they will recognize him as a great and courageous man who is worthy of their respect."

"That is good. It is no less than he deserves." Although Black Wolf's eyes had teared, he smiled.

* * *

While the others returned to the compound, Puh and I went to the little house I had inherited from Great Gran to be sure that everything was in good order and squirrel-free.

Nothing had changed, except that some of the greenery Muh and Gran had placed inside was now somewhat withered and someone—probably Little Fawn—had unpacked Morning Star's belongings.

I was relieved to see no sign of Great Gran's pets.

"The squirrels have not come back," I remarked.

"No." Puh said in a very definite tone.

"Did…um…did anything happen to them?" I sensed that Puh was leaving something unsaid.

"Yes." Puh answered.

"Such as?"

"Such as they met with a sudden and decisive end. Your pup Raena found them curled up together soon after Gran moved in with us and the dog made rather short work of them."

"Oh. Raena never did like those squirrels." I then wondered if Gran had witnessed this unfortunate happening. "Poor Gran. Was she there?"

"Luckily, Gran was out with Ty looking for spring cabbages. Your Muh was able to clean up the remnants of the attack before their return. But Gran knows. She has not asked, but she knows. However, it is just as well. Your Muh could not abide Gran's squirrels. She has enough to cope with without those pests."

I thought of my mother and how upset she had been earlier.

"Until I saw Muh's distress upon our homecoming, I had never considered what fate might have befallen our family if we had not come back," I said.

Puh turned and looked at me, contemplating his words for a moment. Puh knew from personal experience what happened when both the father and oldest son were lost. I could see various emotions at work on his face: the grief brought on by memories of the events he had witnessed that took first his brother Bror, and then his father, and the untold hardships and hazards he and Uncle Mror had endured as they learned how to take their places as providers for their family.

"Yes, your mother was scared," Puh began. "Women have the most difficult role in the family. They are the ones who must wait and worry. It is true that if we had been killed, they certainly would have faced tough times." Puh read my guilt-ridden expression, and continued, "Your mother also knew that we had to leave. Whether it had been Morning Star, your sister Ru, or anyone else who had been stolen, we would have gone after them. She knows that every time we go out our doorway we might never come back. That is the way of it. But regardless, I like to think we have the instincts, the intelligence, and the skills to work through most situations…" Puh put a hand on my shoulder and gave it a squeeze, "…and that together, you, Black Wolf, and I can handle just about anything that might come along." Puh was silent for a moment and then went on, "and besides, your Muh is also more emotional than usual at this time because she is pregnant."

This was not surprising news to me. Three winters old Saree had recently been weaned and the withdrawal of the older of the two nursing tots always seemed to be a precursor to the start of a new baby. Plus, Muh had certainly seemed more introspective and irritable as of late. Little Mi would not be the baby of the family for much longer.

"So," I said, "this will be the tenth child that Muh has carried."

"Eleventh," Puh corrected me.

"Eleventh?" I looked at Puh, taken aback.

"Yes. There was one prior to you," Puh informed me.

"Before you were paired?" It just popped out of my mouth. I was instantly chagrined at my inadvertent impudence. I had never before questioned Puh like this, but the shock of his revelation had made me blurt out the words.

Puh blushed.

"I am sorry, Puh," I added quickly. "I should not have said that."

"There is no need to be sorry. It is an honest question. It went against all tradition, but the only excuse I can give is that I was so besotted from the first moment I met your mother. She was different from any other female I had ever met—not that I had met very many. But she was so exquisitely pretty, so tall, with such lovely dark red hair, the likes of which I had never seen before. She had a certain grace in her walk. She had an aura of serenity about her." Puh looked over at me suddenly as if a thought had just occurred to him. "I must sound ridiculous."

"No, Puh." I shook my head. "I can appreciate just what you mean. I feel much the same about Morning Star, except that I admire her *black* hair and, well, she is not particularly *tall*…nor is she exactly *serene*."

Puh and I smiled at one another with mutual understanding, but then Puh sobered.

"And also, I probably was not right in my mind. Besides being madly desperately in love, I had just lost my brother and my father and I was incredibly sick at heart. But, yes, it was before we were paired. It was back when we had first decided that we would never love anyone else but each other." Puh gave me a sidelong glance. "Apparently, I had not your restraint.

I have long admired how patiently you waited for Morning Star."

"The thought of incurring Black Wolf's wrath inspires a certain amount of restraint." I grinned at Puh but then became serious again. "Actually, I did not think that I would ever win Black Wolf's, Little Fawn's, or Morning Star's approval. Otherwise, I definitely would have made my affections for Morning Star officially known many years sooner."

"Your Muh and I have very much sympathized with your dilemma," Puh nodded. "We did not have her family's approval at first, either. They told us that we were too young and they forbade her to see me anymore. They had hoped to pair her with one of her cousins. I did not know it at that time, but she was already pregnant. When her clan would not allow her to spend time with me, she refused to eat until they finally relented. They still have no use for me and nor do they care to see your Muh. That is why you have never met any of your Muh's kin."

Puh's voice was calm, but I detected a hint of anger in his tone. I was startled to hear this. I had always been a bit envious at what I had perceived as Muh and Puh's freedom to give and receive their love for one another without the worry of social complexities such as those Morning Star and I faced. But now that Puh shared this little-known history with me it seemed that they had experienced their own trials.

"All the same," Puh went on, "I was very sad to find that your Muh had suffered a miscarriage while we were kept apart. We never told anyone about the child, since she lost it early on. But that was long ago, over eighteen years past, as a matter of fact. Let us go and rejoin the others. The food should be ready by now and your new mate will be wondering where you have gone."

"Before we leave," I started, "I have one more question. "What did you say to Muh that so calmed her? When Morning Star was crying just now, I had no notion of what to say to her."

Puh smiled at me.

"You must have said the right things, because she soon recovered."

"Well," I shook my head at the thought of my inadequate attempt at consolation. "That was more due to her strong constitution than any glibness on my part."

"Yes," Puh acknowledged. "Morning Star is much more than she seems. Snow Leopard was extremely unwise to take her and to ever think that she would simply give up to him and agree to be his mate. She is a very spirited young woman."

"But what was it you said to Muh?" I persisted. "She seemed so heartened by your words."

Puh looked over at me with a slight twinkle in his eyes.

"It will not be long before you will know that some things are only spoken between a man and his mate," Puh replied. "But I can tell you a little of what I said. I told her that everything was going to be all right. That there was nothing this side of death that would ever keep me away and she can be sure that I will *always* come home to her."

* * *

The aroma of roasted duck greeted us as we neared the small clearing before my family's dwelling. Blazing flames in the outdoor fire pit lighted and warmed the now well-populated space. No one minded that we were crowded as we sat or reclined on the same mats that we had used during my pairing ceremony feast. I was surprised to see that such a bountiful array of both hot and cold foods had been assembled with such little notice.

It was apparent that Black Wolf, Puh, Morning Star, and I were not the only ones who were very hungry. We all set upon the abundant victuals with great enthusiasm.

The somber mood from Eagle Owl's graveside dissipated as we ate and there were many animated conversations going at once. The children created much noise as they frolicked and the dogs begged for morsels.

I ate well, especially since Morning Star hand-fed me just as she had done during our pairing ceremony, despite the fact that I was feeding myself very efficiently.

"I find it very charming to be fed by so lovely a mate," I said, "but I do wish that you would concentrate on feeding yourself first."

"I am eating," she assured me. Morning Star obligingly allowed me to put a large piece of duck meat in her mouth. After she had chewed and swallowed, she went on. "I just want to be sure that you get enough to fill your stomach. I do not want you to grow to be as raw-boned as your father. I want you to be as robust as a red buck at the end of summer."

Morning Star had spoken in low tones in hopes that no one would overhear, but Black Wolf, sitting at our backs, gave my shoulder a few solid thumps.

"I have a difficult time imagining Tris to look anything but robust," he said. "I do not think that you need to worry, my daughter."

I could see that the slash on Black Wolf's injured hand had at last been treated and wrapped.

Black Wolf then turned to Little Fawn.

"While we were away I heard a most disturbing rumor that I am paired with a cannibal," he teased, "a vicious man-eater!"

His eyes sparkled with merriment as Little Fawn laughingly grabbed him by his whiskers and lightheartedly drew him in for a kiss, too pleased at having him returned to her and at the success of the rescue mission to be annoyed at his jest

"Oh, you!" Little Fawn exclaimed.

"I shall have to sleep with one eye open now, lest she be stricken with hunger pangs in the middle of the night." Black Wolf said with a laugh.

"Yes," said Puh, "but are you going to tell her the rumor we heard about *you*?"

"Ack," began Black Wolf, "she probably suspects worse."

Muh wore a happy expression, but I noted a strained look of grief that lingered on her face when in unguarded moments, her eyes rested on Puh. However, there was no doubt that she was elated to have him at her side once more. They leaned against one another throughout the meal and after the food had been devoured, Puh reclined with his head in her lap, contentedly receiving her fond caresses. As I watched them, it occurred to me to hope that my pairing would still be as full of love when I was old and scarred like Puh, and that my mate, my beautiful Morning Star, would still dote on me with such tender devotion.

We were all well sated. The festive atmosphere was beginning to slowly dwindle and the youngest children were starting to tire. My eldest sister Ru had attempted to deliver a droopy and complaining Baby Mi to Muh, but Puh gingerly took her from Ru and now Mi lay peacefully on Puh's chest. Both parent and child looked as though they might fall asleep at any moment. Before too long, everyone would be seeking a place to rest for the night.

I turned to Morning Star and caught her eyes. I held her gaze and smiled. She nodded and smiled, too. We stood and wordlessly slipped from the gathering. Only Gran noticed our departure. She grinned and touched my arm as we passed by her with a nod to bid her good night.

The waning moon was high in the sky. I took Morning Star's hand and guided her up the hill, leading the way through a serene landscape of muted nighttime colors, accompanied by the undercurrent of sounds made by the low croaking of the frogs and the gentle rustling of the wind playing in the new spring leaves.

* * *

Early the next morning, I lay still joined with Morning Star. She softly dozed in my embrace. I had not slept at all, yet. We had made love all through the night and she had only now drifted off to sleep. But just before, she had whispered to me: "Tris, my love, I always knew that we would be together."

And then, as I kissed her lips, I felt her answering pressure on my mouth gradually ebb away as she fell fast asleep. My own eyelids are growing heavy.

* * *

I see Morning Star as she holds an infant to her breast. Her smooth black hair shines in the sunlight and her lovely dusky skin glows. She is surrounded by playing children, some are as dark as she is, others have my fair skin and bright hair. She is laughing.

~finis~

 **Author's Note** 

First, the obligatory disclaimer: any resemblance to persons either living or dead to any character in this novel is purely coincidental. I have been asked whether these portrayals are based on anyone I know. Nope. I can only say that there is a bit of myself, however minute, in each character.

Second, regarding the description of how Tris and his Puh retrieved honey from wild bees: I have based this on my own experiences. Naturally, my bee keeping was not complicated by a wardrobe made of animal skins, but after a period of tending to my bees in the typical apiarian suit of the 1980s, I found that rig to be rather cumbersome.

Gradually, I whittled down the beekeeper's suit, piece by piece, until it was completely discarded. I found that I could work the hive much easier by simply wearing clean clothing and making sure my person was free of scent. I used slow, deliberate movements and liberally doused the bees with smoke. My bees then more or less ignored me; they may have walked all over me, but I was never stung by my own bees. (However, I have been stung by wild bees.)

I would *never* advise anyone to approach or attempt to access a hive without using the proper gear unless they also have the experience and confidence to do so. Those who choose not to wear protective clothing during these processes do so at their own peril.

Third, although considerable effort was put into making this work as historically accurate as possible, the constant influx of new discoveries and ever-changing theories make it impossible to ensure that the novel's details will hold up to the test of time.

There are a few aspects in which I did take advantage of artistic license. There is no way of knowing the actual appearance of the Neanderthal and the Cro-Magnon peoples, even with considering the basic clues provided by fossil remains and DNA testing, since they only provide data for those few individuals. Much of my character description is based that data, but I found it necessary to fill in the gaps with my own visions of early men.

Also, as of now, the hard evidence of canine domestication goes back approximately 33,000 years, but I have pushed this timeline back a bit for the sake of the plot.

Since many peoples of both the Cro-Magnon and Neanderthal probably did not have much contact with those from outside their home ranges, they were apt to be culturally unique in their isolation. There may have been great differences in their traditions, survival tactics, languages, artistic expressions, etc.

And lastly, to elaborate on the Introduction, this book reflects my personal (admittedly unscientific) opinion, but I believe that these early peoples were probably much more advanced than is often thought.

I think that peoples' life skills must have ebbed and flowed throughout history as climate and habitat changes contributed to the waxing and waning of their living conditions.

As the world offered a warm, reasonably wet place for people to live, they thrived, and no doubt contrived to discover ways to improve their quality of life. Their numbers may have increased until the climate became less friendly, when both they—and the flora and fauna on which they depended for their survival were stressed, leading to the deaths, if not the extinctions of many species, both human and animal.

Discoveries were lost until times were again favorable for people, and then forgotten technologies were embraced by a whole new population.

At the time this story takes place, temperatures were generally ten to twenty degrees lower than they are today; indeed, the last Ice Age pushed many forms of life to their extremity of survival. Many species did not persist to the present day, including the Neanderthal, whose numbers were never very great at any time. In this novel, I have graced these people with the intelligence and the means to support themselves in ways I think they would have needed to survive an Ice Age setting. They would have required warm clothing, not just the haphazard hide wrapped around the waist or thrown over a shoulder as they are often depicted in art or the media. They probably erected some sort of shelters for protection from the elements, which would have been essential when they migrated seasonally as they followed game in order to feed themselves. It would not have been practical to reside in caves except as temporary sanctuaries, since caves are not always available in convenient locations and were definitely not transportable. They also would have had to heat whatever they were using as a home. They would have needed tools that were sophisticated enough to accomplish these tasks and sufficient communication skills to work together. It is pretty incredible to think that even with the necessary proficiencies and tools, that anyone was able to persevere through such challenging times. Surely, the fact that humans still live on this planet is a testament to our intellect and tenacity.

The Neanderthal may not be with us as a distinct people, but I do not think that they went extinct. I believe they were assimilated into populations of Cro-Magnon peoples. Nature may have selected against certain Neanderthal traits in ways that would help modern man survive, such as, for example: a slighter physique that would not require the great caloric and protein demands needed by the Neanderthal, but they, or at least portions of their DNA, are with us even yet.

* * *

This book is the first of *The Dreamer* series. Tris, Tor, Black Wolf, and their families and friends have many more journeys on which to embark and many more adventures to experience. It is my hope that readers will enjoy this saga. Writing is a solitary task and as satisfying as it is, it is so much more meaningful when you find that through it, you have (hopefully) managed to reach into the minds and hearts of others.

Before I close out this note, I must offer my most heartfelt thanks to all those who so generously gave me their encouragement and feedback. I love you all and I am indebted to you in a way that I will never be able to adequately express.

With warmest regards,   E. A. Meigs

Index of European Ice Age Animals

Antelope (Saiga Antelope) These small antelope (24 to 36 inches tall at the shoulder weighing approximately 80 to 140 pounds) ranged over a good part of the northern hemisphere. They are exceptional in appearance due to their unusual muzzles, which feature a long, flexible snout that looks much like a truncated elephant's nose.

Aurochs (Extinct) Predecessor of domesticated cattle. Size varied between 61 to 71 inches at the shoulder, with weights of 1500 to 3300 pounds. Their horns could reach up to 31 inches in length. Sometimes aurochs is spelled "auroch", but from

my readings, I am lead to believe that but the "s" is often included even when the animal is referred to in singular form because it is an alternative form of spelling "ox" and isn't intended to indicate plurality.

Boar Wild boars are the plows of the animal world. They are built for digging. Their heads and massive

shoulders make up a good part of their bodies and their large, sharp tusks, which continue to grow throughout the life of the animal, are very effective at turning over soil. The largest adult male boars can reach weights of nearly 800 pounds and attain a shoulder height of 49 inches. Sows (females) are much smaller and they lack the mane and thick shoulder/back "shield" of the boars. Their tusks are also of a more modest size. The coloring of their coats varies from anything between white and black, but most tend to run towards darker shades.

Brown Bear
(Eurasian Brown Bear) Although this bear is called a "brown bear" its color can range from black to a tawny light brown. Males average 550 to 650 pounds but very large specimens can exceed

1000 pounds. Females weigh 330 to 550 pounds. During pre-history, the brown bear did consume some plant matter, but it was generally carnivorous.

Cave Bear (Extinct) This was a very large, stout bear. The average male weighed in at 880 to 1100 pounds. Females averaged a little over half that (495 to 550 pounds). Despite their size, bone analysis and other indicators suggest that cave bears were primarily herbivores.

 Cave Lion (Extinct) (European Cave Lion) These efficient feline predators were some of the largest known cats in animal history. Based on skeletal

remains, it is speculated that the males may have reached 11 ½ feet in length from nose to tip of the tail, and weighed over 880 pounds.

Chamois A medium-sized goat/antelope. They are 28-31 inches tall at the shoulder and range in weight from 55-132 pounds. Besides being a fine source of meat, their hides were used to make garments.

Crow (Carrion Crow) A large black bird, approximately 18 to 21 inches in length with a large, heavy beak that is well adapted to catching and eating small prey such as mice, frogs, insects, etc., and scavenging off the kills of other animals.

Elk (Eurasian Elk) ("moose" in North America) A medium-sized elk/moose, now extinct in many parts of Europe. They average from just over 600 to just over 1000 pounds, with shoulder heights at 5.6 - 6.9 feet.

Fallow Deer A medium-sized deer, about 30 to 37 inches at shoulder height and weighing 66 pounds (small doe) to 220 pounds (large buck), although unusually large bucks may tip the scales at 330 pounds. Their winter coats are brown, but they are

freckled with white dots on their backs and sides during the summer.

Giant Deer (extinct) (Irish Elk) The giant deer was one of the largest deer ever to walk the earth. Commonly, it has mistakenly been called an Irish elk, although it was neither exclusive to Ireland nor an elk.

This huge deer averaged nearly 7 feet in height at the shoulder and carried antlers with a spread that could span 12 feet. They are estimated to have weighed nearly 1200 to just over 1300 pounds but larger individuals could have reached upwards of 1500 pounds.

Horse The Eurasian Ice Age horse came in many

different varieties. They were more than likely the size of modern ponies and appeared in all colors, spots and stripes. They may have resembled the Przewalski's horse that still exist today or the now-extinct Tarpan horse.

Ibex (Alpine Ibex) A moderate-sized, dun-colored mountain goat. The bucks' horns sometimes reach 39 inches in length. The does' horns may grow to a length of nearly 14 inches. Similarly, bucks achieve a much larger body size (35 to 40 inches at the withers and weighing from 150 to over 250 pounds) than the does (29 to 33 inches at the withers and 37 to just over 70 pounds).

Lynx (Eurasian Lynx) The biggest of all species of lynx. Approximately 24 to 30 inches at the shoulder, and including its short tail, it may be 31 to 51 inches in body length. The largest males weighed nearly 100 pounds, but the typical lynx will run between 18 (very small female)

and 66 pounds (good-sized male).

Marten (European Pine Marten) A small, weasel-like animal with dark brown fur, often with blond markings or a blond bib on its chest.

At a little less than 3 ½ pounds and about 21 inches in length, the marten was hunted for its beautiful, silky fur.

Mink (European Mink) A small mink,

even the largest is just under 20 inches in length and only about 1¾ pounds. They have been prized for their dense, luxurious winter coats.

Porcupine (Old World Porcupine) This rodent wears an impressive coat of quills, some of which may be up to 14 inches in length (Crested Porcupine). These species of porcupines come in a variety of sizes: the smallest adults run from 11inches to 34 inches long, and may weigh between 3.3 to 60 pounds.

Red Deer (European Red Deer) Another very large species of deer. The buck weighs in at 350 to 550 pounds (48 inches at the shoulder) and does run 260 to 370 pounds (45 inches at the shoulder). These deer, unsurprisingly, are known for their

reddish coats. During autumn, the males often have a short mane on the backs of their necks.

Red Fox The biggest of the fox species, the adult ranges from 14 to 20 inches tall at the shoulder and weigh from 5 to nearly 40 pounds. These animals were often harvested for their fine fur.

Reindeer (Also known as caribou) This important game animal consists of several different subspecies and varied in size from 120 to 550 pounds. Color varied as well, but all subspecies shared many of the same basic characteristics, such as a fairly

impressive set of antlers (in most reindeer, both the bucks and the does grow antlers) and a two-layered coat of fur, featuring a woolly undercoat that thickens dramatically each winter and an overcoat of longer, coarse, hollow hairs.

Roe Deer (Western Roe Deer) This small deer averages just over two feet to two feet, 6 inches at the withers, and a mere 33 to 77 pounds. Nonetheless, they were an important source of meat for prehistoric humans.

Sheep The actual breed(s) of ancient sheep that roamed Ice-Age Europe are unknown, but it is recognized that sheep were hunted and eaten by early man. It is possible that the Mouflon (shown in image) is the modern day link to prehistoric sheep. The Mouflon have a shoulder height of less than 3 feet and weigh from 75 to 110 pounds.

Snow Leopard This beautiful cat is well adapted to life in a cold, mountainous habitat. It has a stout build and long, dense fur that varies in color from white to pale gray, with dark gray to black spotted markings. It is about 24 inches at the shoulder with a weight of 60 to 120 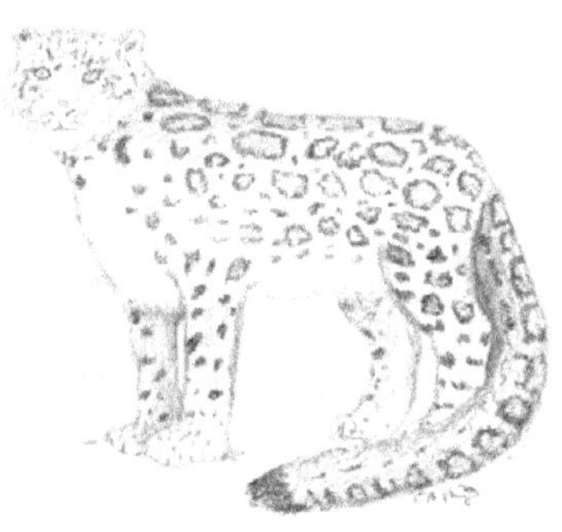 pounds, although larger males have been noted at 165 pounds. Their fur was considered to be very desirable and they have long been hunted for their pelts.

Vulture (Eurasian Griffin Vulture) This large scavenging bird may have a wingspan of over 9 feet and weigh as much as 33 pounds, although most individuals range from 14 to 25 pounds. It is known that early men consumed the meat of vultures. 

Wisent (European Bison) An impressive animal, the  wisent is the heaviest land animal that still resides in modern day Europe. Fully grown specimens range from 5 to 6 ½ feet at the shoulder and weigh 660 (small female) to more than 2000 pounds (large male). The wisent was an important source of food and hides for prehistoric humans.

Wolf (Eurasian Wolf) These are the largest of the  European or Asian wolves. Their sizes vary greatly from 70 to 212 pounds. Although their coats could be black, white, or even reddish, by far the most common color was a grey/buff and white combination of medium length, dense fur.

Wood Grouse (Western Capercaillie) This Eurasian bird is the largest of the grouse species, weighing as much as 15 pounds. The cocks have an average weight of 9 pounds and a wingspan of 36 to 48 inches. The hen is considerably more modest in size, with a weight of

approximately 4 pounds and a wingspan of 28 inches.

 Woolly Mammoth (Extinct) This large mammal lived in Eurasia and North America, and was similar in size to today's African Elephants, but with considerably longer tusks, a shorter tail, and much smaller

ears. The males of this huge species could attain heights of up to 11 feet at the withers and weigh over 12,000 pounds. Females were somewhat smaller, although still impressive in size at up to 9½ feet at the shoulder and weights up to nearly 9000 pounds. Their hairy hides came in a wide range of colors that could be anything from blond to quite dark. They were protected from the extreme Ice Age weather conditions by a double fur coat that consisted of a short, dense, woolly undercoat and strands of long outer guard hairs.

Woolly Rhinoceros (Extinct) Looking much like a  modern rhinoceros in a heavy fur coat, the woolly rhinoceros sported two horns on its long snout and carried its thick body on short, stout legs. This animal averaged about 4000 to 6000 pounds, with a shoulder height of about 6½ feet. The larger front horn that grew from the woolly rhinoceros' nose could reach lengths of 24 inches.

About the Author
E.A. Meigs

I was raised on Cape Cod (Brewster, Massachusetts, USA) at a time when the Cape was still a rural area made up of woodlands, marshes, beaches, streams, and ponds. There, my life was divided between the land and sea. My father was a commercial fisherman, backyard boat builder, and an outdoorsman; so I had an early introduction to boats, working in the commercial fishing industry and spending lots of time in the local fields and forests. When I wasn't on a boat or roaming around the great outdoors, chances are I was reading or writing. I have been a compulsive writer literally since I could first put words on paper, producing my first full length novel at ten years old. Even at that age, my goal in life was to someday find a way to combine my love of nature, the outdoors, and writing.

After raising a family and embarking on a long and varied career that included many years working on and around boats and in the commercial fishing industry; a stint with Florida Fish & Wildlife in a small field office; and other jobs that actually allowed me to use my writing skills, I awoke one day with *The Dreamer* in my head. I began writing the novel with the intention of producing just one book, but as the story progressed it became apparent that the plot would require much more than one volume to tell the tale.

I have two wonderful adult daughters and eight delightful grandchildren. I am an avid camper and I strive to get out hiking as often as possible, daily, when my schedule allows.